# Never Let Go

## Luna Peters

Published by Luna Peters

Copyright © 2025 Luna Peters

All rights reserved. No portion of this book may be reproduced in any form without permission from the publisher, except as permitted by International copyright laws. For permissions contact author : lunapetersauthor@gmail.com

No part of this book may be used to create, feed, or refine artificial intelligence models, for any purpose, without written permission from the author.

The characters in this book are entirely fictional.

Any resemblance to actual persons living or dead is entirely coincidental.

Although the author and publisher have made every effort to ensure that the information in this book was correct at press time, the author and publisher do not assume and hereby disclaim any liability to any party for any loss, damage, or disruption caused by errors or omissions, whether such errors or emissions result from negligence, accident or any cause.

Cover Design by Artscandare Book Cover Design

Formatting: Jac Franklin

Developmental editing: Jac Franklin

Copy/line Editing and Proofreading: Stacey's Bookcorner Editing Services

ISBN: 9798317336554

Independently Published and Printed in Great Britain by Amazon

First Edition

# Contents

| | |
|---|---|
| Playlist | VII |
| Content Warnings | IX |
| Dedication | X |
| Quote | XI |
| 1. Lauren | 1 |
| 2. Caleb | 6 |
| 3. Lauren | 11 |
| 4. Caleb | 18 |
| 5. Lauren | 22 |
| 6. Caleb | 27 |
| 7. Lauren | 32 |
| 8. Caleb | 41 |
| 9. Lauren | 45 |
| 10. Caleb | 50 |

| | | |
|---|---|---|
| 11. | Lauren | 53 |
| 12. | Lauren | 59 |
| 13. | Caleb | 65 |
| 14. | Lauren | 69 |
| 15. | Caleb | 76 |
| 16. | Lauren | 84 |
| 17. | Caleb | 89 |
| 18. | Lauren | 94 |
| 19. | Lauren | 99 |
| 20. | Unknown | 101 |
| 21. | Lauren | 102 |
| 22. | Caleb | 106 |
| 23. | Lauren | 109 |
| 24. | Caleb | 114 |
| 25. | Lauren | 119 |
| 26. | Caleb | 128 |
| 27. | Lauren | 132 |
| 28. | Caleb | 138 |
| 29. | Lauren | 147 |
| 30. | Caleb | 153 |
| 31. | Lauren | 159 |
| 32. | Unknown | 165 |
| 33. | Lauren | 166 |
| 34. | Lauren | 170 |

| | | |
|---|---|---|
| 35. | Caleb | 177 |
| 36. | Lauren | 179 |
| 37. | Caleb | 186 |
| 38. | Caleb | 188 |
| 39. | Lauren | 191 |
| 40. | Caleb | 197 |
| 41. | Lauren | 202 |
| 42. | Caleb | 208 |
| 43. | Lauren | 213 |
| 44. | Caleb | 222 |
| 45. | Lauren | 225 |
| 46. | Caleb | 231 |
| 47. | Lauren | 233 |
| 48. | Caleb | 237 |
| 49. | Lauren | 243 |
| 50. | Lauren | 247 |
| 51. | Caleb | 249 |
| 52. | Lauren | 252 |
| 53. | Caleb | 256 |
| 54. | Lauren | 260 |
| 55. | Caleb | 265 |
| 56. | Lauren | 267 |
| 57. | Caleb | 273 |
| 58. | Lauren | 281 |

| | |
|---|---|
| 59. Lauren | 284 |
| Bonus Chapter | 287 |
| Acknowledgements | 291 |
| About the author | 293 |
| Stalk Me | 295 |

| | |
|---|---:|
| Bad Things | **I Prevail** |
| The Downfall Of Us All | **A Day To Remember** |
| The Devil You Know | **Stone Broken** |
| Falling Apart | **Papa Roach** |
| Downpour | **Our Hallow, Our Home** |
| My Heart's To Blame | **Falling In Reverse** |
| I Can Do It With A Broken Heart | **Taylor Swift** |
| Karma | **MOD SUN** |
| I Don't Need A Man | **The Pussycat Dolls** |
| Taste | **Sabrina Carpenter** |
| Something To Feel | **Dixon Dallas** |
| Make It Make Sense | **A Day To Remember** |
| Hello Heaven, Hello | **YUNGBLUD** |
| Tears Don't Fall | **Bullet For My Valentine** |
| Broken In All The Right Places | **Lost Kings, MOD SUN** |

# Content Warnings

Never Let Go contains scenes of an adult nature throughout, including a consensual sexual relationship between a college professor and his student. The book also contains adult language throughout. It also contains the following;

Dub-con

D/s dynamic (without full conversations regarding limits)

Unprotected sex

Mention of childhood neglect

Violence (directed at MC)

# Authors note

While this book does have a dark theme, it's not paramount to the story. It's more of a side character who butt in and wouldn't shut up.

This story is predominantly about Lauren and Caleb's journey.

Happy reading.

Luna

To all the women who love a bit of silver with their fox... this one's for you.

'The biggest regret of your life won't be what you did, it'll be what you didn't do.'

**LEE BRICE**

# Chapter One

## *Lauren*

"You have *got* to be kidding me," I groan to the plain white ceiling of my dorm room, placing my head in my hands. "What a shitty fucking day."

Considering how my morning started, you would have thought it would get better, but no.

I woke up with my alarm as usual but fell back asleep, which meant I was late to my first lecture of the day. Now, you're probably thinking, *But Lauren, that's not the end of the world*. I'm just going to throw in about some spilled coffee and a forgotten bag of books—do with that what you will.

So like I said, shitty fucking day.

I'm currently sitting in my room, staring at my bright green eyes and long blonde hair in the mirror, wondering how the hell I'm going to get myself ready and across town for work in the next hour, when the *third* Uber just cancelled on me.

Snatching up my bag with all the essentials—outfit for tonight, hair ties because you can never have too many, and my trusty chalk—I head out into the living room just as my best friend, Sydney, walks through the door.

"What up, bitch?" She glances at me, and I frown before laughing and rolling my eyes at her.

"Your inside voice didn't follow you inside then?"

Sydney's literally the best person I know. We met after being roomed together when we started at Abingdon University and ended up forming this... weird friendship? She's all hugs and kisses and I'm... not.

Sydney flips her long dark hair back, her eyes twinkling with mischief as she gives me a grin. "Bitch, please. You love me," she sasses.

Smirking, I reply, "If I have to."

Sydney's the hottest girl I've ever seen and if I were into them—I'm not, much to Sydney's dismay—then I would totally bang her. Because Sydney *is* into girls. She's got these gorgeous, big, brown doe eyes that most girls fall for and a body to die for—curves and ass everywhere. But she's also the type of girl that's allergic to commitment, choosing to run out the door the next morning, never to see them again.

"You working tonight?" she asks while putting her bag down on the small table we have in the corner of our room.

It's not massive by any means but it does the job. According to Sydney, the plain, beige walls are in desperate need of brightening. She keeps talking about buying a potted plant or picture, and like the good best friend that I am, I nod and agree every time she brings it up—not that she's done anything about it in the two years I've known her.

Our dorm room is one of the bougier ones—not only having separate bedrooms, but a living room and kitchen, as well. Our kitchen is to the left as you walk in with two bedrooms farther down the hall, one on either side. Unfortunately, we share a bathroom with the rest of the floor. As long as you get in there either first thing in the morning or last thing at night, it's usually empty.

I look up from my phone as I reply, "Yeah, Sapphire has me on the early shift." I wave my phone in the air. "I'm just gonna order an Uber."

"Sounds good, babe," she calls out, strolling towards her bedroom. "I've got studying to do tonight, so I'll be here when you get home."

I always thought it was weird that dance majors had schoolwork, but what do I know?

Sydney's the best dancer I've ever seen. Think Jenna Dewan in Step Up and you have Sydney. I keep trying to talk her into coming to work with me at Strokes, but she's always said she doesn't want to dance day and night.

"Catch ya later," I call out as I head to the door.

Let's hope tonight's an easy one.

---

Opening the door and walking into Strokes, I glance around and see it's practically dead. Two guys sit at the front, hooting and hollering at the stage as the waitresses stand at the bar, talking, waiting to be called over. This is standard for a Tuesday night, most men at home with their families, waiting for the weekend to come when they can use lame ass excuses as to why they're home late, and smelling of perfume. It's usually just the singles during the week.

Not that I mind it so much, it gives me a chance to practice on the poles, not worrying about having to give the performance of my life. Not that I do, anyway. Strokes isn't that kind of place.

Since I walked in here nearly three years ago, there's always been this feeling of home, of comfort. Luckily I had no issues with applying for the job. The Midwest State allows you to become a stripper at the impressionable age of eighteen, yet you can't legally drink alcohol... go figure.

Strokes has been done up to a high standard, a black and chrome theme throughout. The stage is front and center with a bar at the back, booths round the edges and tables placed in the middle. Sapphire, the manager, has always let us do our own thing when it comes to our performances. Security's also on hand if there are any issues with unwanted attention.

Strolling through the main bar and out toward the back room, I can hear the girls' laughter as I step through the dressing room door, the door clicking shut behind me.

"Girl, did you see those two guys at the front? They're like a pack of fucking vultures. Tell me why I do this job again?" Esme asks, and I can't help but laugh.

Esme's big, and beautiful with a heart to match. She decided to cut her long blonde hair off a couple weeks ago, opting for a short, pixie cut which she dyed green. Honestly, she looks freaking fantastic and I wish I had balls as big as her.

"Because of the tips, Esme!" Destiny shouts from behind her mirror, where she's sitting applying her make-up.

Destiny's like the mother hen of the group, always checking in on us and making sure we're okay, that we always have a safe person to talk to. Her luscious, coily hair matches perfectly with her tanned skin. She's got a body to die for—boobs and legs for days.

I smile to myself as I think about how much I love these girls. Most strippers I've met are bitches, so it's nice to be around a group of girls who can banter their way out of anything.

"Aw, poor Esme. Did they try groping you again?" I chuckle.

Esme sits down next to me as she fans herself. "Seriously, the guy in the suit nearly climbed up on the stage and pulled me off. Where do they find these loons?!" she questions, as she flings her arms wide in a *what the fuck* gesture. Luckily for Esme, she's a tough girl so stuff like this doesn't scare her easily.

Quickly changing into my outfit for the night—a black lacy one piece that shows more of my ass and cleavage than I'm used to—and touch up my makeup, I go to the long, standing mirror on the wall and check myself over—not bad.

I take my hair out of its ponytail and bend over, fluffing it up, before flipping my head back. Catcalls and whistles start up behind me, variations of "get it girl" and "work it" being thrown my way. I laugh, turning round and shimmying my boobs at them before bowing.

"Lauren, you're up," Sapphire calls from the doorway.

Grabbing my hat—a prop to go with tonight's outfit—I walk toward the stage area. The intro to *Bad Things* by *I Prevail* begins and my hips automatically start swaying to the beat as I strut slowly and seductively. Just as the beat kicks in, I take a running jump at the pole ready to earn some cash.

## Chapter Two

## *Caleb*

"Thanks, everyone. Put your assignments on my desk on your way out. Anyone that needs any extra help knows to contact me during work hours," I call out over the noise of the eager young adults racing toward the door.

*God, I need a vacation*, I think as I swipe my hand through my dark brown hair. *Definitely need a trim, too.* It's grown out longer than my usual short on the sides and a mess of hair on top, meaning that I now look like a darker version of Kurt Cobain.

I've been a professor at Abingdon University for the last year, having moved here for a fresh start. My ex, Samantha, didn't take the breakup so well. Clingy, overbearing, and a Daddy's girl tends to wear thin after a while.

When I took the job, I didn't know how long I'd be here for, but so far, it's not too bad. The pay's good, and the hours go quickly. I begin stuffing my belongings into my satchel when Vince Williams, the Dean of Admissions, walks in.

Stopping to perch on the edge of my desk, he says, "Caleb, glad I caught you." I give him a disapproving look, but the asshole just sits there.

The guy's always given me the creeps with his fake ass smiles and too long, lingering glances toward female students. It gives him that lecherous feel. I mean, the guy isn't even that good looking—his blond hair is slicked back giving off bad Draco Malfoy vibes and his clothes are too nicely pressed. His British accent adds to the lack of charm he thinks he possesses.

Raising an eyebrow, I drawl, "Dean Williams, to what do I owe this pleasure?" If he notices my sarcasm he doesn't respond—*shame*.

"I wanted to let you know that you have a new student joining your class as of next week. I haven't had the chance to bring her in yet, but she needs this class in order to pass. She has excellent grades but still needs an undergrad minor," he states as he folds his arms across his chest. I love the way he's trying to intimidate me but unfortunately for him, his short, tubby stature is nothing compared to my muscled 6'2" frame, so it doesn't work.

Turning my back, I continue packing my shit so I can get the hell out of here. "No problem. My TA, Brad, can handle her assignments and catch her up."

Out of the corner of my eye, I see the dean tense at the clear dismissal—*like I give a fuck*—and a smirk pulls at my lips.

"Thank you," he all but sneers as he stands up and straightens his jacket. "I'll let you get back to your day." With that, he marches toward the door and back to god knows where.

Blowing out a breath at the always awkward impromptu meeting with the dean, I pick my satchel up off the desk and sling it across my body before locking the door and heading out to my black Mustang Shelby GT350. I saved up every single cent I earned as a sixteen-year-old kid—washing cars, mowing lawns, washing dishes in the back of diners, you name it—to be able to afford her. I throw my satchel in the back seat and turn the ignition on, my baby purring to life.

I'm meeting the guys at Bucky's, the bar just off campus, for a beer. It's close enough for us to meet—the only downside being college kids frequent here, as well. If I had a dollar for every time I was hit on by a college student, I'd be a rich fucking man.

The décor leaves much to be desired, though. It's your typical dive bar that you really should stay away from but love all the same.

Parking in the lot, I make my way in, spotting the guys at a table in the corner with a round in front of them.

"Here comes trouble!" James shouts as he reclines back, putting an arm across Theo's chair.

"I haven't been 'trouble' since I was eighteen, asshat," I joke as I stride closer to the table. Noah moves over so I can sit next to him, waving at a barmaid so I can order.

We catch up, ribbing each other as friends do. I mean, I've known these guys for most of my life, there isn't anything they don't know about me. How our friendship has lasted this long, I'll never know, but I'm grateful for their crazy asses all the same.

Taking a sip of my lukewarm beer, I grimace, nodding at Noah as I ask, "How's high school life?"

A strange look passes across his face, there one minute and gone the next—interesting.

"Same old shit. Kids think they know everything." He shrugs, not saying anything else.

I chuckle at the typical Noah response. Noah's the quiet one of the group; he's the type who sits back and watches everything around him, silently taking notes. He's tall and lean with a mop of dark hair. Think gothic, moody, and grumpy, and you have Noah.

Next there's Theo—the jokester. The one who's the most likely to get picked up by the cops for some prank he's pulled. His long, blond hair is swept up in a man bun, the sides looking freshly shaved. Theo's got this scary looking Viking thing going for him but he's just one big cuddly teddy bear.

Then there's James—the playboy of the group. Where I'm all nerd, he's all sophistication and suaveness. I mean, the guy can talk his way out of everything and *into* anything. He's the 'love em and leave em' type. His dark hair and shocking blue eyes give him an edge, that so far, no girl has been able to resist.

*Insert eye roll here.*

After a few hours of shooting the shit, James stands up, his chair scraping against the tiles on the floor, before slapping me on the shoulder as he passes by. "Well guys, it's been fun, but I gotta bounce. I gotta check on Andrew's daughter. Said I would swing by on my way home and make sure she's okay." He throws some money down on the table as he walks off.

"Tell her I said hi," Theo calls after him. Without turning around, James flips him the bird.

"I'm off, as well. Got an early start tomorrow. We still on for Saturday night?" I ask Theo as I drain the last of my beer and put my jacket on.

"Yeah, Strokes at 8 p.m. I can't believe my soon-to-be brother-in-law let me talk him into having his bachelor party there. Christie's gonna go nuts," Theo laughs. "It's gonna be *epic*." He rubs his hands together in glee, and I bark out a laugh. The image of Christie's reaction plays in my mind, and I can't help but feel sorry for Dan and the loss of his balls when she gets hold of him.

"Dude, you're gonna be just as fucked when she gets hold of *you*."

I grin as his face falls, the realization finally kicking in at the horrors of what his sister's going to do to him. Christie once put laxatives in his drink after Theo slept with her best friend and never called her back. Needless to say, Theo never went after any of Christie's friends again. I cringe remembering the aftermath.

"Fuck."

I laugh and say my goodbyes before heading to my car.

Opening the driver's door, I get in, the leather creaking under me as I settle myself in. The engine purrs as I start her up, sending goosebumps down my arms. *Damn, that never gets old.*

Driving down the neighboring streets, their freshly mowed lawns and white picket fences all blend into one. My windows are down, the wind blowing softly through my hair as *The Downfall Of Us All* by *A Day To Remember* blasts through my speakers. I may be turning thirty-seven this year, but it was never a phase, Mom.

I pull up to my modest two-bedroom house, which is conveniently near campus, and park in the garage. Walking in through the side door, I throw my keys down and take my shoes off, heading into the kitchen and swiping a beer from the fridge.

I take a swig and look around, appreciating how far I've come from growing up in a trailer park. Spoiler alert—I'm a poor boy from the wrong side of the tracks who managed to claw his way out and become an English professor at one of the most prestigious universities in the country. Hard work does pay off.

Finishing my beer and putting the bottle in the recycling bin, I head up and take a quick shower before removing a pair of sweats from the drawer and getting into bed. Alarm set, I'm ready to crash and start it all again tomorrow.

# Chapter Three

## *Lauren*

*I got called into the dean's office.*

*I'm not freaking out, you are.*

*Why the fuck did I get called into the dean's office?*

I'm internally freaking out while Sydney's lounging on the sofa, clearly nonplussed by my meltdown. I'm an A grade student, I never get into any trouble—well, not since being at college, anyway—I work, I pay my taxes. What. The. Fuck?

Not bothering to glance up from her laptop Sydney says, "Babe, you're gonna be fine. Stop freaking out." Her pen dangles from her mouth as she drags a hand through her hair, concentrating hard on the screen in front of her.

I gape at her incredulously. "Stop freaking out? Why the fuck am I being called into the *dean's* office?" Yep, I'm hyperventilating now. The nervous sweat begins to bead along my brow and my breath starts to come in short bursts.

"Why don't you go over there and find out, hmm? Instead of asking me the same question and getting the same answer." She gives me a pointed look and smirks. "I know you're not that dumb."

*Bitch.*

"Fuck you and none of your help, Syd. I hope your favorite face cream stops being made," I snark at her, trying to hold back my laughter at the look of outrage on her face.

"Get the fuck out of here," she shouts while throwing a pillow in my direction. "I hate you. I don't even know why I keep you around," she grumbles but there's no real heat in her words.

We both know we'd be lost without each other. She's my soul sister. The one who keeps me grounded when all else fails. She's the one I lean on the most, and who I know will always have my back, no matter what.

Blowing her a kiss, I reply, "Because you love me." I give her a wink just for good measure, and continuing my internal freak out, lift my bag off the peg and leave, hoping and praying that everything will be okay and that I'm worrying over nothing.

As I amble across campus, I can't help but look at Abingdon University with awe—the old buildings covered in ivy, the hustle and bustle of students racing to get to their lectures in time. The warm autumn breeze gently blowing the trees lined on each side of the path lending it that typical American college look. I continue my trek toward the admissions building and my impending doom.

*Okay, that's a little bit of an exaggeration but work with me here.*

I've been here for the last two years, studying English. Someone I went to high school with had dyslexia. I saw how much she struggled, how much she was constantly told she wasn't good enough and it broke my heart. I wanted to help, to show others that having dyslexia doesn't mean they're stupid, or they can't do what everyone else can, it just means they need a bit more TLC. What school I'll end up at is still a mystery to me, one I'll look more into toward the end of the school year.

Walking into the admissions building, I take a deep breath and try settling my nerves. The receptionist looks up from behind her desk—an aging older woman with gray hair and a questionable fashion sense.

"Hello, dear. How can I help you?" she asks with a kind smile.

*Okay, I take it back... she has a lovely fashion sense and I'm just being a terrible person.*

"Uh, hi. I'm Lauren Taylor. Dean Williams wanted to see me?"

*Dammit why am I acting like I stole cookies from the cookie jar? Man up, woman!*

"Ah yes, he's expecting you. Go on through, dear." She gestures to the door in front of her, her smile never leaving her face.

*Into the lion's den I go*, I think trying to put my big girl panties on. Slowly walking up to the door, I knock, entering when I hear a voice call out, "Come in."

The dean's office is nice; spacious and filled with light, the floor to ceiling windows giving it that light and airy feel. Bookcases line an entire wall to my right, I can't see the titles from here but they don't look like anything I'd read. Casting my gaze to his desk I notice a framed photo—the two point two quintessential all-American family, mom, dad, son and daughter.

A throat clears and I whip my head up to meet the gaze of Dean Williams, his eyes cold and calculating as he peruses me, sending an unpleasant shiver down my spine. He's sitting behind his desk and I've never, in this moment, been more thankful to be farther away from him.

"Miss Taylor. Come in, take a seat," he says, gesturing to the chair opposite his desk. His eyes never leave me as I sit, and I can feel a line of sweat moving down my spine. Shifting uncomfortably in the chair, he continues to stare at me, not saying a word.

*Is it me or is it hot in here?*

Finally, he leans forward, saying, "I'm sure you're wondering why I've called you in?" *No shit, Sherlock.* "You only have one major, and you need another alongside it to pass this semester. I have taken the liberty of placing you in an undergrad class with Professor Anderson. You have excellent grades, Miss Taylor, but in order to pass you must take this extra class," he explains.

The feeling of discomfort the longer I'm with him continues, I mean it could be his British accent—they all sound weird to me. The leering look on his face, almost like he's checking me out could also be another reason. Unfortunately for him, I don't do older men, especially teachers. Ew.

I swallow and exhale slowly. "Okay, thank you. When do I start?" I inquire.

Dean Williams steeples his fingers together. "Monday morning. The class has been added to your schedule and Professor Anderson's TA, Brad, I think his name was, will ensure you have everything you need to get you started." With that he gives me a smile and nods toward the door dismissing me.

Leaving his office, I take a slow walk back to my dorm room. Sydney's at class so I let myself in and flop down on my bed, trying to shake the gross feeling of Dean William's gaze on me. I mean, is he allowed to act like that with students? All leery and weird. Or was it just me reading the room wrong? I rub a hand over my eyes, a headache forming.

My phone starts buzzing in my pocket, all thoughts of Dean Williams and his creepiness fleeing my brain as I shift around on the bed like a fish out of water—whose idea was it to make skinny jeans so *tight*?—I finally manage to slide my phone out and I unlock it to see a message from Sapphire:

> Sapphire
>
> I need you to work Saturday night. Big bachelor party, so all hands on deck - S x

Ah, fuck! There goes my quiet weekend. I'd asked for the weekend off to catch up on assignments. I have a photographic memory—it's kinda the main reason why I was able to get into such a good university and keep up my 4.0 GPA, without breaking a sweat. But I'm still like every other college student—I get caught up binge watching TV shows, I work—so sometimes I fall behind and need to catch up.

It's a weird and not altogether pleasant experience, if I'm being honest. I can vividly recall every single memory I have, almost like looking at a picture and seeing everything—names and faces, dates, *everything*. I only need to meet or see something once and it's there, stuck. The downside is I can be triggered easily—music, nightmares—if there's a memory attached to it. I've learnt over the years to control it but it's still hard.

I quickly message Sapphire back knowing I don't have any other options:

> Me
>
> Fine, but you owe me double time and another weekend off.

She replies instantly:

> Sapphire
>
> Done.

Setting my phone down, I lug out my books and walk to the living room—the lighting's always been better out here—and get to work.

I don't know how many hours pass before Sydney comes barreling through the door. "Oooooh girl, I am *exhausted*," she exclaims as she throws herself down next to me. "Are we ordering in tonight because there ain't no way I'm cooking."

"Only if we can order Chinese, I swear I had a bad stomach after eating from Bill's Pizzeria," I groan, remembering the discomfort.

"Sure," Sydney laughs. "I'll change and then order. Same as usual?" she asks, already stripping off her top as she walks into her room. The girl has no shame.

"Yeah, please. I'll just finish this off and tidy up."

We sit and watch a film while we're eating. Spending quality time with Syd is few and far between, our schedules being so busy, so I enjoy it where I can.

"I thought we could go out Saturday night? We haven't been out in ages," Sydney says around a mouthful of chicken chow mein.

"Can't. Sapphire called me in, apparently, they have a big bachelor party coming and I'm needed." I cringe at the thought. I love my job, I really do, but bachelor parties are no fun. Fights get started, drinks get spilt, and someone always ends up either puking or crying—no thanks.

Sydney pouts. "Boo. You're no fun anymore."

"I know," I sigh. "She promised me another weekend off though, so we'll do something then, okay?" At this point I'm giving her the puppy dog eyes so she doesn't turn this into one of her dramathons.

"Ugh, whatever." She points her fork at me. "Drinks are on you though." The devilish glint in her eyes means I'm in for one hell of a bill at the end of the night.

"Love you," I sing as I walk to the kitchen and place the empty containers in the bin. "I'm heading off to bed."

She waves her hand at me, too engrossed in Henry Cavill. "Night, bitch," she says.

"Night, asshole."

I showered and changed earlier so all I have to do is crawl into bed and hope sleep claims me quickly.

# Chapter Four

## *Caleb*

This bachelor party came around too quickly. I mean, I'm happy for the guy but a strip club? Really? Could Theo have been any more cliché with it? I internally roll my eyes at the thought and check the guys out. We're all here; me, James, Noah, Theo, Dan, and a few of Dan's friends who I've met on occasion. I have to give it to the guys, they've scrubbed up well, including Noah who doesn't usually care much for how he's looking.

"Let's get this party started, motherfuckers," Theo hollers as he slaps Dan's back, who not only visibly winces from the slap, but his face becomes paler knowing he's in for a shit storm when he gets home to Christie. Poor fucker.

For a strip club it's not that bad, it's my first time here, not usually making a habit of frequenting places like this. I'm the type of guy who's happy to either use my hand or find a willing woman in a bar for the night when I need to.

The lights are low and the music's loud as we stroll in, getting placed at a table in front of the stage. A couple of scantily dressed waitresses stand at the bar, waiting for us to get settled. The guys are eating it up. The only ones who don't appear to be enjoying it are me and Noah, and by the looks of it he's more miserable to be here than I am.

"You good, man?" I shout over the music. Noah just nods.

I'm not in the mood to get shit-faced tonight so I've paced myself, only having had two beers whereas I lost count after the tenth shot the guys did. I smile to myself knowing the state they're gonna be in tomorrow and having little to no sympathy for them.

We've sat through two girls' routines in the time we've been here—one who went by the name of "Esme" and another called "Destiny." Who knows if they're even their real names or not.

---

It's mayhem in here. Dan started begging to go home about an hour ago and I can't help but laugh at the way his face pales every time his phone goes off. Theo keeps shouting "shots" every five minutes and James is putting the moves on a waitress.

We're like any other typical thirty-six-year-old men—we game, we drink, we mess around. Which is why people find it difficult to comprehend when they discover we're professors, high school teachers, billionaires and lawyers. That we don't sit at home smoking pipes and drinking Cognac. Honestly it couldn't be farther from the truth.

Take me for instance. I'm a nerd, always have been, and I'm proud of that fact. One of my other loves apart from gaming is music, metal to be precise, preferring the nights where I'm at a gig instead of a strip club. So as you can imagine, my ears feel like their bleeding after being subjected to the harsh tones of drum and bass all evening. Hearing the starting track for *The Devil You Know* by *Stone Broken*, I sit up, taking notice that finally, *finally* a decent song is being played.

Turning around in my chair, I peer over at the stage. A light shines on a pole in the middle and I'm not gonna lie, I'm intrigued. A petite, curvy blonde struts out and grabs the pole just as the heavy notes start to kick in. She's wearing more than what the previous acts were, but the added clothing just makes her more alluring.

Her black corset cinches in at the waist, showing off her curves, and images of my hands on her waist as I grab her from behind invade my mind. She's wearing heels, but not ridiculously high ones, ones that look like they give her a bit more height, without the potential to break her neck. She's wearing black boy shorts to finish the outfit, and that ass in those shorts has my dick standing to attention for the first time tonight.

I watch as she spins delicately, one leg wrapping around the pole and the other flicking out behind her. She swings her back leg round in a graceful arc, bringing it forward onto the pole before climbing up to the top and rolling herself into a ball before dropping down at an alarming rate.

I jump up from my chair, ready to shout for help when she stops just before she hits the deck. My heart's thumping, matching the tempo of the music blaring from the speakers. I'm completely mesmerized by this woman. Utterly amazed at her talent.

Sitting back down, hoping no one saw me jump up, she slides down to the floor, coming to land flat on her stomach as she pushes her front half up and kicks her leg up in the air, her ass sticking out, causing her to come into a seated position. She looks up, my eyes locking with hers and the breath leaves me as we share a moment just between the two of us.

She's fucking stunning.

The bright green of her eyes makes me want to drown in them, her face slightly hidden by her hair but from what I can see she looks like she has the face of an angel—*The fuck? When did I become such a sap?* I mentally facepalm myself, but I'm still unable to look away.

She continues on until the end of the song, moving her body in various ways that isn't helping my dick any. Which, might I add, is currently pushing against the confines of my black jeans and urging me to take a closer look. The goddess on stage doesn't look back at me and for reasons unbeknownst to me, it starts to piss me off—I want her eyes on *me*. Surely, that moment wasn't just one sided, right?

She begins walking off the stage and I realize—to my utter dismay—that her act is over.

I hear a commotion behind me, having been completely oblivious to the guys and what they've been up too since seeing her—Dan looks like he's about to puke, James is chasing after yet another waitress, Noah is glued to his phone and Theo is taking it all in with a huge shit-eating grin that says, "my job here is done."

I drain the rest of my beer and go in search of the mystery woman.

## Chapter Five

## Lauren

After getting off the stage, I grab a towel and a bottle of water to try and cool off. Even after spending the last four years pole dancing, I still work up one hell of a sweat. It's the only way I'm able to keep my curvy body in shape with all the food I eat.

Swallowing the last of my water, I throw the bottle in the trash and stroll to the dressing room. The other girls are all flitting around—hair, make-up, applying body glitter—which is *so* hard to wash off, by the way.

Esme's in the center of the room yanking her leggings on before she heads home. "Motherfucking, bastard things," she grumbles under her breath causing me to snort.

"Uh, Esme? You okay there, hun?" This girl has always had the ability to make me cackle with her crazy antics.

"Whoever invented these fucking things had to have been a man. Do you know how hard it is to put my beautiful thick thighs into these things? I feel like Ross from Friends with the leather pants. Hey,

Destiny... find me some talc will ya!" she shouts, her hand slipping and slapping her on the forehead.

Annnd I'm done.

The laugh I've been holding in can no longer be contained, bursting free as I laugh so hard tears stream down my face, ruining my makeup at the image of Esme greasing herself up.

Once I've managed to compose myself, I stand up and change out of my corset, putting my bra on before deciding that I really need to use the restroom. The water I'd drunk, apparently, going through me rather quickly.

As I'm heading down the hallway I hear a noise. Everyone is either out front or in the dressing rooms, so I'm hit with a feeling of apprehension.

*I swear these hallways need better lighting because, fuck, it's dark out here.*

I spin around trying to find where the noise came from, when I see a tall figure appear from the shadows. I can't see him clearly, but I can tell from his build and the way he holds himself that he's one of the guys here with the bachelor party tonight. They all had this kind of... aura about them, and he's giving off the same vibes.

"Fuck me sideways. Give a girl some notice before you sneak out of the shadows like that. I'm all for shadow daddies but for fuck sake," I shriek, clutching my chest and wondering if I'm going into cardiac arrest—I hope not, I'm too pretty to die.

I'm not even going to *think* about the oversharing of my love for shadow daddies. If he's creeping around in the dark, he's got to expect me to react that way, right?

"Sorry," the mysterious man chuckles. "I saw you on stage and—fuck, I don't even know what I was going to do," he says as he swipes a hand through his hair.

He steps further into the light, and I gasp. My mouth falls open and I stand there stunned. I'd caught glances of him while I was on stage and we may have even locked eyes for a moment, but between me dancing and the flashing lights, I wasn't able to get a good enough look, and fuck if I don't stare.

*The man is freaking gorgeous.*

Tall, muscular, tattooed, dark hair—did I hit my head and wake up in one of my romance books because, *damn*.

He looks older than me. I'm twenty but I'd put him in his late thirties/early forties. I've never been into older men before, but I suddenly feel like I could be converted.

His dark hair is closely shaved at the sides, a mop of hair on top which is just begging for my hands to be run through it. Blue eyes surrounded by dark eyelashes that rest on high cheekbones and full, luscious lips complete the absolute god that stands before me.

I pick my jaw up off the floor and clear my throat. "Erm, yeah... I mean... okay," I stammer, my brain clearly not engaging with my mouth as I gape at the gorgeous specimen in front of me. "I'm finished for the night and we don't offer private rooms," I tell him quickly, before he gets the wrong idea. I've been propositioned too many times to count, but something about the guy in front of me is different. He doesn't creep me out the way other guys do. Why? I don't know.

"Good to know," he laughs as he stalks further forward, hand outstretched. "I'm Caleb."

I stare at his hand for longer than is probably polite, I blame my pussy for taking over my brain. I'm no virgin... I mean, I lost my virginity to Chad Montgomery in the back of his SUV when I was eighteen, but it was so uninspiring I never did it again.

Shaking my head from my errant thoughts I place my hand in his, a bolt of something, almost like static shock, races up my arm at the contact. *What the fuck?* I quickly remove my hand from his grip and hold it to my chest, taking a step back and bumping into the wall behind me.

"Lauren," I say, and I wonder if maybe I should start using an alias while I'm working, like the other girls do.

Caleb moves in closer, the blue of his eyes becoming brighter the closer he gets. Eyes that, I swear to god, I lose myself in for a minute. The nearer he gets, the more I need to look up at him. I'm 5'4" but he's got to be 6'2" easily. I crane my neck to get a closer look—chiseled jawline and dimples. *Fucking dimples.* Caleb smirks at me, catching me checking him out. He's so close now that if I were to stand on my tiptoes our lips would touch.

*When did he get so close?*

I take in a deep breath to slow my racing heart, but my eyes roll to the back of my head instead. The man smells amazing—leather, wood and cinnamon. I don't think I've ever smelt anything like it before. I love it and my pussy agrees.

I open my eyes and see Caleb watching me, lust filling his gaze before resting his hands on either side of my head, and leaning in to whisper, "Fuck, you're beautiful."

I'm not sure whether my brain decides to take a leave of absence, and my pussy takes over or if it's him that makes the first move, but suddenly we're kissing—hands groping, teeth clashing, tongues dueling—kinda kissing. My hands tangle in his hair, and I press myself closer to him, deepening the kiss.

Caleb groans into my mouth and I don't think I've heard a sexier sound. My panties are soaked, and my pussy is throbbing, begging for him to touch me.

He brings his hands down to grab my waist when footsteps and laughter bring me back to the hallway—fuck, the hallway!

I drag myself away from his lips, gasping for air. Caleb gazes down at me, his pupils blown wide with desire and I gulp at the intensity. I disentangle myself and take a step back.

"Sorry, uh—fuck," I manage to choke out. "I'm gonna"—I gesture behind me—"go."

I swivel on my heel and run the hell away. I hear "Wait" being shouted behind me but I keep going.

Basically jogging to get away from the mind shattering encounter, I grab the door handle to the bathroom, practically ripping it off its hinges in my haste to get inside. I slam the door behind me, rushing to the sink and splashing cold water on my face.

*What the fuck just happened? I don't do shit like this.*

I peer up at my reflection, my hair's a mess, my pupils wide and my makeup—that I'd painstakingly reapplied after the Esme laughing incident—is smudged. I breathe in and breathe out slowly.

There was something about Caleb that I just couldn't say 'no' to. The attraction that I'd felt toward him as soon as he stepped out of the shadows was instantaneous.

Don't get me wrong, I've dated since Chad and his SUV. Hell, I've been hit on at the club more times than I can count but nothing like this has happened—the overwhelming *need* to be as close to someone as possible. Usually after two dates I'm done. I just don't feel... anything. But with Caleb, I wanted to climb him like a damn jungle gym.

The bathroom door opens pulling me from my thoughts...

# Chapter Six

## *Caleb*

The fuck?

I watch, dumbfounded, as Lauren runs off. I scrape a hand down my jaw and grasp the back of my neck, pacing the small hallway and debating whether to go after her or not.

*That kiss.* I've never had such an intense reaction to someone before. My dick is rock hard and I'm desperate to get my hands back on her, to feel her supple skin—that I only had a short taste of—beneath my hands. I'm warring with myself, weighing up the pros and cons until...

"Fuck it."

I race down the hall and shove open the door that Lauren went into. She's standing at the sink still wearing most of her stage outfit, though she's swapped out the corset for a barely there bra and boy shorts. She spins around, surprise on her face as she sees me.

Without looking back, I lock the door behind me.

Lauren raises an eyebrow and crosses her arms. "What are you doing in here, Caleb? This is the girl's bathroom." She uncrosses her arms and starts pacing, pointing at me as she adds, "I don't even know you."

Shaking my head, my smile widens. "Oh, baby girl. In about thirty seconds you're going to know me *real* well." She visibly swallows at the term 'baby girl.'

I stride toward her, my long legs eating up the distance between us as I grip a handful of her hair and tug her toward me, crushing my lips to hers and just like the kiss in the hallway, I become lost in her. The smell of strawberries and vanilla quickly becoming a taste I could get addicted to, even after one kiss.

And she's mine. At least for tonight, anyway.

Lauren initially tries to push me away but quickly changes her mind, pulling me closer by my shirt. My cock is aching and if I don't get some relief soon, I'm gonna be coming in my pants like a prepubescent teenager.

Her whimpers spur me on as I trail my other hand down her collarbone to her chest before landing on her right breast—just the perfect amount to fill my hand. I tweak her nipple, causing a delicious moan to escape her pretty lips.

"That's it, baby girl. Let me hear you," I command as I tug her bra down, her breast popping out as I lower my head and take the hard bud into my mouth. Lauren arches her back, her hands grabbing my hair, trying to bring me closer. I let go of her nipple with a pop.

"Caleb," she whines.

"What do you need, sweetheart? You need me to make you come?" I ask as I drop to my knees and hook one leg over my shoulder. She gasps as she puts one hand on my shoulder and the other back in my hair, guiding me to where she wants me.

"Please," she whimpers.

"Please what?" I ask again, placing kisses along her thigh. "I'm gonna need your words here, sweetheart. What do you need?"

"Make me come. I need you to make me come."

*Your wish is my command.*

I shove her boy shorts and panties to the side where I can see her juices glistening, my mouth instantly watering at the sight. I lick a line from her ass to her clit, Lauren's breathy moans sounding like music to my ears as I dive in like a man eating his last meal. Sucking her clit, my eyes roll back in my head at the taste of her. Her musky, sweet smell sends me into a feral frenzy as I lick and suck her clit in varying patterns before adding a finger into her tight cunt.

I pump my finger in and out, my tongue never leaving her clit. Adding in a second finger, I curl it around to find her G-spot, reveling in the way she tightens around me as I hit that spot deep inside her.

"Fuck. Caleb," she moans. The sound is so fucking erotic that it makes me groan in response. "I'm gonna come."

"That's it, come all over my face like a good girl," I growl, my warm breath blowing on her clit.

Lauren's legs shake as her climax gets closer, her breath coming in soft, uneven gasps just before she comes with a long, loud moan. Not wanting to waste a single drop, I keep tongue fucking her, almost smothering my face in her cunt. She starts squirming and gently trying to push me away, so I reluctantly wrench myself back, wiping my face, and glancing up to see a blissed-out expression on her face.

Gradually setting her leg back down on the floor, I hold onto her trembling body, kissing my way back up to her neck before I grab her ass and lift her up. I manage to undo my belt and unzip my jeans with one hand as I dip my head down and take her exposed nipple in my mouth. Lauren starts whimpering, rubbing her pussy against my

T-shirt as I take a condom from my wallet—no easy task when you have a beautiful woman writhing in your arms.

Pulling my leaking cock free, I roll the condom on before lining it up with her entrance, gritting out, "Last chance to back out, baby girl."

Lauren gazes at me through hooded eyes, the corners of her mouth quirking up into a smirk. "Just fuck me already, Caleb."

I don't give her any warning as I thrust into her, both of us groaning. Her pussy's like heaven and I'm two seconds away from busting a nut—*grandma, smelly socks, paper grading*, I chant in my head.

Kissing my neck, she breathes out, "Caleb? I really need you to move."

Finally getting myself under control, I gently ease my way out of her before pushing back in, her little mewls of pleasure making me thrust into her harder, faster. I grab both her ass cheeks and fuck her against the wall like my life depends on it, like she's the oxygen I need to breathe and without her, I'll suffocate.

I suck at the curve of her neck, my voice thick with desire as I growl, "Fuck, Lauren, you feel so good. I need you to come one more time for me, baby girl. Can you do that for me?"

I feel her walls fluttering around my cock and I know she's close. My hips slam forward as I reach down and rub her clit that's still slick from my tongue.

"Shit, I'm gonna come again," she pants out, just as she climaxes, her walls pulsing and squeezing around me, making her already tight pussy even tighter.

A tingle starts to form at the base of my spine and my balls draw up. "Fuck... Lauren," I roar, my vision going white as I paint the inside of the condom with my cum.

I capture her lips in a heated kiss, both of us still breathing heavily. I slowly pull out, watching as Lauren winces and lower her down onto shaking legs. Clutching some towels from the nearby dispenser, I go to clean her up.

"I can do it," Lauren says sheepishly, her eyes bloodshot, her lips puffy and her hair a tangled mess, giving her that thoroughly 'I just got fucked in the bathroom' look.

If I could go again right now, I'd be seriously tempted to bend her over the sink and take her from behind, making her watch in the mirror as I completely ruined her.

"Baby girl, let me do this." She must be able to hear the determination in my tone as she nods her head, giving me permission to take care of her.

Once I've finished cleaning her up, she straightens out her clothes while I get my own back in place, noticing a wet patch on my T-shirt from where she was rubbing against me earlier.

Suddenly there's a knock on the door, making Lauren jump. "Hello, is there anyone in there?"

She whips her gaze to me, a horrified expression on her face, before swallowing and shouting, "Sorry, Destiny. Be two seconds." A flush spreads across her cheeks and she smirks. "Well... this has been fun."

I laugh, bending down to kiss her softly. "Yeah, baby girl, it was." I drag myself away from her, grinning.

Her lips curve into a soft smile and she tucks a stray hair behind her ear before passing me by and sauntering to the door. "See ya around," she calls over her shoulder as she slips into the darkness of the hallway.

I stand there with a goofy smile attached to my face until I realize I never got her number, and by the time I head back out into the club to find her, she's gone.

## Chapter Seven

## *Lauren*

Waking up the next morning, I roll over, checking the time and wonder why I'm so sore, wincing at the ache in my lady bits. Then it comes rushing back to me—Caleb and our dirty bathroom sex. I flop back onto the bed and replay everything over in my head. The man made me come not once, but *twice*. I can't even do that by myself with my vibrator.

Sighing, I throw back my covers and swing my legs out of bed, padding to the kitchen in desperate need of coffee. Sydney must be up because there's a fresh pot brewed. Have I already said how absolutely amazing she is?

I sit on the sofa, sipping my coffee, trying to wake myself up when Sydney breezes through the door, fresh from her shower.

"Morning," she sings. Did I mention Sydney's a morning person? She's like sunshine and rainbows this girl. I'm not even remotely human until I've had at least three cups of coffee, but I guess that's why we work—opposites attract and all.

I yawn, before grumbling, "Morning." Leaning my head back on the couch, I watch Sydney rummage through her stuff looking for god knows what.

Stopping what she's doing, she walks over to the kitchen and pours herself a coffee. "How was last night?" she asks, leaning against the countertop and blowing on the mug.

"Good. One of the waitress's said the bachelor party got drunk, started a fight and one of them puked over security as they were being led outside. Just your usual Saturday night." I let out a very un-lady-like snort at the reminder.

Sydney chuckles. "God, I don't know how you do it, girl."

"You know I'm only there for the money. The tips are good, and the hours suit me." I shrug as I finish the last of my coffee and move to grab another cup. "Are you rehearsing this week?"

"Yeah. The showcase is coming up soon, so I need to make sure I've got everything perfected. It just sucks with this new dance instructor. She's a complete bitch, Lo! I swear she's trying to make my life hell one plié at a time," she groans, throwing herself dramatically onto the sofa. "I don't even know what I did to offend her but offend her I did." She rolls her eyes before they land back on me. She sits up abruptly, a calculative expression on her face. "Erm, Lo? What's that on your neck?"

I lift a hand to my neck, confused. "Huh?"

"That! The great big fucking hickey on your neck! Bitch, have you been holding out on me?" she asks as she jumps up from the couch and runs over to me, moving my neck from side to side to get a better look.

"Get off," I laugh, batting her hand away and ducking out of reach. "It's nothing." I have two options: tell Sydney the truth about my hookup or deny everything. "Erm... I fell over?" I pose it as a question, hoping like fuck she'll believe me.

Unfortunately, she knows me well enough to know when I'm lying. Which means she's currently standing in front of me, hands on hips, waiting for my reply.

"Spill it," she demands, quirking an eyebrow.

"Fine! I might have, sort of, hooked up with someone from the club last night." The last part tumbles out in a slew of words that get quieter and quieter as I speak.

Sydney screams and I have to cover my ears to save myself from her screeching. "Oh my god!" She jumps up and down, her arms flapping around like a bird about to take flight. "Tell me everything. You haven't gotten laid since Whatshisface, so I'm gonna need all the details here."

Sighing, I tell her how I met Caleb in the hallway, how he followed me into the bathroom and what happened after.

Once I'm finished, Sydney asks, "Are you gonna see him again?"

"Of course not!" I exclaim. "It was a complete one off. I don't even know what came over me, Syd. I don't do that sort of thing. I swear I was dickmatized. He just flashed those damn dimples at me, and I was a goner, my pussy doing all the talking for me." I groan, slapping a hand to my face in mortification. I can only hope he doesn't return to Strokes to remind me of my blatant hussy ways.

"I mean, I don't see a problem here personally. Sounds like you had a good time with a hot guy. I approve," Sydney replies with a nod and a wicked smile. I'm debating on whether to slap her or kiss her... I'm leaning toward the former.

"You would, Syd. You'll fuck just about anything that moves," I tease.

"I resent that statement," she cries in mock outrage. Walking over to the couch she sits down before saying, "But seriously, are you gonna see him again?" She looks at me expectantly, hand under her chin as she leans against the arm of the sofa.

"No," I sigh, sitting down opposite her, with my coffee. "I didn't get his number. It was epic sex but that's it. I'm not looking for anything."

Now it's Sydney's turn to sigh. "Just remember that there's more to life than books, okay?" she softly says, a look of concern passing across her face.

"Okay," I agree, because really, what else can I say?

Growing up all I had were my books. I'm the typical trailer girl who worked hard to get a scholarship to a university miles away from home. My mom was never around and my dad? I never met him. Mom said I was the product of a one-night stand, or that was what she told me when she was sober and around long enough to actually have a conversation with me.

Sydney pushes up from the sofa and places a comforting hand on my arm before grabbing her bag and discarded coffee from the counter. "Right, I've got rehearsals, so I'll be out until later."

I just nod, lost in thought.

---

I spent the rest of Sunday poring over my books in the hopes that I'd forget about Caleb, but it didn't happen. Flashbacks of his hands on me, gripping my ass while his face was shoved between my thighs on a constant repeat. My vibrator had never seen so much action before and after the fifth attempt to get myself off, with no result, I gave up.

*I'm just destined to become a nun.*

Monday rolled round quicker than I'd like, my alarm going off at an ungodly hour to get ready. Once showered, I quickly get dressed in my leggings and Bullet For My Valentine hoodie—a staple in my wardrobe. The sleeves are now frayed slightly and the logo has faded due to so much wear.

I shove the books I need for the day into my bag, going over my class schedule in my head—my first lecture with Professor Anderson is this morning. Groaning at the thought, I decide to treat myself, so I take a slow walk to the new coffee shop that's opened on campus—The Honey Pot.

The place is heaving when I get there, many students and professors with the same idea—grabbing a coffee before their first class of the day. I order a coffee—black, like my soul—in the biggest cup they sell, grab it and start the small hike to class.

Bringing the hot coffee to my mouth, I blow on it before taking a tentative sip, not wanting to burn my tongue. The slight breeze rustles my messy bun and causes a chill to run down my spine. *I should have worn a coat.*

I take Psychology 101 in one of the smaller, more tight knit classrooms while this class and English lit are in one of the many auditoriums. I hate Psychology, wanting to take literally *any* other course, but my high school guidance counsellor advised me to take it.

Marveling at the inside of Abingdon University never gets old, with its sleek and modern inside, this is the kind of stuff I could only dream about as a kid.

Holding my coffee in one hand, I use the other to open the door into Professor Anderson's class and take a seat in the middle row. The large room starts filling up, the hustle and bustle of students opening their bags, talking, and getting set up ringing in my ears as I slowly drink my coffee.

I rest my head back and close my eyes when I hear a *very* familiar voice.

"Everyone, assignments are due this week."

Fuck! It can't be!

I jerk my head so quickly I'm pretty sure I've just given myself whiplash. Rubbing my neck to ease the ache, I then rub my eyes, hoping like fuck I'm dreaming. I give myself a swift slap for good measure.

Nope. Not a dream.

Because standing front and center is none other than Caleb. What the hell? My heart hammers in my chest, giving me that tight feeling as the realization hits me... hard—I slept with my professor.

"We have a new student joining us today, and you know how much I love to embarrass people," he chuckles. "Miss Taylor, would you stand up and introduce yourself please." Caleb glances around the room searching for the newcomer's face—*my* face.

I shrink down in my chair, cursing myself that I didn't think to put my hood up to hide myself further. His eyes finally settle on me, and if it wasn't for the shit storm of a situation we now find ourselves in, I'd laugh at his expression because it can only be described as a cartoon with its eyes bugging out.

His friendly expression shuts down quickly, his features neutral as he clears his throat. "Miss Taylor?" Caleb pauses, watching me before slowly running his tongue across his bottom lip. I'm so entranced with the act that I end up mirroring him and running *my* tongue across *my* bottom lip. I look up from his mouth, finding his gaze still firmly on me and the world seems to stop.

Suddenly breaking our eye contact, Caleb moves to shuffle some papers around on his desk before saying, "See me after class for any missed assignments." With nothing else said, he shifts the conversation onto the upcoming semester.

I finally let out the breath I'd been holding, my ears ringing and my vision going blurry from the clusterfuck of a situation I've got myself into.

*Caleb is Professor Anderson? Professor Anderson is Caleb?*

I spend the rest of class unable to concentrate, the low timbre of his voice going straight to my clit. I'm lucky Caleb doesn't glance my way again because I don't think I'd be able to hide the emotions on my face. No matter how hard I try, I can't get the image of his head between my thighs to budge. I'm completely tense and I'm pretty sure I'm gonna have to change my underwear before my next class. Which is really freaking annoying seeing as the man is completely untouchable now.

When the bell rings, I hastily put everything into my bag, but a pen drops to the floor before I can catch it. Dropping down under my desk, I grab the runaway item and I shove it in my bag. As I stand up, I notice that the auditorium has all but cleared out, leaving Caleb and I alone.

*So much for getting out before he saw me.*

"Miss Taylor, a word please."

Slowly turning round to face him, I plaster a fake smile on. "Erm, sure."

Cal—Professor Anderson strolls around his desk, perching on the edge, his arms moving to fold across his chest as he looks at me, his face stoic and unreadable. My heart races, as my gaze lingers on him. It should be illegal for this man to look as good as he does. He's wearing a white shirt with the sleeves down, hiding the tattoos that I kno—*stop, Lauren. Do not check out your professor, even if he did give you the best orgasms of your life.*

He continues staring at me, an eyebrow now raised as he catches me eyeing him up and I suddenly wish I was a mind reader—I have no clue how this is going to go.

I bite my bottom lip—a nervous habit I've had since forever—and Caleb's eyes darken, his gaze following my movements.

"Is your name even Lauren?" he asks as he stands to his full height, anger radiating off him in waves and causing me to curl in on myself. Confrontation isn't my thing, preferring to run away at all costs.

"Yes, I don't use a stage name like the other girls," I reply, wringing my hands together, my head toward the floor unable to meet his gaze.

Caleb goes quiet as he rubs his hand across his chin, like he's mulling over what I've said.

*This is so awkward right now.*

I start shuffling from one foot to the other, waiting for him to say something, but as soon as he does, I wish he'd kept his mouth shut.

"Hmm," he muses. "Do you sleep with all of your clientele?" he asks, and my hackles rise.

Swinging my head toward him, I snap, "Excuse me? Where the hell do you get off talking to me like that?"

What the fuck? I know this is an awkward fucking situation to be in but who the hell does he think he is? My cheeks are bright red, I can feel the heat blazing from them, both from anger *and* embarrassment. I mean, who sleeps with their professor? Okay, I didn't know he was my professor when I slept with him, but still.

He exhales roughly, running a hand through his hair. "Look, I'm sorry alright? It's not every day the best sex of my life happens to be one of my students," he explains, his tone softening.

"Still doesn't excuse being an asshole though," I snark, before blowing out a breath and relaxing my body slightly. I know this isn't *all* his fault. The blame lies with me, as well.

He nods. "No, you're right. I'm just a bit thrown off. This could seriously damage both of us—my job, your scholarship—if this was to get out," he states.

I sigh, rubbing a hand across my forehead. "I know," I whisper, the fight from earlier leaving me. "I don't plan on telling anyone if that's what you're worried about. Plus it's not like it's going to happen again." I look at him pointedly and I swear his jaw clenches.

"Definitely not happening again," he agrees, and I'd believe him if it wasn't for the same desperate hunger in his eyes that he had *that* night. I try to ignore the heated flush that spreads over my cheeks *again*. I swear that's all I do around this man.

This is *wrong*. On so many levels. I cannot lose my scholarship. Everything depends on me passing and making a good life for myself. I refuse to end up like my mom.

I'm breathing heavily, my hands clammy as we both lock eyes, neither one looking away as I wait for him to say something.

Finally he says, "So, we act like this never happened."

"Yes," I agree. Even though that couldn't be farther from the truth. How do you forget a night that's seared into your brain? A night that you will relive over and over in your head for the rest of your life?

He clenches his jaw again, a decision being made behind his eyes as he announces, "You need to catch up on assignments. My TA, Brad, is busy so you'll need to come in once a week for extra sessions with me." He goes to his desk and shuffles some papers around, before handing me a sheet of paper. "Here is this semester's reading material. Look at it and we'll meet next week to discuss it."

Clearly I've been dismissed. Annoyed, I turn and leave, heading for my next class. I wish I could say it didn't hurt, because it does. In no world will we *ever* be together. I just need to forget about Caleb and move on with my life.

# Chapter Eight

## Caleb

"Fuck," I shout as I ram my fist into the boxing bag hung up in my garage. I needed some way to get out the excess rage that's been boiling away since Lauren waltzed out of my class a week ago.

Seeing her that first day was like a punch to the gut. I'd been obsessing over her for the rest of the weekend, resolved come Sunday night to go back and find her again, to get her number and ask her out. But I'd gotten so caught up in grading papers that I didn't make it back.

I'd be fucked, though, if I had any inkling that the woman who rocked my world on Saturday, is a fucking student—*my* fucking student.

I hit the bag again before snatching up my towel and water and heading inside for a cold shower.

Once showered and dressed in a loose fitting T-shirt and gray sweatpants, I head into the kitchen, pulling out the many takeaway menus from the drawer next to the oven. Brushing a strand of wet hair out of my face I prop myself up against the counter, crossing my arms, thoughts of food put on hold, as the situation with Lauren really fucks with my head.

I'd spent my life busting my ass to get to this point—becoming a professor and making something of myself. Getting a scholarship to Harvard University was a game changer for me. Because of my good grades I was able to start teaching and worked my way up to professor in only a few years. Another reason why things with me and Samantha didn't work—I was more interested in my academic career than being a boyfriend and socializing. She wasn't the one. I knew it then and so did she, but we kept going, hoping things would change—they didn't.

My phone rings, jerking me out of my reminiscing.

"Theo, what's up, man?" I answer.

"Boys are meeting for a beer. You in?"

Pushing myself off the counter, I pace around my kitchen, contemplating the idea. "I'm not sure. It's been a long week and I just wanna crash."

"No problem, I told em you wouldn't be up for it anyway. Strip clubs ain't your scene," he guffaws.

My ears perk up. "Strip club?"

"Yeah, James is in a funk over some chick," he scoffs.

"I'll meet you there." Could Lauren be working tonight? I can turn around and leave if she is.

*Keep telling yourself that.*

"Wow, dude. That was a quick change of mind," he laughs. "Everything okay over there? Should I be worried?"

"Yeah, all good, man. Just decided to change my mind is all," I chuckle. "I'll get changed and head over." I hang up, not wanting to answer any more questions, because honestly, I don't even know why I'm going either.

# NEVER LET GO

Lauren is strictly off limits. Forbidden. Not allowed. So why can't I stop thinking about whether she'll be there tonight or not?

---

Striding into Strokes I see the guys sitting front and center—typical. Heading over to the wannabe frat boys, I notice they've already ordered for me, knowing I was on my way.

Noah lifts his head as I sit down next to him, giving me a confused look. "Why the change of mind?" he asks, hands free of his phone for once—how unusual.

"Just needed to get out. It's been a rough week." Running my hand down my face, I sigh before taking a long swig of my beer. "Where's James?" I ask no one in particular.

"Chasing some barmaid. I swear that boy's dick is gonna fall off one of these days from overuse," Noah says.

"Woah, Noah... do I detect a hint of jealousy there?" Theo pipes up.

Noah raises an eyebrow and leans back in his chair, crossing his arms as he smirks. "I get more action than you do, fuck face. When was the last time you got any... that wasn't your hand?"

Theo starts spluttering and I bring my hand up to my mouth to hide my smile. Theo fell in love years ago but we don't talk about it. Since then, he's sworn off women, using his pent-up energy to get himself and *us* into trouble whenever he can.

The lights dim and the next act comes on. It's not Lauren. I know I shouldn't feel disappointed, but I do. My career is everything to me, I refuse to lose it over a student, even if she's the hottest thing I've ever seen. Regardless of whether Lauren's of legal age doesn't matter, people will assume I've groomed her, coerced her.

James comes back to the table and basically throws himself down in his chair. "She's not interested," he huffs, clearly put out that someone would dare say "no" to James Smith—shock, horror.

I clap him on the back. "Better luck next time, bro." You'd think these guys were twenty-something not coming up to forty with the way they act.

I stay for another couple of hours and even though I'm with the guys, my best friends, my mood starts sinking lower and lower every moment that passes when Lauren doesn't show. Leaving the guys to the rest of their evening, I head home and wallow in peace.

# Chapter Nine

## *Lauren*

After my run in with Caleb last week, I've tried to keep my head down. He's not been back to Strokes, or not on the nights I've been working, anyway.

I've been over the reading list he gave me and it seems easy enough. I've got my first 'session' with him today. I'm not relishing the idea of being alone with him considering the one and only time we were together, we ended up fucking in a bathroom. Apparently, we can't be trusted.

I don't bother wearing anything fancy, opting for my trusty sweatpants and hoodie with my hair thrown up in a messy bun. Checking the time I realize I need to leave soon, and if I'm really quick, I can make a stop at the Honey Pot on my way.

I get to the coffee shop and order my usual, even going so far as to push the boat out and treat myself to a Danish.

I make my way over to Daniels Hall, where I'm meeting Caleb, quickly eating on the way. It starts drizzling, so I tug my hood up and hunch in on myself. For a stripper, I'm not overly confident, I show people what I want them to see at Strokes, but outside? Outside, I'm quiet and generally not a people person.

Entering the building, I place my bag on the floor, and take off my hoodie, shivering from the cold that's seeped in. Tying the hoodie around my waist, I sling my bag back over my shoulder and resume the walk to Caleb's office. I stand outside taking a couple of deep, calming breaths before raising my hand and knocking.

"It's open," I hear muffled from within. My hand tightens around the door handle and I push it open.

Caleb's sitting at his desk—*holy fuck! Is he wearing glasses?* I do a double take and sure enough he is, which only adds to his appeal. *Stop it!* I internally chastise myself. *He's your professor, he's your professor*, I chant over and over.

He looks up and when he sees it's me, takes his glasses off, pointing at them. "I, uh, only wear them for reading."

*Is he blushing?*

He stands up and gestures to the chair in front of his desk. "Have a seat."

Sitting down, I lay my bag on my lap and wait for him to continue. My gaze strays to the window as he sits in his own chair.

"Did you manage to look over the reading material I gave you?" he asks.

I glance back at him and nod my head. "Yeah, I did."

"Good. Is there anything that you're unsure of?" he questions. I watch the gentle curve of his lips as he speaks, mesmerized.

"Uh, one thing I didn't get," I say as I rummage through my bag. Finding what I'm looking for, I hand him a piece of paper with the reading materials on it. "This."

Caleb rounds the desk and bends down to look, and my heart stops at how near he is. He looks over what I've pointed to and I take the time to study him—his day-old stubble, his strong jawline, and the gray hairs that have started to pepper his temple—something I missed while at Strokes.

He turns his head to look at me, our faces inches apart, breaths mingling as our lips nearly touch. Caleb clears his throat, and I gaze up at him, only just realizing that I was staring at his lips.

Our gazes are still locked as he whispers, "Lauren."

I feel like I'm in a dreamlike state as I hum in response. "Hmm?"

"You, uh..." He trails off, staring at me.

"What?" I breathe out.

"You have something on your face." He smiles and I sit bolt upright, hastily wiping at my face for the offending item.

Caleb laughs at my behavior, and when I say Caleb laughs, I'm talking full-on belly, clutching at his sides, tears in his eyes, kinda laughter. And I. Am. *Mortified*.

I watch Caleb, noticing how handsome and carefree he looks. How much younger it makes him seem, and a warm pool of *something* settles in my stomach. His eyes hold a world of knowledge and I'm suddenly desperate to know him.

"I'm so sorry, Lauren," he gasps between breaths. "Your face." He doubles over with laughter again and it makes me chuckle with him.

"Stop it," I laugh. "It's not funny."

Once Caleb has managed to stop laughing, he grins at me. "Oh, but it really is." His blue eyes twinkle with mirth, those fucking dimples making a show, and I'm floored. Stunned speechless. No man should ever look this good.

Chuckling, Caleb tilts his head and begins explaining about the assignment. I zone out as he talks. My eyes wander to his hands, that are placed on the desk in front of me, as he points to the words. The veins on them are raised, making me want to trace every single one of them with my tongue.

"Hopefully that makes sense?" he asks, standing up to his full height and taking a step back.

I feel my cheeks grow hot as he looks at me. I swallow knowing I need to agree with what he's said, but in all honesty, I didn't catch a word. "Erm, any chance you can repeat that, please?" I duck my head away from his gaze, embarrassment clear in my tone.

He eyes me like he knows where my thoughts had gone but doesn't call me out on it. *Thank fuck.*

"So this will need a ten thousand word dissertation on why *Pride and Prejudice* was advanced for its years, along with your thoughts on the book. What you liked. What you think could be improved on the writing technique and storyline."

I gape at him. "But Pride and Prejudice is one of the greats. It's impossible to try and say what's wrong with it—*nothing* is wrong with it," I state incredulously.

"Ah, see that, right there"—he points a finger at me, his eyes lighting up— "is the beauty of writing, Lauren. Just because *you* loved it, doesn't mean that others will. Some say that it's a superb piece of writing. Others will argue that it's not. I want to see what *you* think could be improved on. Think outside of the box. Look at it from another person's perspective. Find the stuff you *don't* love about it and go from there. Writing is subjective, Miss Taylor, tell me why."

Leaning my head on my hand, I have to know. "What do *you* like and dislike about it, then?" Sitting up, I add, "For research purposes, of course."

"Well for starters, I love the fact that it was written by a woman, in a time when writing was incredibly taboo. Women were only allowed to have babies and to speak when spoken to."

I nod my head in agreement. "Jane Austen was ahead of her time, that's for sure," I muse.

"Absolutely. One thing I didn't like... Mr. Collins." Caleb visibly shudders and I laugh. "That man was a complete menace to society."

Watching Caleb talking so animatedly about one of my favorite things, makes my stomach flutter and my chest warm. It's easy to see why people gravitate toward him, he has this... energy about him that keeps you wanting more.

Caleb notices me staring and almost like a light has gone off in his head, he clears his throat and says, "I've got to go. I have a meeting." He looks at me for a minute, his hands in his pocket—like it's a nervous habit—his gaze unreadable. "Same time next week?"

I nod. "Of course. I'll just grab my things and go. Thank you for... this." *This? Thank you for this?* What does that even *mean*?

I stand up and start backing toward the door, my bag dangling from my hand as Caleb stands by his desk, watching me leave, and I'm suddenly struck with the thought that I wish he wasn't my professor at all.

# Chapter Ten

## *Caleb*

Why does it feel like Lauren's always walking away from me? First in the hallway, then the bathroom at Strokes and now here. I lied when I said I had a meeting. I could've sat there with her for hours, forgetting that she was a student until it hit me that she was, in fact, a student. One that I had to get away from quickly, lest I do something I'll regret—like kiss the living shit out of her until we're both a panting mess.

Sitting at my desk, I run a hand through my hair, thoughts of our—brief—time together going through my mind. I haven't laughed with someone like that in… well, ever. The guys don't count. I'm talking about someone of the female variety. The way she smiled at me made my heart pound in my chest and I never wanted her to stop looking at me like that.

If she was *any* other woman I'd be asking her on a date, wanting to know more about her and what makes her, *her*. The tension that I've felt for the past week gone—poof, like it never existed and it's all down to her. But I know this isn't going to end well. Us riding off into the sunset together isn't an option, and I need to get my head out of my ass.

It. Can't. Happen.

I straighten out everything on my desk when there's a knock at the door. "Come in," I call out.

Dean Williams walks in looking as smarmy as ever and I internally roll my eyes. The one person I could really do without seeing right now. It's like he knows.

Sitting down in the chair opposite my desk, he crosses one leg over the other and leans back like he owns the place. "Caleb. I just wanted to check in and see how things were coming along with Miss Taylor?"

*They're coming alright*, I think, but don't voice my thoughts.

"Good. She's starting to catch up with everything and seems to be a great addition to the class."

The dean smiles and nods his head once. "Excellent. Anything of concern that should be noted? An errant boyfriend, perhaps?" He looks out the window as he asks the question, almost trying to give off an uninterested vibe, but he's not fooling anyone.

The dark look that crosses his features has me clenching my jaw and I hope to fuck it's not because he's thinking about Lauren. Why the fuck does he need to know if Lauren has a boyfriend or not? It's none of his damn business.

I eye him cautiously, trying not to give any kind of emotion away—something I had years of practice with as a kid. "Not that I'm aware of," I reply warily. "She seems to enjoy her own company from what I've heard."

Dean Williams claps his hands together and stands up, striding to the door. Just as his hand lands on the door handle, he turns back to me with a twisted smile and says, "Thank you for your time. I'll check back in soon."

*I really hope you don't.*

## Chapter Eleven

## *Lauren*

I'm in a daze as I walk out of Caleb's office, the seriousness of the situation not lost on me. Shame over feelings I fear I'm starting to catch are pulsing through my body, slamming into me with the weight of a sledgehammer. Taking a minute, I prop myself up against the nearest wall and take a few calming breaths.

I hear footsteps and I look up to see Dean Williams striding my way. My intuition tells me that I need to keep as far away from this man as physically possible, which is why I quickly move to the nearest room and wait for him to pass. Once he's gone, I check the hallway, and seeing it's clear, I run toward the exit.

Luckily I'm working tonight so I don't have time to go down the rabbit hole that is Caleb. I need to get home, grab clothes and head in, ignoring any and all thoughts about a certain sexy professor.

Once I get to work, I put myself through my usual routine—hair, makeup and outfit. I chose a more daring red tonight, compared to my usual black. The push up bra, showing my small B cups to perfection and my boy shorts showcasing my ass.

I glance around the dressing room, with its white walls and harsh lighting. Over the past couple of years each of the girls has brought in something to make it feel less sterile—plants, pictures, a fridge, and even a couch with pink fuzzy cushions, though don't ask me where it came from, I prefer not to know.

It's early evening so there's only me and Destiny in until the rest of the girls show up at various other times throughout the night.

Steve, our security guard, is making his rounds. The guy's an absolute sweetheart, even if he's a bit rough around the edges. Steve's the strip club's version of a knight in shining armor—easy on the eyes, too.

Destiny comes off stage and I know I've got about ten minutes until I'm on. Taking a drink from the fridge I sit on the sofa, scrolling through social media. Noticing Sydney posted a picture about an hour ago, I like and comment on it before shutting the app down and putting my phone away.

"It's dead out there tonight, hun," Destiny says as she walks into the dressing room and grabs a bottle of water. "There's one guy in the side booth though, kinda creepy looking." She shudders.

"I thought it would be, it's not kicking out time for the blue collared boys yet," I laugh. "I'll keep an eye out. Steve's around somewhere."

Standing up from my chair I head toward the stage. I've always loved dancing, I'm no Sydney though—that girl can move—I'm more of the 'I know how to dance in a nightclub' kinda girl. I remember walking home from school when I was sixteen and seeing a new gym had opened up. I don't remember how long I stood there for, I just remember being so enamored by the women and how they moved, unable to take my eyes off them as they spun and twirled around the poles.

After a few weeks of watching at the window like a perv, the owner came out. Leah was lithe and beautiful, she had the kindest smile so when she asked me if I wanted to join in, I couldn't say no. Well, I did at first. I couldn't afford the lessons, but she agreed to me cleaning for an hour after each visit. I ended up being there every day it was open. Leah taught me everything I know and leaving her was the only thing I got sad over when I left for university.

The opening notes to *Falling Apart* by *Papa Roach* starts, pulling me out of my thoughts and I move across the stage, slowly moving each foot in a wide circular motion as I walk. My arms move in a wavy motion that almost makes me look like a fairy. Once I hear Jacobi Shaddox start singing, I grab the pole and gyrate up against it, before squatting down and bringing myself back up with my ass sticking out.

I swing my blonde hair around, moving my body fluid with the music. Out of the corner of my eye as I'm performing my routine, I see a man sitting in the front row, the only seat with low enough light that I can't make out his features.

I slide myself to the floor, crawling towards him in an overly dramatic fashion before rolling onto my back and scissoring my legs in the air. I roll myself up, flinging my head back, and standing. Gracefully gliding over to the pole I grab it, spinning around in what's known as a 'fireman's spin'—one hand holding low on the pole, one hand high and my feet together as if I'm sitting cross legged.

I can feel his eyes on me the entire time I'm dancing. I know I'm a stripper and I'm *meant* to have eyes on me, but this is the first time in two years that I've actually felt uncomfortable. A shiver runs down my spine and a sense of foreboding takes over. *Shit, now I'm starting to sound as dramatic as Sydney.*

Finishing off my set, I head backstage, hanging with the girls until I'm on again.

At the end of my shift, I throw on my trusty sweats and hoodie, gathering my hair into a messy bun. I've already ordered an Uber so I head to the main entrance to wait, passing Steve on my way out. "Night, Steve," I say, giving him a small wave.

He stands up from behind his desk, where the cameras are, and says, "Let me walk you out, Lauren."

"Steve, I'll be fine, honestly. The Uber is just round the corner, and you're needed here." I've never felt unsafe in this area, so it doesn't occur to me not to be okay with waiting outside on my own.

"Lauren," he drags out my name, clearly not happy. "I don't like it."

"I love you for wanting to look after me, but I promise I'll be fine… I'm a big girl, Steve." I wink at him.

"Fine. But the minute there's even a slight issue, you get your butt straight back in here. You get me?" He raises an eyebrow at me, crossing his arms over his broad chest to let me know he's serious.

I lean up and kiss his cheek. "You worry too much, but I promise. Any sign of trouble and I'll be straight back." I smile up at him and he just rolls his eyes.

Strolling outside with my phone in one hand, my keys in the other, I breathe in the fresh night air. I quickly make my way through the car park to the main road, so it's easier for my ride to find me.

The streetlights are illuminating the path ahead of me and I stop outside a closed bookshop, leaning my back up against the wall as I check my phone for any updates.

I hear a noise behind me and I jump. Turning to look, I find a dark figure approaching me. *Don't panic, don't panic.* But the closer he gets, the more I recognize him.

Holy fuck.

It's the dean. What's he doing here? I try to conceal my shudder. I've said it before, I'll say it again—the guy gives me the creeps.

He's dressed in an all-black suit, making it easier for him to blend into the shadows. He's got a strange look on his face that only adds to the creepy vibes he's giving off. I tighten my grip on my keys, preparing myself for the worst possible outcome. I'm not saying that he'd do anything to hurt me, but I've heard enough horror stories growing up to know I always need to be prepared.

"Hello, Miss Taylor," he says, a grin pulling at the corner of his mouth giving him what can only be described as a sinister look.

Shifting uneasily, I rush out, "Dean Williams, you scared me."

He steps closer to me, his body lit up by the streetlights, giving him an eerie vibe that has me swallowing hard. "I apologize, that wasn't my intention," he says, his gaze boring into mine.

I gesture to my phone, waving it around slightly. "Uh, I'm just waiting for my ride." I'm now beginning to regret my decision for Steve to wait outside with me.

"Indeed." He nods, smiling toothily at me, a somewhat deranged look in his eyes. "You were fabulous tonight, my dear," he compliments.

"Th-thank you?" It wasn't really a question, but it came out as one. Was he the guy sitting in the front row? Was he the one who spent the entire night watching us and making us feel uncomfortable?

Luckily, my ride turns up before he can say anything else. I wave awkwardly because, really, what else could I do? And jump into the Uber, glad to get away from the unsettling encounter.

# Chapter Twelve

## *Lauren*

"You're gonna be there, right?" Sydney asks nervously the next morning.

I smile at her. "Of course, I wouldn't miss it for the world."

Sydney's midterm showcase is coming up in a few weeks and I know how stressed out she's been with it. I've never missed one of her shows, and I'm not about to start now.

We're sitting in the front window of the Honey Pot, people-watching before class. The place is a small outbuilding on campus, which tends to be more of a takeaway coffee shop than a sit-in one, so the seating's minimal. I love the atmosphere here, though, with its quirky décor and mismatched furniture. It makes the place feel warm and cozy.

"Do you want another one?" I nod towards Sydney's nearly empty cup.

Draining the last of her drink, she holds it out to me. "Please."

Standing up, I take a slow walk over to the counter salivating at the sweet treats, sandwiches, and pasta. Forgoing those I wait for the barista to finish serving another customer when a stunning redhead, with curves to die for, and green eyes brighter than mine, comes and takes my order.

"Hi, what can I get you?"

"A large black coffee and a large, no fat latte, please."

"No problem. Lauren, right?" she asks as she writes my name on the cup.

I smile at her and laugh. "Do I come here that often?"

"Oh, no, not at all," she stutters, her eyes going wide at the thought I might think she's stalking me. "I just meant I've seen you around, in a non-weird, nonsexual way," she fumbles, her face going bright red from her embarrassment.

"It's okay. I get what you mean," I chuckle, and watch as her shoulders relax.

A small smile curves at her lips as she holds out her hand, and I eye it like it's the beginning of the plague. "I'm Raven."

I place my hand in hers as I reply, "Nice to meet you, Raven."

We stand chatting for a few minutes while she makes the coffees—Raven's a physio major working at the Honey Pot part time. I hate talking to people, it's why I don't have many friends, but Raven has this gentle manner about her that has me talking to her like I've known her for years. The last person that happened with was Sydney, so I take it as a good sign.

We're just finishing exchanging numbers and promising to meet up when a voice from behind breaks in.

"Small macchiato, please."

I freeze at the low tone, unmoving before coming to my senses and turning around.

"Ca—Professor Anderson." I swallow, trying to dampen my suddenly dry mouth.

Caleb stands before me wearing a tight white T-shirt, jeans, and black sneakers. He runs his tongue slowly over his bottom lip and I can't help but track the movement, completely enthralled by such a small act. My pussy decides to wake up at that point and I clench my thighs together to dampen down the need for him, but it doesn't work, especially when the corner of his mouth quirks up in a small grin.

I feel like we're in our own bubble, the outside world having faded away as we stand there drinking each other in.

"I'll just get that for you, Professor Anderson," I hear Raven say, but I still can't take my eyes off the man in front of me.

*Heaven help me—stop looking at him!*

"Miss Taylor." He nods as he reaches to pay for his drink. He's close enough that I get a hint of his leather and cinnamon smell. Raven hands him his drink, pulling us out of our staring contest and I watch as he takes a sip, entranced by his Adam's apple as he swallows.

*Why is an Adam's apple just as hot as the veins popping on a man's hands and forearms? I need a new hobby.*

My errant thoughts are interrupted by Sydney. "Woman, where's my coffee? You've been—Dear god, who is this gorgeous man?" she gasps as she eyes Caleb. Even though Sydney's into women, she's always been able to appreciate a man when she thinks he's good looking and, apparently, she thinks Caleb is.

"Erm, Syd, this is my English professor. Professor Anderson."

Caleb grins and offers his hand. "Nice to meet you."

"You didn't tell me he was hot, Lo," Sydney says out the side of her mouth, just loud enough for everyone to hear. Raven stifles a laugh behind her hand.

"Nice to see you, Professor. We need to get going." I grab Sydney by her arm, abandoning the coffees, grabbing our bags and heading for the door, calling out to Raven that I'll text her soon.

"What was that all about?" Sydney exclaims as I try to get us as far away from the shop as quickly as possible.

"Oh, nothing. I have a paper due, and I didn't want him to remember and ask me for it," I stumble out. Guilt for lying to Sydney starts churning in my gut, threatening to bring up my coffee.

I heave out a sigh. Seeing Caleb again is confusing. I mean, he's never far from my thoughts. I have one class with him a week and now my extra lessons, but I can't help how my body reacts to him. It's as if I'm the lighter fluid, and he's the match, ready to burn me with a single look. And even though my dating history is extremely short, I've never reacted this way to *anyone* before.

"I'm going to the library to study," I tell Sydney. "I'll meet you back at the dorm later." I give her a quick kiss on the cheek and make a run for it before she can ask any more questions.

---

Getting to the library, I unpack my bag and place my books on the table. I've put myself in a corner by the window, rows of bookcases surrounding me and shutting me off from everyone.

Lost in my assignment, I jump when the chair in front of me moves, and someone sits down. I peer up, annoyed that someone would disturb me, only to find Caleb eyeing me.

I put my pen down and lean back in my chair, crossing my arms. "You shouldn't be here," I tell him.

He gives me a teasing smile. "I just came to check on how your assignment was coming along," he replies.

I exhale slowly. "Caleb, we can't be seen together. What if someone were to say something?" I sit forward, frantically searching the library to see if anyone's looking our way.

"I'm a professor talking to my student, just as I would in my office, Lauren." Caleb brings his hand to his mouth to hide his smirk. "Call it this week's session."

I sigh and run a hand through my hair, thinking better of it and putting it up in a ponytail. Caleb watches me, his gaze darkening with my movements and staring at my neck for far longer than he should.

He leans back, sprawling out in the chair, arms wide in a relaxed pose. "I read your file. You have a photographic memory." He states this as fact, rather than asking. "Why didn't you get through school earlier? I would have thought you'd have been fast tracked."

Sighing, I place my head on my hand and gaze out the window. "They didn't know. They knew I was good, but I kept it quiet. I didn't want the hassle of people looking into my home life."

"Why not?" he questions, his voice sounding genuinely confused as to why I'd kept it a secret. I glance back at him, his blue eyes drawing me in, begging me to spill my deepest, darkest secrets. But I can't, so I go with vague.

"My home life was... less than desirable shall we say. I kept my 'episodes' to a minimum as best as I could and kept my head down."

He looks thoughtful, before saying, "That must have been very lonely."

"It is what it is." I shrug. "What about you? How did you end up as a professor here?"

"I ended a relationship and needed a fresh start." He shrugs, as if that's answer enough.

I know I shouldn't be interested. I know I shouldn't ask my next question, but I do anyway. "What happened?"

"We weren't right for each other." Caleb shifts slightly in his chair and clears his throat. "I applied for the job and never looked back."

"Would you ever go back? To where you're originally from, I mean?" I'm curious about him. What makes him tick, what makes him... *him*.

"No, I have nothing there. My only real family are my friends, and they slowly followed me out here. Noah's a high school teacher. Theo's a lawyer and James is... I don't actually know what James does, I just know he's a corporate douche." He smiles as he talks about them, his face lighting up, and causing flutters to appear in my stomach.

*No, Lauren. Stop.*

A comfortable silence descends around us when the librarian, Mrs. Rose, comes over, whispering, "Professor Anderson, I'm sorry to bother you but I'm having some trouble with the printer. Would you be able to help me?"

Mrs. Rose is an elderly woman who, from what I've heard, has been here since she left college. She's as tall as I am—meaning not tall at all—with her greying hair pulled back into a severe looking bun, and her dress hanging off her thin frame.

Caleb stands up and turns toward Mrs. Rose. "Of course, Moira." Tapping the table with his knuckles, he glances back at me and softly says, "I'll see you same time next week?"

I nod, wanting him to stay, wanting to talk to him more but knowing we can't. All I know is that no matter how hard I try, I can't seem to shake Caleb Anderson.

# Chapter Thirteen

## Caleb

I'm the closest to Noah, having been best friends with him since we met in kindergarten. Another kid was trying to steal his lunch money so I stepped in, and we've been joined at the hip ever since, which is why I'm now sprawled out on his couch nursing a beer I've barely touched. He's the only one I'd be able to talk to about this, or I hope he will be, anyway.

Noah moved here shortly after me and has been living in the same apartment since. Not many guys would follow their best friends across the country, but he did, not that he had much to give up back home just like the rest of us.

James was the only one of us who was born with a silver spoon in his mouth. Born to rich parents, he had the life we all wanted but thought we could never have. Noah, Theo and I grew up in a trailer park. I'm still not sure how we ended up being a foursome… James was just there one day and that was it, still here over twenty years later.

"You gonna tell me why you're here?" Noah says as he sits on the couch opposite me, leaning back and crossing his ankle over his knee, before taking a sip of his whiskey and giving me the eye.

Thoughts of Lauren have been on a constant loop in my head since I saw her. The shame of wanting her, warring with the need to have her. To make her mine.

I throw my head against the seat, sighing as I rake a hand down my face. "I fucked a student," I blurt, not bothering to look him in the eye knowing what's coming—he's gonna yell at me. Tell me I'm a fucking idiot and to find a new job, but he's silent. Too silent.

I lift my head up and finally look over at him, his face a mask of stoicism. Bracing my forearms on my knees, I play with the wrapping on the beer bottle—*why is this so satisfying?*

He takes another sip of his whiskey. "Did you know she was a student at the time?" he enquires with a tilt of his head.

"No. I met her the night we went out for Dan's bachelor party. One thing led to another and—"

"You ended up balls deep in her," Noah finishes for me.

"Something like that," I mutter. "What the fuck do I do? I can't seem to stay away from her."

Noah swirls his drink around before downing the lot. "You need to cut her loose, man. I'm sorry but you know this will fuck both of you over if you don't. No pussy is worth it."

I tense a little as the words leave his mouth, hating the way he says it. Lauren isn't just some random piece of pussy, and it just proves how fucked up I am over this girl for it to affect me so much. That, and the way he says it makes me wonder if something's going on with him.

"You're right. Fuck, I know you're right," I admit, it's just a lot easier said than done.

With a nod of my head I make my decision—I need to stay as far away from Lauren as possible. How I'm going to do that I don't know, but I'm going to have to find a way, because the alternative doesn't bear thinking about.

---

After I left Noah's, I went home, showered, graded some papers, and caught the tail end of a football game. I've never been one for sports, but I like to keep up every now and then, just so I don't glaze over when the guys bring it up.

Making my way upstairs, I look around, a sudden feeling of melancholy taking root and for the first time ever, I feel lonely. The walls are bare of any family photos. No kids toys everywhere waiting for me to stub my toe on them. No wife waiting in bed for me. I have no fucking clue where these feelings have materialized from, but they can fuck off. I'm happy with my life. Right?

*Maybe I need to start dating.*

This might be the dumbest thing I've ever done but once I'm committed, I go all in—downloading a dating app and questioning my life choices.

I set up a profile and add a picture—one that Samantha took of me a few years ago, so I still look halfway decent, less bags under my eyes and definitely less grays—and add a bio. I'm not expecting miracles but it's a start.

I mindlessly swipe through not really paying attention. Just as I'm about to close it down, fed up with the same thing—'likes long walks,' *do you really?* 'Loves food,' *I'm pretty sure everyone does,* when I come across a woman around the same age as me—blonde hair, green eyes, and I quickly swipe right. The screen lights up with 'match' and I send her a message. Completely unoriginal, of course:

Caleb2612

**Hey, how are you?**

If I could punch myself, I would.

I don't get a reply, so I keep scrolling for a few more minutes, the urge to delete the app growing with every passing second, my tolerance for it slowly waning.

Putting my phone on the side, I turn out my light and lie in the dark contemplating how my life got here. Where I went wrong with relationships, and why they never worked. Or more importantly, why I picked the wrong women.

I drift off into a fitful sleep dreaming of a different blonde-haired, green-eyed beauty.

# Chapter Fourteen

## *Lauren*

I've got a rare weekend off. Sapphire owed me one for the bachelor party, so Sydney and I are currently getting ready to paint the town red. Margaritas have been flowing for the last hour and I'm trying to do the zip on my dress up but failing miserably.

"Syd," I yell. "Heeelp meee."

Sydney, who is in the kitchen mixing up more drinks, shouts back, "Coming."

I don't know why I leave her to make the drinks, there's usually more alcohol than mixer which is why I'm feeling slightly tipsy already.

She comes in looking like the absolute goddess that she is. Her long dark hair curled to perfection and one side pinned back, her smoky eyes and red lipstick compliment the black skinny jeans and red corset.

"You're so pretty," I sigh, leaning my head on my hand.

"And *you* are drunk," Sydney laughs. "I might have to cut you off or we'll never make it out of here." She comes to stand behind me, doing the zip up.

I've reused this dress more than I care to admit but honestly... I love it. It's a green A-line dress with short cap sleeves; the front's low which is perfect for giving me the slightest hint of cleavage and ends just above the knees. I know, I know... why would I dress so prim and proper when I'm a stripper? For that exact reason. I spend most of my time in various states of undress so when I go out for me, I kinda like to be covered up a bit more.

"All done," Syd says as she moves to sit on my bed, the one currently littered with clothes and shoes.

I look at myself in the mirror hanging on the wall. I've styled my hair similar to Sydney's, but I don't have mine pinned back, just flowing in soft waves. I went light with my makeup—mascara, blush, and some bronzer. I'm not a lipstick kind of girl so I'm going bare tonight.

"Uber's ten minutes away," Sydney calls as she walks into the living room, most probably to make us another drink before we head out.

"Coming," I holler as I grab my clutch and shoes.

---

Illusion is heaving when we get there, the line of people waiting to get in going down for half a block. It's up the street from Strokes, so we don't have to wait, heading straight in.

We push our way through the crowds, the DJ playing *Downpour* by *Our Hollow, Our Home*. One of the main reasons why I love Illusion—it's a rock bar. It's your typical dive bar that has paint peeling off the walls, a weird smell, and your feet constantly stick to the floor, but it has such a great atmosphere.

Other than a few odd tables dotted around, there's no other furniture in here, leaving room for the dance floor. And yes, it's totally possible to dance to metal. The bar's on the left and there's always plenty of servers on hand, so it never takes long to get a drink.

Strolling to the bar I order a Jack and Coke, needing a change of pace after Sydney's margaritas, and sobering up on the ride over. I lost Sydney to the dance floor the minute we walked in.

One song after another has played since getting here, so time has lost its meaning. All I know is that I'm hot and sweaty as I stumble to the bar and ask for a glass of water to cool myself down. I finish gulping it when someone bumps into me.

"Sorry," I shout over the music. A blonde woman who looks to be in her late thirties smiles at me.

"My fault," she shouts back. I smile and continue watching the crowd when she leans over and says, "I feel so old being here. All I want to do is ask them to turn down the music so I can hear myself think."

I laugh, knowing I've never had that problem. When I listen to music it has to be loud, so loud that I can't hear myself think. "I can't say I agree."

I glance back to the dance floor when I catch the outline of another person standing next to the blonde. I grab my clutch to check my phone when I knock it on the floor, the contents spilling everywhere. "Fuck."

I reach down to get it when another pair of hands starts helping me.

"Thank you..." My words trail off when I look up and stare into blue eyes, blue eyes I know very well.

*Caleb.*

My breath catches and I realize I've been staring for too long. Quickly grabbing the rest of my things, I shove them into my bag before standing back up, swaying slightly from the head rush. The blonde from earlier comes over and puts a hand on his arm. My eyes zero in on that one move, and jealousy flares within me. I look back at Caleb, who reaches behind his head to rub his neck, a blush creeping up his face.

I know I don't have the right to be jealous. He's on a date. He's a free, single, good-looking guy, but it feels like a punch to the gut anyway. I place a hand on my neck where the mark that Caleb left still lingers faintly. Will he leave a mark on her neck at the end of the night when he takes her home? Will he forget all about me as he's fucking *her* into oblivion?

*Shit.*

I turn away ordering a shot of tequila—I'm gonna need something stronger to get me through this. I down the shot, foregoing the lime and salt and walk over to where Sydney's gyrating against a tall brunette. As I'm walking my hips start swinging as I get into the beat of the song. I lift my hands in the air and dance like no one's watching, but I know they are, I can feel their eyes roaming all over me. Or more specifically, *his*.

I open my eyes and, sure enough, Caleb's watching me, not paying attention to his date. His jaw's clenched and if he squeezes any harder, the glass he's holding will shatter.

He looks gorgeous though. His dark hair has been gelled, giving it that almost run through look. His black skinny jeans offset the white band T-shirt he's wearing along with black sneakers, and his tattoos are only adding to his allure—*this has got to be my favorite look of his so far.*

I wipe the drool from my mouth that's gathered at the sight of him. The alcohol has caused my inhibitions to lower, and my pussy begins to pulse, knowing exactly what he feels like.

A hand wraps around my waist, and I look down—definitely a man. I gaze up at the newcomer, allowing him to move my body with his. He's cute—blonde hair, tall, lean. Not my usual type, but I'm going with it.

Looking back at the bar, I notice Caleb still watching me, his date obviously trying and failing to get his attention because it's all on me. I get a sick, twisted feeling that he's just as jealous as I am, but brush it off quickly. I'm not that girl. I don't intentionally set out to make anyone jealous, least of all my professor who is entirely off limits.

"Wanna get out of here?" the guy asks over the music.

I nod in response, quickly texting Sydney to let her know I'm heading back to the dorm. I'll see her in the morning, no doubt she'll be doing the walk of shame. I don't plan on going home with this guy but seeing Caleb and not being able to touch him, feels like its ruined my night. My alcohol fueled brain is starting to dull my mood and honestly, I just want to go.

We walk hand in hand to the exit, bodies now crushing together making it difficult to move around. Several times I wonder if I'm going to get dragged into one of the makeshift mosh pits but manage to avoid them.

*Definitely time to go home.*

Once outside, I turn to the random stranger and utter, "Thanks, I'm off now."

"Huh?" He looks confused for a moment, his eyes glazed over. "I thought we could go back to yours for a night cap." He winks.

I'm not sure how a dance equates to a nightcap, but whatever. "Nope, I'm out. Thanks for the dance."

As I turn to leave, he grabs my arm. "Where do you think you're going?" he sneers. His grip is tight enough to leave a bruise and I struggle in his hold, wishing I'd stayed inside with Sydney.

"You're hurting me, get off," I hiss, trying to yank my arm away from him. Tears spring to my eyes when he clutches even harder, all the fight I'm giving him useless against his strength. "What part of 'no' don't you understand, dickwad?"

I'm looking around for security when I notice they're dealing with another drunk, so I'm on my own. *Great.*

Noticing where my line of sight has gone, dickwad smiles a toothy grin. "Looks like it's my lucky day, babe." He grabs my arm harder and starts pulling me away to the back of the building.

I manage to kick his leg, nearly toppling over at the same time. He stops, turning to face me. "There's more where that came from," I snap, "so get your hands off me and walk away before I call for security and have them deal with your skanky ass."

"Try it babe, and see what happens," he laughs, clearly not thinking I'll do it, but little does he know. I take a deep breath in but before I can make a sound...

"Get your fucking hands off her," I hear growled from behind me. I swallow and the guy physically winces, dropping my arm like it burnt him.

"No harm, no foul, man. I was just talking to my girl here," he jokes, trying to brush it off, not realizing who he's talking to.

"She isn't your fucking anything, *man*. So, unless you want me to rip your arm out of its fucking socket and shove it up your ass, I suggest you let her go, right. The. Fuck. Now."

I whimper at the tone Caleb uses. I really shouldn't be turned on by it but I am. The way he's coming to my defense, the way his veins are popping on his forearms and hands as he clenches and unclenches them. I should be classing him as a walking red flag, but I don't. I take one glance at Caleb, seeing the rage, anger, and concern swirling in his eyes and run straight into his arms.

# Chapter Fifteen

## *Caleb*

I'd been messaging Olivia, the woman I'd matched with, on and off for the last week. Nothing deep or personal, just the usual basic questions, 'why are you on a dating app,' 'favorite place to vacation,' 'what would you do if you weren't in your current job.' Boring, mundane questions, but I guess I have to start somewhere.

We agreed to meet up for a drink, so I suggested Illusion. It's a hole in the wall bar but the music's good. I've showered and shaved—my two-day stubble not being a good look. I don't want to look like I'm trying too hard, so I've put on a white band T-shirt, black jeans, and my sneakers. Could I have made more of an effort? Probably, but I'm just not feeling it.

I've gelled my hair and as I look at myself in the mirror, I'm seriously contemplating cancelling. Taking a deep breath, I walk out of the bathroom, running down the stairs and grab my keys and jacket from by the door.

Sliding into my car, I start the engine, the blaring notes of *Obey* by *Bring Me The Horizon* causes me to jump.

*Fuck, last night's me is not tonight's me.*

I reverse out onto the main road and head towards Olivia's place. I offered to pick her up and I'm kinda regretting that decision now. What if the date goes bad and I need to bail? I'll still have to take her home.

*Fuck my life.*

I go to run my hand through my hair and cringe when I remember the gel. I pull my sticky hand away and wipe it down on my thigh.

Olivia lives in an old apartment complex on the other side of town, meaning that she's completely out of the way. When I offered to pick her up, I was hoping she'd say no. Note to self: don't offer next time.

Driving slowly through town, I see burnt out cars, graffiti on walls, and houses boarded up. Finally getting to Olivia's, I leave the engine running—I should probably go and knock, but I don't, I sit in the car and text her.

Me

> I'm outside.

It takes a few minutes, but she messages back.

Olivia

> Oh, okay. Be down in a minute xxx

The last couple of days I've noticed she's started putting kisses at the end of her messages. It started off with one every so often, slowly adding more in, to the now three that I receive. I don't do kisses at the end of my messages. Never have. I'm not even invested in this date, so when a thought of Lauren pops into my head, it catches me off guard—*nope, not happening, dickhead.*

I don't think there's been a single relationship that I've ever given my all to. Does that make me an asshole? Yeah, I guess it does. It's never my intention to lead anyone on, I just get stuck in situations hoping that one day it'll stick—news flash, it doesn't. Samantha was my longest relationship and that felt like pulling teeth on the daily.

A tap on the window pulls me from my thoughts—Olivia. I lean over and open the passenger door for her. I'm the original gentleman.

"Hi," she breathes out as she gets into the car. Olivia's wearing a barely there red dress, her long blonde hair down and her tits nearly spilling out. If I was James or Theo I'd be all over that but it just turns me off. "Thanks for coming to get me." She smiles, and all I can muster is a small tilt of my lips in return.

*Get it together. It's not her fault you're a fucking idiot who has the hots for his student.*

"Yeah, no problem."

Her face drops slightly, probably from my lack of enthusiasm before she pulls her shoulders back and beams a smile.

We make small talk on the way over and by small talk, I mean, she talks and I grunt every so often, keeping my eyes on the road.

Getting to Illusion, we head in. I feel a brush of a hand against mine and I quickly put my hands in my pockets. I'd already called ahead so we don't have to wait in line and I usher her inside, finally trying not to be an ass, and placing a hand on the small of her back. The music's loud and for once I'm glad I can't hear myself think.

We make our way to the bar and order our drinks. Olivia stands next to another woman, but I'm too focused on paying to take any notice.

Something drops to the floor by my feet, bending down to pick it up, I see it's a woman's clutch, the contents spilling everywhere. I look up, doing a double take as I come face to face with Lauren. *My* Lauren.

*What's she doing here?*

Okay, that's a stupid question. Apart from Bucky's and Strokes, this is the only other bar in town.

"Thank you..." She trails off as she glances up, noticing it's me.

She stares, her mouth gaping open before she, apparently, comes to her senses, grabs the rest of her things, stuffs them in her bag, and strides away to the dance floor. I watch as her hips start swaying to the music and I can't help the way my gaze lands on her ass—which looks fucking great by the way—and my cock begins to stir.

Lauren starts dancing, her hands up in the air, and just like that first night at Strokes, I'm mesmerized by her. She's so damn enigmatic, that she just draws you in with her beauty. I'm too busy watching Lauren and her sweat glistening body that I don't notice the hand that's on my arm.

"You okay," Olivia shouts in my ear. I reluctantly turn my gaze away and glance at her, a look of concern showing on her heavily made-up face.

I gently move my arm out of her grip, giving a nod of my head as I reply, "Yeah, I'm good."

Looking back toward Lauren, rage hot and heavy begins clawing its way through my veins as some fucking cunt touches her. My jaw's clenched so hard, I'm pretty sure I just broke a tooth. I watch as his hands wrap around her waist, his head nuzzling into the side of her neck, rubbing against her. My blood boils at the sight. All I can think of is peeling every single one of his fingers off her and bending them backwards until they break.

I'm about two seconds away from ripping the asshole off her, when I remember I can't—she's not mine, she never will be. She's my *student*, I emphasize the thought to remind myself she's off limits.

"Do you want another drink?" Olivia asks, following my line of sight to see what I'm looking at.

Raking a hand down my face and sighing, I glance at Olivia. "I'm sorry, this was a mistake." Guilt for treating Olivia like shit and guilt over Lauren starts to make me feel nauseous.

"Yeah, I got that." Olivia gives me a small smile as she puts her hand on my arm and squeezes gently. She doesn't look upset, more like... disappointed. "I'm gonna call a cab and head home."

I just nod, feeling pretty confident that dating isn't for me. But the little voice in the back of my head pipes up, *or is it because you're with the wrong woman*? Glancing back over to the dance floor, I search the crowds but Lauren isn't there.

*Where did she go?*

Frantically looking around, I try to think of where she could have gone. Fear enveloping me at the thought that something could have happened.

*Think Caleb. Where could she have gone? Bathroom?*

Rushing to the women's toilets, I shove my way through the door—women scream at me to get out but all I'm focused on is finding Lauren.

*Where the fuck is she?*

I race to the exit, pushing my way through the crowds of people, my heart pumping along to the beat of the song that's currently playing. Sweaty bodies are crowding around me as fear grips me. I physically start pushing people out of the way in my haste to find Lauren. A drink gets spilled down my T-shirt but I couldn't give a shit—the T-shirt can be replaced. Lauren cannot.

I burst through the door, people in the queue staring at me as I continue my search, my panic rising with every moment I don't find her.

"You're hurting me, get off," I hear Lauren cry to my left. I run as fast as I can toward her voice, finding her with the same asshole from earlier, grabbing her arm.

"Get your fucking hands off her," I growl. I'm two seconds away from pummeling this motherfuckers ass. I glance over at Lauren who looks fucking livid—*same, baby girl, same.*

"No harm, no foul, man. I was just talking to my girl here."

I swear to fucking god. His girl? *His fucking girl.* I'm gonna kill him.

I clench and unclench my hands, seething. A full on murderous rage beginning at the audacity of this prick. "She isn't your fucking anything, *man*. So, unless you want me to rip your arm out of its fucking socket and shove it up your ass, I suggest you let her go, right. The. Fuck. Now."

The asshole, seeing that I'm not fucking around and he's away from the safety of security, let's go of Lauren, stepping back and holding his hands up in an 'I surrender' gesture. He saunters off back into the bar, probably to try it on with another unsuspecting victim.

Lauren comes running to me and I open my arms for her. She buries her head in my chest, wrapping her arms around my waist.

She's shaking as I pull her closer, inhaling her vanilla and strawberry scent, calming all my previous murderous thoughts. "Hey, baby girl. You doing okay?" I murmur, stroking the back of her hair.

She gazes up at me, her mascara smudged from nuzzling her head into my chest. The pool of unshed tears making the green of her eyes pop more than usual.

"I'm okay now, thank you," she sniffs, and I don't think I've ever seen her look more beautiful. "I just need to go home."

"Of course, sweetheart. Let me take you, my car's parked over there," I say, nodding toward the parking lot.

She doesn't say anything, but the fact that she lets me lead her to my car without a word, I take as permission.

I open the passenger door for her, waiting until she gets in before bending down to secure her in. I brush a stray lock of hair behind her ear, and she leans into my hand.

Lauren gives me a small smile, her bottom lip wobbling as she says, "Tha-thank you... for helping me." Her eyes begin to water and I haul her into me—as best as I can, with her strapped in—giving her a hug.

I swallow the lump that's formed in my throat, choking out, "Let's get you home, baby girl."

After getting the information out of Lauren about where she lives, I drive her back to campus. Neither one of us says anything, just comfortable in the silence. I know it's not right but I put my hand on her thigh anyway, just to offer her that little bit of extra comfort. She grabs my hand entwining her fingers with mine, leaning her head back onto the seat and gazing out the window.

I keep my eyes on the road but every so often I rub my thumb across her hand, just to let her know I'm here.

We get back to campus and I park outside her dorm, my tinted windows giving us some sort of privacy. Lauren fell asleep on the drive back, her soft snores soothing my frayed edges. I turn off the engine and gaze down at her, her mouth slightly open, and I can't help but tenderly run a finger down her cheek to her lip, wishing things could be different.

"Lauren," I gently coax. "We're here, sweetheart."

She opens her eyes and looks around, the alcohol in her system causing her eyes to unfocus slightly and confusion to settle in.

"Oh, right. Thank you." She undoes her seatbelt before turning to me. "Thank you for, uh, coming to my rescue?" She chuckles lightly;

the situation not lost on her, but what's that age-old saying? If you don't laugh, you'll cry.

"Anytime, Lauren," I gruffly say.

We continue staring at each other, and I take in all of her beautiful features, filing them away. Neither one of us makes a move, not wanting the other to leave.

Finally I come to my senses, clearing my throat and leaning back in my chair, looking through the windshield as I basically dismiss her.

"Right. Thanks again," she awkwardly says before getting out. I watch as she stumbles toward her dorm, everything screaming in me to run after her, to make sure she gets to her room okay, but I can't.

Once she's through the door, I start up the engine and drive home.

# Chapter Sixteen

## *Lauren*

Wiping a hand under my eye to get rid of the excess mascara, I let myself into the dorm room. Sydney isn't back yet and with any luck, she found some random girl and won't be back until morning.

I rub my arm where that asshole grabbed me, bruises starting to mar my skin from his tight grip. My thoughts are completely jumbled, not only from the alcohol still flowing through my bloodstream but from the assault and Caleb. I don't have the brain power to deal with the chaos of emotions I'm currently feeling, so I take a quick shower, removing all traces of the night and crawl under my covers.

Hopefully tomorrow I can make more sense of what the hell happened.

I wake up to a drilling sound in my head. I try to open my eyes but the harsh sunlight from my open blinds causes me to shut them again. I roll over onto my back and try not to puke.

*Did I drink that much last night or am I just a lightweight now?*

I reach over and grab my phone, checking the time—10:01 a.m. Shit, I should really get up and check if Sydney got back okay.

I shuffle into the living room and put the coffee on while I find some Advil in the drawer. Popping a couple, I pour my coffee and head to the sofa, putting on a movie to pass the time. I must have dozed off as I wake up when Sydney comes through the door.

Sitting up, I rub my eyes. "Hey," I croak, my voice still having the reminisce of sleep attached to it. "You're back late."

Sydney blushes and walks to her room with her head down. "Uh, yeah. I, uh, went for breakfast," she mumbles low enough for me to hear.

I get up slowly, my head better than it was, but still pounding as I amble toward her room, propping myself up against her door frame. "Okaaaay... you're being really weird right now. You good?" I ask.

"Yup." She pops the P, still not looking at me.

Crossing my arms, I raise an eyebrow. "Alright." She moves around her room, tidying up. "I'm gonna grab some food then study. Wanna watch something later?" I ask.

She finally looks up at me, a small smile on her face. "Sure," she replies.

I'm worried about Syd, but I don't push her. I sigh, grab my book bag from the table and head to my room.

We didn't watch a film last night. Sydney never came out of her room, so I finished my assignments and fell asleep.

My lectures don't start until this afternoon so I got up, showered and dressed in my usual leggings and hoodie and walked down to the Honey Pot, hoping to catch Raven.

I push through the door and her head pops up from under the counter. "Lauren, hey," she greets with a smile.

"Hey, Raven," I reply, giving her a small wave.

Grabbing a cup from the back counter, she asks, "Your usual?"

"Please."

Once Raven's finished making my coffee, I grab the cup and head to one of the tables out front. I haven't had any time to sit and work through what happened on Saturday night, and in all honesty I didn't have the energy to. It's exhausting trying to field emotions when they pop out of nowhere—sat on the toilet, thoughts of Caleb. Making a coffee, thoughts of Caleb. The man has implanted roots into me and I can't cut them out. So I sit, gazing out across campus as I sip on my too hot coffee and try to compartmentalize.

First—asshole. Did he scare me? Absolutely. Will I let his actions worry me and hold me back? Not a chance. I'm not going to let some guy who can't take 'no' for an answer get to me. He's not worth it. Taking the time to reflect on my actions, I know that the alcohol in my body had caused me to act emotionally, which is why I clung on to Caleb when he 'saved' me.

Once I've decided that the asshole has been dealt with and filed away, my thoughts stray to Caleb—how he came to my defense, how he held me after, how he drove me home. It shouldn't give me butterflies to think about him and how he dealt with the asshole, and it definitely shouldn't make my pussy clench at how low and dark his voice had gotten. Nope, definitely not thinking about *that*.

He's my professor, a man who's completely off limits, a man who's sixteen years my senior. *Fuck sake, I need to get a grip on my emotions.* Why couldn't he be literally *anyone* else?

"Lauren, right?" a voice asks from behind me, startling me. I glance over my shoulder seeing a gorgeous guy looking straight at me. He's got to be at least six feet with dark brown hair and a killer smile.

"Yeah...?" I ask because I have no clue who he is and how he knows my name.

He blushes and grips the handle of his satchel that's across his shoulder. "Sorry, I'm Brad... Professor Anderson's TA."

"Oh, I've heard so much about you." I smile at him and gesture for him to take a seat.

We chat for a while before I notice the time and start gathering my things.

"I can always help with any missed assignments if you need it," Brad offers, as he stands up. I freeze instantly.

*Huh?*

Standing to my full height, I turn toward him, my brows furrowed with confusion. "Oh, I was told you were too busy."

Brad scratches the back of his neck, looking just as confused as me. "I don't know who told you that but I tutor other students so I have the time to help... if you want me to, of course."

*I swearing to fucking god. That absolute asshole.*

I'm angry. No scratch that, I'm fucking fuming. Why would Caleb lie to me about Brad not being able to help when he clearly can?

"I would love that, thank you."

"I thought it was weird when Professor Anderson said you didn't need any help and you would catch up by yourself."

*I beg your fucking pardon?*

I give a barely there smile and hope he doesn't pick up on the fact I'm about to kick Caleb's ass.

As we're heading in the same direction we walk together. The weather's unseasonably warm for this time of year causing me to take off my hoodie, leaving me in just a tank top.

Brad's a good conversationalist and even though Caleb's flittering at the back of my mind, he's not at the forefront like usual. Brad makes me laugh with his dry wit, so when he asks to see me again, I can't help but say yes. We exchange numbers and a somewhat awkward half hug and say our goodbyes.

I get to class, sitting in my usual seat, pulling my laptop out and fire up my emails:

---

To: ProfessorAnderson@abingdonuniversity.com.

From: LaurenTaylor@abingdonuniversity.com.

Subject: Services No Longer Required.

Dear Professor Anderson,

I had the pleasure of meeting your TA, Brad, today, who has kindly informed me that he is available to undertake helping me catch up with my studies.

Due to this, I will no longer require your tutelage.

Best wishes,

Lauren Taylor

---

*Stick that in your pipe and smoke it, Caleb.*

With a sick satisfaction, I close down my emails and concentrate on my lecture.

# Chapter Seventeen

# Caleb

I woke up this morning and chose violence. I'm still fucking raging over what happened with Lauren at Illusion. My mood went from bad to worse after I looked out of my office window to see Lauren and Brad laughing and, what looked to be, the exchanging of numbers. Shortly after, I received an email from Lauren saying Brad was going to be teaching her from now on.

*I think the fuck not.*

The only reason why I chose to tutor Lauren myself was to be around her. Fucked up, yes. Brad could've easily done it and I definitely wasn't thinking clearly when the words tumbled out of my mouth—my dick did all the talking there.

I all but stomp into the classroom, slamming my satchel down on the desk—with far more force than is necessary—causing the pens to rattle and the papers to lift. The loud mutterings between students comes to an abrupt halt at my act of aggression.

"Books out, page twenty," I bark. "Someone tell me what Hemingway was trying to say here." I perch on the edge of my desk, arms folded, waiting for an answer.

Some asshole pipes up, "That he needs to get laid."

Closing my eyes, I pinch the bridge of my nose. One, two, three... Nope, can't do it.

"Get the fuck out of my class," I bellow. The kid looks at me, eyes wide, before scrambling to collect his stuff, and runs out the door. "Anyone else got any smartass remarks?" I question as I glance around the room. "I don't relish the fact I have to ask this *yet again*, but what was Hemingway trying to say *on page twenty*?"

I shouldn't, but I peer at Lauren, her face a mask of shock—eyes wide, lips slightly parted. The rest of the class have varying degrees of intrigue and shock. I'm usually all jokes and banter but right now? Right now, I'm about to explode.

Clenching my jaw, I bite out, "Miss Taylor, care to explain what Hemingway was saying here?"

She tilts her head to the side, giving me a challenging stare. "He's telling us to write more concisely. Long sentences avoid readers from enjoying the script. So, in a sense, Hemingway wanted to teach people how to write effectively."

*Game on.*

"Miss Taylor, my office after class," I snap, and her challenging stare morphs into anger in an instant. Good. I need her to hate me. "The rest of you, use this time to prep for a pop quiz next lesson." The groans echo around the auditorium but I'm past caring.

Class drags by in a murmur of hushed tones as I try and fail to concentrate on the work before me. By the time the bell rings, my mood still hasn't lifted and I storm into my office, throwing my bag on the sideboard as I pace around.

I'm restless and irritable and I know why. It's *her*. She's clawed her way in without either one of us realizing it and seeing her with Brad was the straw that broke the camel's back. I've never been a violent person until her. Now I'm mentally killing every fucker that goes anywhere near her.

I continue pacing, taking—what I hope is—deep, calming breaths to get myself under control. I gaze around my office to distract myself. I've always liked it. It's compact with only a desk, a chair, and a sideboard, but it's mine.

There's a knock on the door and I pause, raking a hand through my hair as I call out, "Come in."

The door slowly opens, and Lauren's face emerges. "You wanted to see me?" She poses it as a question but the attitude behind it is close to her getting her ass spanked.

I gesture to the chair opposite my desk. "Have a seat, Miss Taylor."

She sits down, looking around my office as I take a seat in my own chair, giving me the opportunity to take her in. She's got her hair up in a messy bun, no makeup, a black vest top—which gives me a fantastic view of her tits—and black leggings which hug her ass and thighs. As Lauren turns to look at me, she bites her lip.

*Sweet baby Jesus.*

Blood rushes to my cock as I imagine her lips wrapped around me.

"Care to explain what the fuck that email was about?" I glare at her, the anger that I thought I'd got rid of, coming back in full force just thinking about the damn thing.

"Care to explain why the fuck you lied?" she retorts.

"I didn't lie. I just... stretched the truth slightly."

"That's what you're calling it? You are un-fucking-believable, Caleb," she hisses. "You had no right to do that. But I guess the jokes on you now because I no longer need you." She raises her eyebrow at me and jealousy floods through my body.

"Watch your tone. I'm still your professor," I snap.

Lauren scoffs. "I think we're well past that now, *Professor*, but whatever."

*This fucking girl.*

I pinch the bridge of my nose, for what feels like the hundredth time and try to breathe through my anger. "You are to continue having your scheduled lessons with me as planned. Are we clear?"

"No, we're not fucking clear. Why? Brad can help me. I don't need you," she sasses.

There's that fucking word again—*need*. "Regardless of what you think you need or don't need, Miss Taylor, this is what I'm telling you."

"Well, you can tell me all you want, Caleb, but the fact of the matter is, Brad will be helping me... not you." She smirks, like she's enjoying being a brat.

My control is slowly slipping, threatening to send me into territory we can't come back from. But then again, I think we're way past that now.

"Accept what I'm telling you, Miss Taylor, or get the fuck out."

Lauren's green eyes blaze with defiance, her posture matching it when she crosses her arms over her chest and places her right knee over her left, raising an eyebrow at me. "Come again, Professor? It sounds an awful lot like you're trying to tell me what to do."

Mirroring her posture, I reply, "You forget who's in charge here."

"Is that so?" she purrs.

"On your knees, Miss Taylor," I grind out. I shouldn't be doing this, it's wrong, unethical, and anyone could walk by, but my stupid fucking mouth ran away from me *again*. Am I being unprofessional right now? Yes. Can I get fired for this? Also yes. Do I care? Not in the fucking slightest. This girl has pushed me far past my limits.

Lauren's breath hitches, her eyes going slightly wide at my demand, a flush spreading across her cheeks and I know I've got her. I can see the desire in her eyes, the way she's unconsciously leaning toward me and biting that damn lip.

"Caleb?" she questions, tilting her head to the side and taking me in. I don't know what the fuck she's asking me for but I'm taking what's mine.

"Baby girl, I'm not going to ask you again. Get. On. Your. Knees."

Just when I think she's going to call me out, she stands up and drops to her knees and fuck if my cock doesn't go from semi hard to rock hard in 0.2 seconds flat. The sight of her nearly sending me feral.

"Crawl to me," I command.

Doing as I say, Lauren crawls to me, staring up at me with her soulful green eyes, and for a moment I get lost. Her hips swaying from side to side like she's on stage, her movements exaggerated, knowing the effect she's having on me. I rub a hand over my cock to ease the discomfort and I can feel the pre-cum leaking in my boxers.

She comes to a stop between my legs and with a slight glint to her eye, Lauren asks, "What now?"

"Take my cock out like the good girl I know you are."

Lauren's breathing becomes faster, her thighs clenching.

*Oh, she definitely liked that.*

She runs her hands up my thighs, her gentle touch causing shivers, before getting to my belt buckle. She quickly undoes it and reaches in to take my cock out, it springs free from its confines as her hand fully wraps around me and I groan at the sensation.

Leaning forward, her grip on me loosens slightly. I tuck a finger under her chin, bringing her eyes to meet mine. "Suck my cock."

# CHAPTER EIGHTEEN

## *Lauren*

"*Suck my cock.*"

Let's get one thing straight, if any other asshole had said this to me, they'd be getting a headbutt straight to the dick right about now. But when Caleb says it? I want to say, "Yes, sir." This man has my pussy whipped and I can't say I'm mad about it.

I'm fuming with Caleb, not only with the whole Brad thing, but also with what happened back in class and the way he spoke to me. But I can't deny that when he told me to get on my knees my body obeyed his command like the traitor it is. The fact that we're both angry, we know this is wrong and that we both could lose everything is only heightening the feelings.

I peer up at Caleb, his blue eyes filled with both anger and lust as I lean in and gently run my tongue from base to tip. He raises an eyebrow at me and I just smirk, continuing my teasing strokes. Caleb grabs a handful of my hair suddenly, pulling me off him.

"Quit playing around, Lauren, and suck my fucking cock before I gag you on it," he growls.

Deciding not to poke the bear, I place my mouth around his cock, the groan that leaves him can only be described as orgasmic. He tilts his head back as I suck him further into my mouth. I move my head up and down, circling my tongue around his tip, bringing my other hand halfway up until it meets my mouth, essentially jerking him off with both my hand and mouth. His hands tangle in my hair, the bite of pain causing my thighs to clench together again.

"Just like that, baby girl," he grunts, causing me to tighten my grip on his cock and suck harder. "Ah, fuck."

I'm slowly losing my mind with his grunts of pleasure, he's got me wound so tight, and I'm desperate for some sort of release. With the hand that's wrapped around him, I reach into my leggings and circle my clit, whimpering, which causes Caleb to push me down further as he thrusts up into my mouth. I gag, saliva starting to pool at the base of his cock and my eyes water from the luscious attack on my throat.

I peer up through wet eyelashes and find Caleb with a look of pure ecstasy etched on his face, so I do what any other girl would do in my position—I rub my clit faster.

He suddenly pulls me upright, my chest heaving as I wipe the drool from my chin. Caleb stands and I follow suit, craning my neck to gaze up at him.

He grabs me by the throat, dragging me to him. "I tell you when you get to come, Lauren," he commands.

*Heaven help me, why is this so fucking hot?*

He crashes his lips against mine and I sink into the kiss. There's no tentative, slow kissing here. It's full of passion, of need, of want and *I am here for it*. I thread my hands through his hair and tug him closer to me, trying to rub my pussy against him to ease the pressure, to stop the pulsing ache that only he can relieve.

Caleb draws back and I chase him, trying to find his lips once more. "Bend over the desk, Lauren."

So what do I do? Why, I bend over the desk, of course. He roughly pulls my leggings and panties down while my face is pressed against the desk, my hips digging in as the cool air helps bring my body back to a temperature that isn't burning hot for this man. He doesn't bother removing my clothes completely, just leaves them in a pile at my feet, before gently nudging my legs further apart.

"You've been a bad girl, sweetheart. You've tortured my every waking thought and dream since I met you." He leans down to whisper, his breath hot on my face. "Do you know what happens to bad girls, Lauren?"

"N-no," I stutter, my brain having gone haywire from his touch.

"Good girls get rewarded, bad girls get spanked."

*Wait? What? Spanked?*

I attempt to stand up, but a resounding *smack* echoes throughout the room, and it takes a second for my brain to catch up before the intoxicating pain comes through. I shouldn't like it, I really shouldn't but *fuck me*. It's like a direct line to my pussy and I'm begging for more.

He leans back over me, growling in my ear. "Tell me to stop, baby girl."

*Absolutely fucking not.*

"Tell me you don't want this. That you want me to go," he breathes out as he places kisses along my neck and his hand snakes down to my ass, caressing it slowly. "That this is wrong."

"Caleb, please," I whine and another smack to my ass nearly has me coming. Caleb finds my clit and begins to circle it with his thumb, before pushing a finger into my pussy. "Fuck yes," I cry out though it's muffled by my arm.

Caleb bends over me, trailing kisses along my neck before his mouth lands on my shoulder, his teeth sinking into my skin. "So wet for me, baby girl. Does my naughty girl like being spanked, hmm?"

At this point I think I said, "Yes" but it could've also been incoherent nonsense as far as I know. Because as long as Caleb keeps doing whatever it is that he's doing, I'd agree to just about anything. The sounds my pussy's making is enough to make a sailor blush.

He reaches under my vest and pulls down my bra, cupping and tweaking at my nipple. I whimper at the combined pleasure and pain impact it has on my body.

"You think you deserve to come, Lauren? After what you've put me through? The torment? The sleepless nights? The *disgrace* at lusting after a student?" he tsks.

His fingers thrust faster, and my moans get louder, so loud in fact that Caleb clamps his hand over my mouth to keep me somewhat quiet, not realizing I'd moved my arm.

"Please... please let me come," I beg, not even the slightest bit ashamed. He carries on circling my clit, faster and faster, and just as I'm about to come... he stops.

I move my head to the side, glaring at him but the asshole just smirks. He smacks my ass one more time before he grabs a condom—from fuck knows where—rolls it on, and thrusts into me. I cry out, thankful that he'd taken the forethought to cover my mouth back over—I'm not sure if that was to stop me from mouthing off or...

"I swear to god, your cunt is like heaven. I don't think I'll ever get enough," Caleb rumbles, his tone low and dark. And I have to admit, I don't think I'll ever get enough of him either.

Caleb's thrusts get quicker, harder and before long, I'm coming completely undone, gripping his cock with my pussy in a vice-like grip. Caleb slows down, moving in and out at a slow and tortuous pace.

"Fuck, baby girl, watching my dick slide in and out of this pretty cunt almost has me blowing my load," he grinds out and I moan at his filthy mouth.

He must decide that he can't take it anymore as he begins pounding into me relentlessly, causing another orgasm to work its way through my body. Three more thrusts and Caleb joins me, roaring out his release. He collapses on top of me, crushing me between him and the desk as both of us try and catch our breath.

Caleb grabs some tissues from his desk to clean me up with, and I have a strange sense of déjà vu. Once that's done, I pull my panties and leggings up before tugging my bra and top down. I run a hand through my hair—my hair tie must have fallen out.

Knowing that this was a mistake, an overwhelming need to leave takes over me. "I should go."

Caleb nods, knowing there isn't anything either of us can say that'll make this easier. His blue eyes are void of emotion as he places his hands into the pockets of his black slacks. The white shirt he wore this morning, now crumbled from our... activities.

I grab my bag and move toward the door, giving him one last lingering glance before leaving.

# Chapter Nineteen

## *Lauren*

You ever get the feeling you're being watched? I've felt it for the last few days, the constant eyes on me wherever I go. I'm probably being over dramatic—one too many scary movies with Sydney playing havoc with my brain.

I'm sitting in the back room of Strokes—the one where the girls go to rehearse—because I've had so much pent up energy since Caleb's office that I needed an outlet. The urge to seek him out is becoming harder to ignore. I was going crazy staring at the four walls of the dorm room, so I came to the one place I knew would help.

I've always loved practicing in this room. Three walls are covered with floor to ceiling mirrors so we can watch our posture as we move and the other wall is a large window that overlooks the back of another building. There isn't anything out there, so none of us have ever been worried about being spied on whilst we workout.

I glide over to my favorite pole—the static one. There are two varieties: static and spinney, both names saying exactly what they do.

The static pole stays static and doesn't move. The spinney pole moves so you're constantly spinning around—I get dizzy easily, so that one's out. Plus, I find I get more range of motion with static and I'm more likely to throw myself into a move.

I've been practicing my running into a handstand—I take a running leap, do a front flip and end up upside down, one hand on the bottom of the pole, one hand high up, and my legs in a straight line towards the ceiling. It's a current work in progress.

I'm alone tonight, the other girls are either working out front or having the night off so it's nice to have the place to myself. I hit play on my phone and *My Heart's To Blame* by *Falling In Reverse* starts playing, allowing the tension in my body to start easing.

# Chapter Twenty

## Unknown

She doesn't know I've been watching her from the shadows. The first time I saw her, I knew she was going to be mine. My mother always told me I would find a woman to love one day and it's *her*. I've asked around about her, she doesn't have a boyfriend, and only has one friend, so getting to her won't be an issue. My lips curve up at the thought.

I come here and watch her all the time. She's beautiful as she twists and spins around the pole. I have this unending obsession with her. The need to possess her entirely. She's going to be mine, one way or another. She's stretching, so I should probably think about leaving.

"Soon, my love. Soon," I whisper into the darkness.

# Chapter Twenty-One

## Lauren

After my workout, I towel off the sweat before spinning toward the window, that unsettling 'I'm being watched' feeling happening again.

I get up and walk over, looking out into the dark, but all I see is my reflection staring back at me. I shiver, anxiety pooling in my chest.

*It's fine, everything's fine.*

Finishing up for the night, I grab my bag, and head out to the dressing room. Removing my phone from my bag I notice a message from Brad:

Brad

> Hey, Lauren. Are you free tomorrow night? Thought we could grab dinner while we go over the assignments ☺

I *am* free tomorrow and he seems nice. I could do worse. Caleb isn't an option, so I text Brad back.

Lauren

Sounds great ☺

Brad

Awesome! I'll pick you up at 8.

I order an Uber, which was my original intent when I pulled out my phone, and head to the entrance. Steve's in his usual spot behind the desk, I give him a wave, but don't stop.

I get back to the dorm and Sydney's sitting on the sofa eating ice cream, piquing my curiosity—Sydney only ever eats ice cream when something's wrong.

"Everything okay, Syd?" I ask as I place my bag down and curl up next to her, resting my head on her lap.

"Uh huh," she mumbles around a mouthful of cookie dough. "We still going to my parents for Thanksgiving break?"

I jerk my head up. "Yes! I haven't seen your mom and dad since we got here." The excitement clear in my tone.

I absolutely adore Sydney's parents. Dave and Cynthia Johnson are mom and dad goals. They welcomed me into their home with open arms and I love spending time with them. Dave's a retired fireman and Cynthia's an ICU nurse, she only works part time, says she can't give up the job completely or she'd end up killing Dave.

"Okay, I'll let them know we're still going," Syd says, giving me a nod. "Are you working tomorrow night?"

"No, I've got the night off, but I'm meeting up with Brad."

"Whoa, whoa, whoa! Who the fuck is Brad and why am I only just hearing about it," Sydney yells, placing the carton of forgotten ice cream on the coffee table.

I blush. "He's a TA. He's helping me catch up on some assignments for Professor Anderson." Automatically my mind goes straight to Caleb, but I push them away.

*Nope. Absolutely not. Go away.*

"Girl! Is he hot?" She winks and wiggles her eyebrows at me.

"Shut up," I laugh. "He's... cute. I like him, he seems nice." I shrug. Brad doesn't fill me with butterflies like Caleb does but at least he's a safe option and won't get me kicked out.

Sydney's hounding me with questions by this point. "Where is he taking you? What time is he picking you up? He's picking you up, right? What are you weari—"

"Syd," I yell, but I'm still laughing. "Slow down. I don't know where he's taking me. He's picking me up at eight, so yes, he's picking me up, and I have absolutely no clue what I'm wearing. Probably the same as usual... jeans and a hoodie."

Sydney sits there, mouth agape, staring at me, before she jumps up shouting, "Abso-fucking-lutely not. I will allow the jeans but the hoodie is not happening. I'll grab you something to wear." She rushes out of the living room and into her bedroom. "I will *not* have you looking like some... heathen," she calls.

"Alright, Tan France," I giggle. "Whatever makes you happy." I roll my eyes even though she can't see me.

"I saw that, bitch. Don't you roll those pretty green eyes at me. You'll be thanking me tomorrow when you're having a string of orgasms."

I get thrown into a visual episode of Caleb and I in his office. I completely zone out, reliving every detail as if it was happening all over again. My thighs clench together and I have to bite my hand to stop the whimper that wants to escape. I remember his hands gripping me tightly, the way his cock felt as he thrust into me, over and over again. The way his tongue had me seeing stars—

"LAUREN!" Sydney shouts, distracting me. "Girl, are you okay?" she asks gently, placing her hand on my arm. Sydney knows this happens on occasion and that I don't like to talk about it.

"Yeah, I'm good," I mumble. "I'm gonna... go and lie down." I force a smile and all but run to my room.

As soon as I get there, I grab my trusty vibrator and get into bed. I lift my T-shirt and bra up, rolling my nipple around and pinching it slightly, sighing at the contact. I take my other hand and move it down into my sweats, placing a finger on my clit and rubbing in slow deliberate circles.

*"Does my girl want my cock in her cunt?"*

Images and sounds of Caleb flood my senses and all I can think about is him. I can feel his touch on my skin, his gentle hands as he grips my hips.

*"I love the way you feel around my cock."*

Shit! It's like he's here with me, like he's whispering in my ear. I'm so wet, the vibrator's easing in and out smoothly, the tip hitting my G-spot, the sensation causes me to lift my hips off the bed, trying to chase the feeling. I bite my lip to stifle my moans of pleasure, thinking of Caleb's tongue on my clit.

*"Come for me, baby girl."*

I cry out into my hand, as I climax, my body shuddering with the aftershocks. Coming down from my high, I remove the vibrator and throw it down next to me. I shouldn't have been thinking of Caleb but his was the only face I could see when my eyes were closed, the only voice I could hear. And that thought alone scares the shit out of me.

# Chapter Twenty-Two

## *Caleb*

I haven't been able to stop thinking about Lauren since I fucked her in my office. But I'm angry at her, so fucking angry. If I'd never laid eyes on her then none of this would've happened. We would never have been thrown in to a situation that's completely fucked up.

Another person I'm angry at is Brad. *Fucking Brad*. He gets to be seen with Lauren, gets to touch her, have her number and I have... nothing. I have an email address and even then, that's monitored. Thus fucking with me more as I'm angry for wanting her, but angry for not being able to have her.

My head is one big screwed up fucking mess.

I rub my forehead and rest my head on the couch. I broke out the big guns tonight and poured myself a whiskey, which I've been nursing for the last hour. I'm tempted to get drunk but I don't want to deal with the hangover tomorrow. At the ripe old age of thirty-six, they don't go as easily as they used to, and I'll be on my ass for days after.

Without thinking it through, I get up, put my shoes on and grab my car keys. Unlocking my car, I get in and start her up, reversing out onto the main road. I don't know what my destination is, all I know is that I need to be somewhere, anywhere that isn't staring at the four walls of my house.

---

I end up at Strokes—predictable? Probably. I'm sitting here, engine idling wondering if I should go in, or just head home. Something stops me from going home though, so instead, like the dickhead that I am, I turn the engine off and make my way inside.

It's busy for a Wednesday night but I manage to get to the bar with no problems. I ask the waitress for a bottle of water before turning around, and leaning against the bar, searching.

I'm sipping my water when I catch sight of long, blonde hair weaving through the crowds.

*Bingo.*

I follow after her, catching glimpses when the crowds part so I know where she's going. When I open the door, Lauren whirls around.

"Caleb," she gasps, eyes wide. "Wh-what are you doing here?"

She looks breath-taking in her work outfit—a green, lacy, barely there lingerie set, showing off her curvy body to perfection. My mouth waters at the sight, my cock growing hard beneath my jeans.

"Honestly? I don't know. I was just driving and ended up here." I shrug my shoulders and put my hands in my pockets, rocking back and forth on my feet.

Her face softens. "Caleb," she sighs.

"I know, I just... couldn't stop thinking about you after you left my office."

"We can't do this, Caleb. It's not right," she says, almost sounding like she's forcing the lie out.

"You don't think I know that, Lauren? You don't think I feel disgusted for lusting over my student? A woman nearly half my age?" I exclaim, frustration at the situation simmering beneath the surface. "You think this is easy for me?" I hit my chest, my emotions getting the better of me. "Well newsflash, it's not."

"What do you want me to do here, Caleb? You want me to tell you that I don't feel the same way? That this isn't just as hard for me as it is for you? Well newsflash, it is," she cries.

I can't bear to see the dejected look on her face, the pure sadness that's radiating from her, and in that moment, it's clear as day—I'm falling for her.

"You should go," she whispers, eyes cast down.

I feel like she just punched me in the gut. I want to do anything that'll make this better. I want to do anything to make *her* happy. I take a couple of steps toward her, but she holds out her hand, stopping me.

"Lauren, I—" I start but she cuts me off.

She wraps her arms around herself, still not looking at me. "Please... just go."

I sigh, running a hand through my hair, before replying, "Okay, sweetheart."

Walking back to my car, I inwardly curse myself for going there. Nothing good came of it, other than to make us both feel like shit. One things for certain though, Lauren Taylor has me trapped, and I'm not sure I want out.

# Chapter Twenty-Three

## *Lauren*

I have my 'date' with Brad tonight and after Caleb turned up out of the blue at the club last night, my head's a mess. I *had* to turn him away, no matter what I'm starting to feel for him.

Caleb and I are wrong. We don't fit together, we lead separate lives, not to mention the age gap. Giving Brad a chance is a good idea, the best really. He's my age, we could potentially fit, and no one would bat an eye about us being together.

So why does the idea of me being with Brad cause a knot to form in my stomach? The thought of someone else's hands on me cause me to feel nauseous?

I stare at myself in the mirror, my makeup and hair done, because I want to at least *try*. Try to put Caleb out of my mind. Try to move on from this stupid... crush? Infatuation? I don't even know what to call it.

Taking one last look at myself, I get up and blow out a breath. *What am I wearing?* I tap my lip with my finger in contemplation before going with my usual jeans and hoodie. I know Sydney picked out an outfit and I said I wanted to *try* but give a girl a break, I did my hair and makeup, that's gotta count for something, right?

There's a knock at the door as I'm pulling on my Converses. I head over and check who it is before opening it—safety and all that.

*Brad.*

Opening the door, Brad's standing there with his hands in his denim jeans and a white button up. He's got that bashful boy next door look down perfectly.

"Br-Brad, hi," I stammer out. What is *wrong* with me?

"Hey, Lauren. You look great." He smiles. "You ready to go?"

"Yeah, let me just get my bag."

After locking the door behind me, we head down to his truck—a beat up red Ford F-150—before helping me get in. It's clean and fresh making me wonder if he's just had it detailed or if he's just normally this tidy.

"Thought we could head over to Bucky's? They do some great chicken wings, and the beer's pretty good too," he chuckles.

I smile softly. "Sounds great."

We make the drive over in silence. It's not an uncomfortable silence per se but it's definitely weird. I'm not a conversationalist. I don't know how to make small talk so asking a bunch of questions to fill the silence isn't gonna happen.

We pull up at Bucky's, Brad rushes round to open my door, but I'm already halfway out. We walk through the quiet parking lot where there are a few cars parked around.

The bar itself isn't busy and I honestly don't know whether to be happy or upset. At least if it was busy we wouldn't be able to hear ourselves think, meaning less conversation.

*Some first date I am.*

Grabbing a table, we order drinks and look over the menu, not that I'm particularly hungry, my stomach turning in knots at the weirdness of it all.

Taking a sip of his beer, Brad leans back in his chair and asks, "Do you have plans for Thanksgiving?"

"Yeah, Sydney and I are going to her parents," I reply, glad to be on a topic that I could talk about for days.

"Sydney's your roommate, right?"

"That and best friend extraordinaire," I chuckle and Brad laughs, causing the tension to ease somewhat. "What about you? Any plans?"

"I'm staying on campus. My folks are away so there's no point in me going home."

I nod, completely understanding. Times like these I'm forever grateful that Sydney came barreling into my life with her crazy chaos.

We talk while we eat, the earlier tension completely gone. I've relaxed slightly now I've had a couple of drinks, and even though I thought Brad was easy to talk to in the coffee shop, I guess when you're just sitting talking to someone versus being on an actual date, things get... strange.

I like hanging out with Brad, but there's a part of me that wishes it was someone else sitting in front of me. Does that make me a bad person?

I'm laughing at something Brad says when I look over to the bar door opening. My laughter stops in its tracks when I see who it is—Caleb.

*For five fucking minutes.* Of all the places, he walks in here. I'm beginning to think the universe is trying to tell me something with the way we keep bumping into each other.

I'm attempting not to drool at how good he's looking wearing a tight black Henley, jeans, and black sneakers, his peppered hair in a wavy mess, but I'm failing miserably.

As if sensing I'm near, Caleb glances my way, and I suck in a breath when his gaze locks with mine. At first his eyes brighten as if he's happy to see me but when he looks to see who I'm *with*, his jaw clenches, and his eyes darken with subtle jealousy.

I gulp and quickly look away, trying to concentrate on what Brad's saying—something about a tree and a broken arm when he was a kid. I smile and nod along, trying desperately not to glance over my shoulder and see if Caleb's still here.

All of a sudden Brad pipes up, "Professor Anderson, hi."

I internally eye roll at his overly enthusiastic ass kissing.

Caleb walks over and stands next to our table. "Brad. Lauren." He nods to both of us.

Brad starts talking about an assignment, but Caleb's gaze never leaves mine. The intense look he's giving me causes my pussy to throb and I shift slightly to ease the ache, but Caleb catches it, raising an eyebrow in question.

How Brad is oblivious to the sexual tension between Caleb and I, I will never know. You could cut it with a knife.

"Excuse me," I say as I bolt up from my chair, nearly knocking it over in the process. I briskly walk to the bathroom and exhale a sigh of relief when I enter and close the door behind me.

Taking a couple of deep breaths I walk over to the sink and pat water on my face and neck, trying to cool myself down from our heated encounter.

The door opens and I hear, "We need to stop meeting like this."

I whirl around. "Goddammit, Caleb. What are you doing in here?" I hiss.

"This."

I frown, not understanding when he strides toward me, one hand grabbing my hair before slamming his lips against mine. I lean into the kiss, his tongue gliding across my bottom lip, silently asking for entrance which I allow, my mouth parting slightly. This isn't like the other kisses where it was angry and passionate. No. This is a slow tongue dual and I'm not sure which one I prefer.

I thread my fingers through his hair, deepening the kiss and whimper at the thrill of his hard cock against my stomach. Caleb slowly draws back, resting his forehead against mine, silently breathing me in.

# Chapter Twenty-Four

## *Caleb*

After my colossal fuck up going after Lauren at Strokes, I'd kept to myself. Busied myself with assignments, lectures, reading... *anything* to get my mind off her and how she looked when she asked me to leave. So that's how I ended up here, parking my Mustang outside of Bucky's regretting my life choices after agreeing to meet James for a beer.

I run a hand through my hair and tap the wheel before getting out.

*Here goes nothing.*

Glancing around, looking for James, my eyes land on a pair of very familiar green eyes. I can't say I'm disappointed she's here until I see who she's here with. Fucking Brad. The elation at seeing her quickly turns to jealousy and I clench my jaw at the sight of them. Are they on a date? As friends? Lauren will never be mine, but that doesn't mean that she doesn't *feel* like she's mine and seeing her with another man just rams that point home.

Lauren glances away first and I storm over to the bar, no James in sight. "Whiskey," I tell the barman as I lean my forearms forward and put my head in my hands. If I have to get an Uber home tonight then fuck it, I will.

I down it in one shot and ask for another. I'm still wondering where the fuck James is when my phone goes off. Reaching into my back pocket, I slide my phone out.

> James
> Stuck at work, can't get out. Won't make it.

*Just my fucking luck.*

Pushing myself off the bar, I go to leave when I hear, "Professor Anderson, hi."

Stopping, I roll my eyes and take a deep breath before strolling over to where they're sitting, giving them a slight nod in greeting. "Brad. Lauren."

Brad starts yammering on about something but I'm too busy staring at Lauren. She looks fucking gorgeous. Her hair and makeup done and the jealousy that claws its way into me that she's done this for him and not me, etches away.

"Excuse me," Lauren says as she gets up from her chair and walks away.

Brad's still talking and I'm *still* not paying him any attention. "That's great, Brad," I interrupt. "My friend just got here. I'll catch you later," and head off in search of where Lauren went.

I know I shouldn't be chasing her down *again*, but this seems to be a regular occurrence I can't stop.

Shoving my way into the women's bathroom, I blurt the first thing that comes into my head. "We need to stop meeting like this."

*Really, Caleb? You're an embarrassment.*

Lauren spins around and hisses, "Goddammit, Caleb. What are you doing in here?"

"This."

Confusion mars her pretty face and I take a couple of long strides, reaching out and grabbing a handful of her hair before crashing my lips against hers. I run my tongue over her bottom lip. *Let me in, baby. Please*, I internally beg. She must hear me because her lips part allowing my tongue to slide in.

The kiss is soft and slow, not like our usual heated embraces. I lose myself in her—her touch, her smell, her taste. Lauren threads her fingers through my hair and my cock gets harder, pressing against the confines of my jeans. The bolt of static I always feel when Lauren touches me in full force now that she's so close.

I keep kissing her tenderly, exactly how I imagined our first kiss to be. One where I could take her out on a date and take her home at the end of the night.

But I can't.

I draw back and rest my forehead against hers, breathing her in. "Are you on a date with him, sweetheart?" I ask, afraid to hear the answer, but I have to know.

Lauren opens her eyes, her gaze filled with sadness, and a tinge of lust. She swallows and sighs before whispering, "Yes."

Jealousy rears its ugly head and I'm consumed. The idea of his hands on her, of *any* man's hands on her is enough to send me into a rage.

I take a deep breath, trying to calm myself. "Don't. Don't date him, Lauren," I plead, my hands coming up to cup her face.

"Why? You have no say in who I date, Caleb." She's not angry, just stating a fact.

Lauren steps away from me and brushes a hand through her hair. "Caleb, this is like a broken record now. We see each other, you follow me, something happens, and then we go our separate ways only to repeat it again." She throws her hands up in the air as she starts pacing around. "I can't keep going on like this. Something has to give. I need to find someone of my own age, someone who I can be out in public with." Lauren pauses before whispering the last part, "Someone who isn't my professor."

The guilt is overwhelming. I can't stay away from her but I'm putting both of us at risk. "I know," I sigh. "I just—" I stop, not sure what to say. Sometimes words don't need to be spoken to understand their meaning because I know, just by looking at Lauren, she has the same conflicting emotions swirling in her eyes as I do.

This push and pull that the universe is doing with us. Forcing us together in unlikely situations only to laugh and say 'gotcha.'

I reach into my wallet and pull out my card, holding it toward her. "Take my number. All the students have it for emergencies so it's not like it's favoritism or anything. Just—if you need me for assignments or... whatever." I'm fumbling in the dark here with no idea what the fuck I'm doing or what I'm trying to say.

Lauren tilts her head as if contemplating my request and weighing up all the pros and cons. Just when I think she's going to tell me to get fucked, she reaches out and takes the card from me.

"You should go," I say. "Brad's probably wondering where you are and is about to send out a search and rescue team for you." I smile, though it doesn't reach my eyes.

Lauren chuckles lightly. "Yeah, you're probably right." She heads to the door and stops as she gets there, her back to me. It's barely above a whisper but I hear it anyway. "I wish things could be different, Caleb.

I wish it was you and not Brad." With that she leaves and for the first time, doesn't glance back.

# Chapter Twenty-Five

# Lauren

It's the start of Thanksgiving break so Sydney and I are currently cruising to her parents for the weekend. The windows are rolled down on her blue Mini Cooper, the music's blaring and the wind's in my hair—what more could a girl want? I feel better already, as if leaving campus and all the drama behind me has lifted a weight off my shoulders, making me feel lighter, if only for the weekend.

Sydney's driving so I get to be a passenger princess and DJ. I glance over at her when she starts singing *I Can Do It With A Broken Heart* badly, my face morphing into horrified shock that she would *dare* sing Tay-Tay off key—Swifties everywhere would be mortified at such blatant disregard for our queen. Yes, I love Taylor... bite me.

"*Lights, camera, bitch, smile,*" she sings as she glances at me, laughing at my expression. "What?"

"Who *are* you right now?" I gasp in mock disbelief.

Sydney carries on, laughing as she turns off at our exit.

Not long after, we're pulling up outside Dave and Cynthia's house. It's a modest three bed, with a large front and back yard. It has the most amazing wraparound porch which I've been obsessed with since I first saw it, spending most of my evenings here sitting on the outdoor swing, watching the world go by.

"My baby," Cynthia cries as she runs from the house and envelopes Sydney in a hug. I wince from the impact. *That's gotta hurt.*

"Mom. You're embarrassing me," Sydney whisper yells.

"And this is exactly why I do it." Cynthia winks at me as she comes over to hug me. I lean into her embrace and hug her back. "Hi, honey," she says.

I smile up at her. "Hey, Cynthia."

"Come on, your dad's firing up the grill." Cynthia helps us grab our things and we head in. She's always reminded me of a younger Helen Mirren, including the humor. Cynthia's constantly playing pranks on everyone and if she can embarrass you, her life is complete. If I was to ever have kids… she'd be mom goals.

We end up in the kitchen once everything's put away. Another thing I love about this house? The kitchen. I may have a slight obsession with good looking kitchens. It's all open windows, lots of light and space—the stuff of dreams.

I grab a soda from the fridge and sit at the breakfast bar while Cynthia fusses over Sydney. I'm trying and failing to stifle my giggles as Cynthia tries wiping off a beauty spot Sydney drew on her face to 'try it out.'

"You've got mud on your face, hun," Cynthia says.

"For the love of fuck, Mom. I drew it on, it's not mud," Sydney cries as she runs to the other side of the kitchen island to get away from her.

Cynthia stops chasing Sydney. "Why on earth would you want to do that?" she asks incredulously. "Is this a new 'in thing' that the cool kids do, because honestly... it's not a look." Cynthia purses her lips like she's sucked on a lemon and I'm done. Even Sydney bursts out laughing.

Dave comes in with dinner, raising an eyebrow but doesn't say anything, used to his wife's antics after thirty years of marriage.

We sit at the dining table, catching up on everything since the last time we saw them. Thoughts of Caleb drift in every so often but I push them to the side, not wanting to deal with *that* can of worms, while I'm trying to have a good time.

Syd and I decided to stay in, opting not to be hung over on Thanksgiving. We say our good nights and head to bed. Sydney's on her phone not saying much, she's been in a weird mood lately, but I've just put it down to her new dance instructor riding her ass. She'll talk to me when she's ready.

I take the time to get myself ready for bed and scroll through social media before calling it a night.

---

I'm stuffed, literally stuffed. I can't eat anything else. Cynthia went all out for Thanksgiving today with the amount of food she prepared; at one point I wondered if she was preparing for a zombie apocalypse—the kitchen looked like a bomb had gone off. I chuckle at the reminder.

It's been such a fun, chilled out day though, not even bothering to get changed out of my pajamas, opting for comfort over style. I've always enjoyed spending time with Sydney and her family, nothing's ever forced. You just walk into their home and it's like you've been there your whole life.

Pouring myself a glass of wine, I walk out onto the wraparound porch and curl up on the seated swing, wrapping a blanket around my shoulders to keep warm. The lights from the kitchen creating a warm glow outside as I sit and gaze across the yard.

A noise brings me out of my blissfully blank mind, and I turn my head to see Cynthia coming outside with her own glass of wine in hand.

"Mind if I sit?" she asks.

Moving over to let her sit down, I reply, "Absolutely." Opening the blanket, she huddles in next to me and I lean my head on her shoulder.

"You seem out of sorts, hun. Everything going okay?" she asks, her motherly instincts flowing over to me.

I hum as I take a sip of my drink, unsure of what to say.

Cynthia turns to face me, a look of concern flitting across her features. "You know you can talk to me about anything, right?"

"I know. I just... don't know how to explain it, I guess," I reply, shrugging my shoulders.

"Why don't you start at the beginning?" she offers.

I nod before starting. "I met a guy, found out he was off limits, starting catching feelings, told him to leave me alone, he did but—"

"But you didn't actually want him to stop?" Cynthia finishes for me, a knowing glint to her eyes.

"Something like that," I mumble.

"Why's he off limits?" she enquires.

"He's not someone I can have." Tears begin to fill my eyes. Lying to both Sydney and Cynthia is making me feel like the absolute worst kind of person.

"Hmm," she muses, tapping her glass with her nails. "Did you know that when I met Dave, he was off limits?"

"I think our 'off limits' are slightly different, Cyn," I chuckle.

"He was my best friend's boyfriend."

My eyes go wide, and my mouth drops open in shock. "Cynthia, you little hussy."

"Don't look so affronted, it was the 90s," she laughs. "My point is, sometimes the forbidden can lead to something neither one of you ever thought was possible. I've spent the last thirty years with my soul mate. I lost my best friend that day but what I gained instead? That was worth everything."

Looking at Cynthia and the love that's clearly shining in her eyes at the thought of Dave, my heart squeezes in my chest. Could I have that with Caleb? Could he be the one if I stop fighting it? Stop fighting *him*?

Cynthia stands up, grabbing her glass. "You don't have to make any decisions today, just think it over, hmm?" With that she kisses my forehead and walks back into the house, leaving me to mull over her words.

---

After mine and Cynthia's chat, I needed to get out of my head for a while so after two quiet nights in, Sydney and I decided we're going out, out tonight. I've gone with a cute 50s pin up style—hair up, light on the makeup and heavy on the red lipstick. We went into town this morning and I found a stunning red A-line polka dot dress that matched the vibe.

So here I sit—I'm pretty sure I'm on cocktail number five—with a nice little buzz going, waiting for Sydney. I didn't her about what happened at Illusion, it's not that I was hiding anything from her, it just never came up, so I'm happy knowing we'll be going home together.

"Girls? You ready?" Dave calls out. He's driving, saving us having to get an Uber. Picking up the last of my shit, I add them to my clutch and we make our way downstairs, where Dave is waiting for us, keys in hand. "You both look beautiful," he says, pride shining in his eyes.

Sydney gives him a hug. "Dad, thank you, I love you, but if you ruin my make-up by making me cry, I *will* hurt you."

Dave chuckles, giving her a hug back. "Understood, baby girl."

Tensing at the term 'baby girl,' I give Dave a quick hug and kiss, wiping off the red stain I left behind on his cheek, before we trundle out to his car.

On the ride over Sydney plays DJ, both of us singing badly to anything she can find on her playlist, a mix of everything from pop to metal. When Dave starts rapping to *Limp Bizkit's Rollin'*, Sydney and I lose our ever loving minds—who knew he was so cool?

Once we get to the club, we say our goodbye's, promising to call him if we need picking up, we both assure him we will but should be okay. The place isn't anything like Illusion or Bucky's, it's more your nightclub kinda vibe—strobe lights, drum and bass and sweaty bodies everywhere. Sydney's in heaven… I need another drink.

Perching at the edge of the bar, I order us a couple of tequila shots, my usual Jack and Coke for me and a cocktail for Sydney—something about wanting to try something different, I just think she's gonna end up puking. I down my drink, needing to get my buzz back, and wave down the bartender for another.

Sydney jumped on the dance floor as soon as she finished her drink—surprise, surprise—but I love watching her. This is our thing; I stand at the bar drinking and she goes off dancing.

I feel my phone go off in my bag and reach in to grab it.

> Brad
>
> Hey! Hope you're having a great weekend. It's quiet here without you.

I honestly don't know what to say to this. I mean, yeah, we've been spending time together but I made it pretty clear that we can only be friends. After the whole incident with Caleb at Bucky's I can't—won't do a relationship right now. I tried to go on a date and what happens? The universe throws a curveball at me.

I don't want to be rude so I quickly type out my reply:

> Me
>
> Weekend's great, thank you. Hope yours is okay?

I put my phone away and call the bartender for more shots—I'm going to need something stronger.

The night passes by in a blur of shots, dancing and more shots. Deciding to check the time, I reach for my phone, squinting at the screen as I see another message from Brad. *Dear god, he just won't quit.* I think this is the fifth one he's sent me now and I haven't replied since the first.

> Brad
>
> So you must be really busy not to be able to reply. Just wanted to let you know that Dean Williams want to see you in his office Monday morning. Professor Anderson will be there, as well.

*What the fuck do they want?*

Too much liquid courage and a bad attitude are to blame for what happens next.

> **Me**
> Why do I need to be in the dean's office on Monday morning? And why will you be there?
>
> It's Lauren Taylor by the way.

Short and to the point, because honestly? I need to know why I'd be called in to see them. I'm not expecting a reply to come through as quickly as it does, so I nearly drop my phone when I see his name on the screen.

> **Caleb**
> The dean wants to check on your progress. As your professor, I need to be there.

*Hmm.*

> **Me**
> I find that hard to believe, but okay.

> **Caleb**
> Lauren, I swear. It had nothing to do with me. Are you okay?

Why is he asking if I'm okay? Of course I'm not. I kinda, maybe, sorta have feelings for my professor.

> **Me**
> Yeah, I'm okay. I'm out at a bar with Sydney.

Do I sound like a drunk sixteen-year-old right now? Most probably.

> **Caleb**
> What bar?

Why is this causing butterflies in my stomach? I can feel a goofy grin plaster across my face and I have to give myself a mental slap to stop it.

Me

> Can't remember the name. What are you doing?

*I'm going to hell.*

# Chapter Twenty-Six

## *Caleb*

I'm in my home office when my phone goes off. It's a Saturday night so it can only mean it's the boys wanting to drag me out for a beer. I take my glasses off and rub my eyes. I've barely slept. I'm a law unto myself really, chasing a goddamn college student around like a teenager.

My phone pings again, alerting me to another message that pulls me out of my somber mood. The message is from an unknown number, clicking on it, I open it up.

> Unknown
> Why do I need to be in the dean's office on Monday morning? And why will you be there?

Confusion mars my features as I think of who it could be. As soon as I've read the message, another one pops up.

> Unknown
> It's Lauren Taylor by the way.

I put my glasses back on and do a double take. She messaged me. My heart's pounding as I re-read her message, twice. Ah fuck. This one had nothing to do with me. The dean wants to check in on Lauren and how she's getting on, so that's what I tell her. Her reply comes through instantly.

Lauren

> I find that hard to believe but okay.

I swear to god this little brat. She's lucky she's not here to get her ass spanked. My palm is itching to get itself reacquainted with her delectable ass. Reiterating my response and asking her if she's okay seems like the mature and adult way to deal with things. *Might calm down the raging hard on that's now tented my sweats, too.*

Lauren

> Yeah, I'm okay. I'm out at a bar with Sydney.

The possessive beast within me emerges. Is she being safe? The last time she was out, she got manhandled by some asswipe. I sit up straighter in my chair, my protective instincts kicking in as I message her back, asking for which bar because I'll be damned if she's out alone again.

Lauren

> Can't remember the name. What are you doing?

*What am I doing? I'm going out of my mind right now, baby girl, that's what I'm doing.*

I look down and realize I'm now pacing around my office, running a hand through my hair obsessively. I scoff internally, like it'll make a difference.

Me

> What. Bar. Lauren

I'm slowly going insane. Is this what it's like to chase after a woman half my age—Fuck, is that another gray hair?

> Lauren
>
> I honestly don't know. I'm at Sydney's parents for the weekend so I'm not anywhere near campus for you to come and rescue me. What are you doing?

FUCK!

I can't even get to her if something happens. I don't think. I do. I call her and she answers after the second ring. The first thing I hear is loud music.

"Hang on," she shouts, while doing god knows what. I'm still pacing my office, tension snaking its way into my shoulders.

"Lauren," I growl, my patience hanging on by a thread. I need to know she's safe. It suddenly goes quiet.

"Don't panic, I'm outside. Security's right behind me. Wow, they weren't kidding when they said air makes you more drunk. And I am druuunk right now. Are you drunk, Caleb?" she giggles.

"No, baby girl, I'm not drunk," I chuckle. This shouldn't be so adorable.

Lauren sighs into the phone. "I love it when you call me that."

"Call you what? Baby girl?" I ask, my lips twitching.

"Yeah," she replies wistfully.

I chuckle. "Noted." My tone drops, laced with concern and worry. "Are you safe? After Illusion—"

Lauren cuts me off. "I'm good. Sydney's inside and we're leaving soon. I just—When Brad messaged telling me about the meeting... I guess I thought you had... I don't know... made it up to see me again?"

Shaking my head, even though I know she can't see me, I reply, "I promise you, it had nothing to do with me."

"*Can* I see you again?" she whispers.

My chest tightens at her admission. "Lauren." I drag her name out and run a hand through my hair leaving it in a more disheveled state than it already was. "Why don't we talk about this when you haven't been drinking, yeah?"

She chuckles. "That would probably be a good idea."

"Go back inside," I tell her. "Text me when you get back to Sydney's."

"Okay. Goodnight, Caleb," she breathes out.

"Night, sweetheart."

Lauren hangs up and I resume my seated position, staring at nothing. My cock's painfully hard from hearing her voice on the phone, her breathy tones having an effect on me, and even though I shouldn't, I reach into my sweatpants and grab myself.

I try to think of anything other than where my mind wants to go—Lauren, so I focus on R-rated videos I've watched in the past, but she keeps creeping back in.

Images of her spin around in my head—the bathroom at Strokes, her on her knees in my office. I take my cock out, spitting into my hand as I glide up and down my length. My breathing becomes faster, matching the strokes of my hand. I think of Lauren bent over my desk as I fuck her from behind, her ass bouncing to my thrusts.

I groan as my spine tingles with my impending release, my balls drawing up tightly and I know it won't be long. The thought of Lauren's mouth stuffed with my cock as she looks up at me with her beautiful green eyes sends me over the edge and I come, shooting my release into my waiting hand.

Sprawling in my chair, I blow out a ragged breath, grabbing a tissue from my desk and wiping myself off.

# Chapter Twenty-Seven

## *Lauren*

I wake up to the mother of all hangovers. *Water. I need water.* I smack my lips together. *Yup, dryer than Gandhi's flip flop.*

My throat is scratchy and raw as I groan and sit up, reaching for the glass of water that I'd left on my bedside table before going to sleep. The cool water soothes as it goes down but does absolutely nothing for the woodpecker attacking my head.

Grabbing my phone to check the time—9:47 a.m. Sydney and I aren't due to leave her parents until later today, hoping to avoid traffic. Just then, Sydney comes in with a cup of coffee.

"Good morning, sunshine. Rise and shine," she laughs as she opens the curtains.

I groan as I throw the duvet over my head. "Why do you hate me? Evil woman!" I exclaim.

Not forgetting the coffee I know she has in her hands, I reach one hand out from under the duvet and wiggle my fingers in a "gimme" fashion. Sydney must love me because she hands it straight over. Seeing as I'm curled up in the fetal position, it's a bit difficult to drink so I slowly sit myself up, while still under the duvet.

Once I've sat up and had a couple of long sips of my coffee, I breathe out a sigh of content and finally remove my head from under the duvet.

"We getting on the road soon?" Sydney asks as she sits on the bed.

Her long hair is up and she's in sweats, something she doesn't do unless she's not going anywhere... something about not wanting people to see her less than perfect? I glazed over at that point, Sydney's nothing short of perfect in my eyes.

Finishing off the last of my coffee, I reply, "Mmm."

"Who were you on the phone to last night?" Sydney enquires, a knowing glint to her eye. "Brad?" She smirks.

"Huh? I was on the phone last night?" I have no memory of this. I grab my phone from beside the bed and check my messages.

*Fuck.*

I check my call log.

*Double fuck.*

"I'm guessing by the look on your face someone drunk dialed last night?" Sydney grins and grabs her pillow, holding it to her chest. "Ooooh this is so good. Who was it? Please tell me it was Brad." She leans in for a closer look.

Even in my less than stellar state I move so quickly I end up tumbling out of bed, flat on my back with my legs in the air. "Ouch." I rub my hip where I landed on it.

Sydney's head pokes over the edge of the bed. "Must be good if that's your reaction," she cackles.

"Erm, yeah, it was, uh, Brad," I stutter.

*Because that didn't just give away that I'm guilty.*

"So, what happened?" Sydney raises an eyebrow at me as I slowly climb back onto the bed.

"Oh, he messaged me to say that Professor Anderson and Dean Williams want to see me on Monday morning. I, uh, called him to find out the details."

Fuck, I hate lying to her.

Sydney pouts. "Is that it? Girl, I thought you were gonna give me the good stuff and tell me there was phone sex involved."

I roll my eyes at her. "My apologies for not having better gossip for you."

"Apology accepted," she retorts with a wink. "Come on, get your ass up. We need to start packing before we have lunch with the parents."

I groan but throw the duvet off, shuffling into the bathroom and getting in the shower before packing up the few things that I brought with me. As I'm washing my hair I think back to last night, trying to remember the conversation...

I let out a gasp. *I. Did. Not.*

Oh, but I think I did. I think I asked to see Caleb again. I'm going to do what every self-respecting person would do in my position—ignore it. Act like it never happened. I know nothing. Zilch. Nada.

It'll work... right?

---

We got back from Sydney's parents late last night, so I've had next to no sleep before having to get up at the butt crack of dawn to get to this meeting with Caleb and the dean on time. I push through the door of the admissions building and the same kind lady from before is sitting behind her desk.

"Hello, dear." She smiles as I get closer.

"Hi, Lauren Taylor to see Dean Williams. I have an appointment with him this morning."

"Ah, yes, Professor Anderson is already in there waiting for you. Go on through, dear."

I nod and turn toward the door. Knocking, I hear, "Come in," a few seconds later. Taking a deep breath, I walk in.

The first thing I notice is Caleb. He's leaning against the window and my breath catches. He's not wearing his glasses today and I'm not gonna lie, I'm a little bit disappointed. He's wearing a white shirt and black slacks as usual, his peppered hair messed just the way I like it. He pushes off the glass window and stands to his full height when he sees me.

A throat clearing brings me out of my perusal and I realize I've been staring. I avert my gaze toward Dean Williams and an emotion crosses his face, one too quick for me to decipher.

"Thank you Professor Anderson, but I think Lauren and I have it from here," the dean says without taking his eyes off me.

"I'm good, I don't need to—" Caleb begins but the dean cuts him off.

"It wasn't a request, Professor Anderson. You may leave." He finally glances at Caleb, a dark look spreading across his features.

I watch as Caleb's jaw tightens ever so slightly but gives a small nod. His gaze lingers on me before he strides to the door, opening it and slamming it shut behind him.

Dean Williams stands up from his chair, rounding his desk before coming to stop in front of me.

"I take notice of special students, Lauren. And you are a... special student." He runs his thumb across his bottom lip and his expression darkens.

"Thank you?" It comes out more like a question, my confusion evident in my tone as I try to figure out what's going on.

"You see Lauren, I think you would do well here if you were to... how do I put this? Engage in activities that would *enhance* your education."

I swallow, a feeling of dread working its way up my spine. "I'm not sure I follow, sir."

The dean takes a lingering look at me, lips curved in a thin, sardonic smile. "Do you have a boyfriend, Lauren?" he asks.

"N-no, sir." Where the hell is he going with this? Is he allowed to do this? I squirm in my seat.

"Good, good." He leers at me, almost like he's... happy? Excited that I don't have anyone. He leans in to touch my face and I jerk back, slapping at his hand.

"Wha-what are you doing?" I protest.

"Sorry," he says, not looking sorry at all, his dark eyes shining with cold amusement.

Quickly standing, I blurt, "I have to get to class."

"Of course, I'll be seeing you around... to check on your studies, of course," Dean Williams says, as he saunters back to his desk and resumes his seated position, completely oblivious to the inner turmoil he's caused.

Bolting for the door, I feel his cold stare following me. I don't stop running, even with shouts from admin staff and faculty members telling me to.

I eventually shove my way through the door leading to the exit, folding over myself as I try and catch my breath. The blood rushes to my ears, my fingers tingle and I'm gasping for air. Students continue walking around, completely oblivious to my state of panic. I'm shaking, trembling, as if I'm frozen solid, the adrenaline of the dean's office now wearing off.

Unfolding myself from my braced position, I close my eyes and tilt my head back to the sky, counting each inhale and exhale, until I start feeling like I can breathe easier. Sensing someone approaching me, I jump.

"Hey, it's just me," a soothing voice says. I look over and a sob works its way up my throat, threatening to come out. If I start now, I won't be able to stop. "Sweetheart, you're shaking."

"I-I—" No matter how hard I try, the words won't come. Tears line my eyes.

"It's okay, Lauren. You're okay," he says, standing close enough that I can hear what he's saying, but far enough away that it looks like an innocent conversation. "We need to get you out of here. Can you put your hood up for me and walk to the parking lot? I'll be walking behind you the whole time."

I feel like I'm in a daze and completely overreacting.

"Hey, look at me. Lauren." Caleb steps closer. "Look at me," he demands forcefully as he tilts my chin up and I meet his gaze. He softens his tone as he says, "Put your hood up and get to the parking lot, okay? We'll deal with everything after, sweetheart."

His voice is a soothing balm to my soul and I find myself nodding at him and following his instructions as if my body's on autopilot.

Putting my hood up, I start walking. I have no clue what to do when I get there but just knowing that Caleb's behind me, gives me that little bit of peace to keep moving.

# Chapter Twenty-Eight

## *Caleb*

Every muscle in my body protested at leaving Lauren with Dean Williams. Call it intuition or whatever but something ain't right. The unnerving look he had on his face when he asked—no, told me to leave just made it that much worse. I wanted to stay, to protect what's mine, but if I'd put up a fight, questions would have been asked. I didn't go far though, I made my way to the front of the building and waited for her, hiding under the shade of the nearest tree like a stalker.

What I didn't expect was Lauren to come flying out the doors not long after, bending over to catch her breath. I wanted to run over there, to comfort her but with the amount of students walking around, it was too risky, so I had to bide my time and walk over slowly making it look more like I was a concerned teacher and less like a man running after a woman he's half in love with.

The anxiety at witnessing her having a meltdown was tearing at me. Lauren shut down completely, this wasn't anything like Illusion. Yeah, she was shook up but she brushed it off—or what looked like it. This

Lauren is close to having a panic attack, so I wasn't thinking clearly when I told her to walk to my car. I wasn't thinking clearly when I used my nickname for her. And I sure as shit wasn't thinking clearly once I'd gotten her into my car and had driven her to my house. Which leads us to now—Lauren sat on my couch.

Fuck.

I push my hair back from my face and take a breath before asking her if she wants some water. She declines but I grab one anyway, just to give me something to do. I place it on the coffee table in front of her and sit down next to it. Lauren's reclined back, head against the sofa with her eyes closed. I rest my forearms on my knees and put my head in my hands, waiting for her to say something... anything.

I hear a sigh, followed by a shuffle and then a hand threading through my hair. "Caleb?"

I glance up and gaze into her beautiful eyes, getting lost in them for a moment before I reach for her, hauling her towards me. Lauren comes willingly and straddles my lap, placing her head in the crook of my neck. I wrap my arms around her and just breathe her in, that familiar vanilla scent soothing me in a way nothing ever has before.

"Uh, Caleb? Are you... sniffing me?" Lauren asks.

"Shhhh, baby girl, let me enjoy this for a minute," I groan and hold her tighter. She chuckles softly but snuggles into me more, relaxing in my hold.

I don't know how long we sit here for before she starts talking. "He's so weird, Caleb. Dean Williams, I mean."

"What happened, Lauren? I need to know," I grit out, anger fueling my response at the thought of her being alone with that asshole.

"I don't know, he was just being... disturbing... about stuff. Like he wanted to know if I had a boyfriend and to 'engage in activities that would enhance my education'... whatever that means."

*Oh, I know exactly what he means. Motherfucker.*

"The way he was staring at me, Caleb, it wasn't right. He tried to touch me... so, I don't know. I just freaked out and ran," she says with a shrug. "He gives me such bad vibes, it just threw me off for a minute. I'm okay now though... I feel safe with you," she breathes out.

My eyebrow raises incredulously at her. "Sweetheart, don't bullshit me. You completely shut down in the car on the way back. You were trembling. You are clearly *not* okay." My voice is thick with emotion as I brush a strand of hair away from her face.

Lauren sighs, her shoulders drooping against my chest as she mumbles, "Would you believe me if I said I've forgotten about it?"

"Not a fucking chance." I exhale harshly, the breath blowing a hair into my face.

Drawing away from me, she sits up, playing with the button on my shirt, not looking at me. "You know things were... somewhat difficult at home. I learned from an early age to compartmentalize, to make a list of pros and cons and quickly work through them. The guidance counsellor said it was my way of 'dealing with the trauma of my childhood.'" She scoffs. "Personally, I think it's a load of shit. This isn't like with Illusion, someone grabbing my arm is... I guess... normal? For me. But Dean Williams? That shit was scary. I'm sorry I worried you." She finally looks up at me, stroking my face lightly, like she's tracing the lines of my face. Sadness pulls at her lips, her eyes a dark whirlpool threatening to suck me in.

I kiss her forehead and pull her closer, at this rate she won't be able to breath with how tightly I'm holding her. The protective instinct taking over, the urge to go back to Dean Williams and scare the shit out of *him*, growing more by the minute.

"I'm sorry, sweetheart," I say against her head, tenderly tracing circles on her back, whether it's to comfort her or myself is yet to be seen.

Lauren looks at me, confusion etched on her face. "What are *you* sorry for? You didn't do anything wrong, Caleb," she says incredulously.

Not looking at her, I confess, "I wasn't there to protect you from him."

Gently tugging at my face, she says, "Caleb, look at me." I peer up at her, her bright green eyes shining with resolve. Lauren cups my face in her hands as she says, "You're always saving me. I feel like a damsel in distress at this point," she chuckles, trying to lighten the mood and I chuckle with her. "This wasn't either of our fault." Lauren lowers her gaze and it's now my turn to cup her face and make *her* look at *me*.

"I know, sweetheart." I brush a hair out of her face and behind her ear. "Still doesn't make me feel any better, though," I reiterate, my lips brushing against hers in a tender kiss

*This is a bad idea. Abort. Abort.*

Drawing back, I start apologizing, "Fuck, Lauren. I'm so—" I begin. I've just fucking kissed her when she's vulnerable. What a fucking asshole. Pushing at her gently, I move to stand up but Lauren stops me.

"Please don't," she whispers. "Please don't pull away from me."

"Lauren—"

She cuts me off again. "No Caleb, please. I need this. I need *you*."

My eyes search hers for any indication that she's lying, that I should stop but all I find is the truth and god help me, I'm done for. I block out every reason why this is a bad idea and just follow my instinct. The one that's screaming at me that this is right... that *she* is right.

Lauren wraps her arms around my neck and presses herself in closer, rubbing her pussy against my growing cock, as she continues straddling me on the coffee table. I grab her ass and move her faster, getting her off through our clothes. Lauren's breathing gets faster and she breaks the kiss, allowing me to kiss down her neck, where I find a particularly sensitive spot that has her whimpering.

Her moans get louder, but I stop—I need to move this somewhere that's more comfortable than on a coffee table.

"Wh-what! Caleb, I swear to fuc—"

Grinning at her, my voice drops to a growl laced with desire. "Don't worry, baby girl, I got you." I grab Lauren's ass and push up, and she automatically wraps her legs around my waist.

"Now this, I can get behind," she chuckles as she holds onto the back of my neck and kisses me.

Stumbling to my bedroom, I have to pause halfway up the stairs as Lauren reaches down and palms my dick. I growl at her in warning, ready to fuck her there and then.

Shoving the door open, I stride across to the bed and throw her on it, she squeals and bounces a couple of times before coming to a stop. Sitting up on her elbows, her gaze lands on me, the heat and the desire radiating off her and matching my own.

Lauren comes up onto all fours and starts crawling to the edge of the bed as I take my shirt off, stopping when she sees my naked torso. I'm not a guy with a six pack but I'm also not a guy with a dad bod either, I like to think I'm somewhere in between, both hard and soft. My arms are covered in full sleeve tattoos which finish at my shoulder and go down to my wrists—another reason why I wear long sleeves at work, to hide them.

I slowly undo my belt buckle and slacks as Lauren watches me, biting her lip, before running her tongue along it. I follow the movement with my eyes, wishing it was *my* teeth biting and running along her bottom lip.

Just as I'm about to undress, Lauren suddenly shouts, "Wait." I pause, raising an eyebrow. "Let me," she purrs.

*Fuck. Me.*

I cross my arms over my chest and wait for her next move.

Lauren gets up off the bed and comes to a halt in front of me, trailing her fingers down my arms and taking in my tattoos before leaning in and placing a gentle kiss on my chest. I breathe out a sigh at the contact and tangle my hand in her hair. I don't force her, it's just there, feeling the smooth, silkiness of it.

She gazes up at me as she trails kisses down my chest before getting onto her knees and palming me through my slacks. I tip my head back and groan, my cock painfully hard.

Lauren places her fingertips inside the waistband of my trousers and pulls them down in one movement. My cock springs forward, almost taking out her eye. She places a tender kiss to the head before licking the pre-cum that's gathered there. I groan louder and tug her hair harder. Lauren must take that as an invitation as she fully engulfs my cock with her mouth.

"Damn, you're too good at this," I gasp, the feeling of her warm, wet mouth overwhelming me. She whimpers in response and I swear I see stars.

Lauren starts to work my cock with her mouth, back and forth, faster and faster, before bringing her hand up to jerk off what she can't fit in. She swallows me to the back of her throat—her cheeks hollow, and she sucks like she's trying to draw the soul from my body. My spine starts to tingle with my impending orgasm.

"I'm going to feed you my cum, Lauren, and you're going to swallow every fucking drop," I growl, as I cup the back of her head and thrust into her mouth, she doesn't tap my thigh to stop so I keep going, chasing my own high.

Roaring out my release, I slowly ease in and out of Lauren's mouth, before pulling out altogether, my chest heaving up and down, but my cock's still hard—*that's new*.

She looks so goddamn beautiful on her knees, wet lash line, and drool on her chin.

I reach down, pulling her gently to a stand before crashing my lips to hers, not caring about the taste of my cum in her mouth as the kiss deepens, and I pull her closer. Grabbing her ass cheeks, I lift her up again, moving to the bed before placing her down.

I point at her clothes. "Off."

She begins removing her hoodie, T-shirt, and bra. I grab my cock, giving it a couple of tugs at the sight of her pebbled nipples, begging me to put my mouth on them. Lauren quickly removes her jeans and underwear, leaving her bare to my gaze.

I slowly get on the bed and crawl towards her, trailing kisses along her legs before getting to her glistening cunt. I run one finger up her slit, gathering her juices before rubbing her clit in circular motions.

Lauren's breath hitches as she moans out, "More."

I smirk at her. "I'm not sure what gave you the idea that you're in control here, baby girl." I tap her clit to emphasize my point.

"*Agggh*," she cries and I do it again only for her back to bow off the bed, hands clutching at the sheets.

*Hmmm, guess she likes that.*

I slip one finger into her cunt and slowly bend down, licking a slow line from her entrance to her clit, thrusting a finger into her pussy before sucking her clit into my mouth. Lauren's moans fill the room and I know she's close. I add a second finger and she comes, screaming my name, her hips lifting off the bed and her hand clutching my head, pushing me into her further, almost suffocating me.

*Not a bad way to die.*

Lauren comes down from her orgasm but I keep going.

"Caleb, I-I can't," she pants out, pushing me away.

"You can and you will, sweetheart. Give me another one," I demand. No sooner do I say this, that she comes again. "So responsive, baby girl." My voice is low and strained as I speak.

I lean over and grab a condom from the nightstand. "Do I need this, baby girl?" I ask, because even though we've gone without a condom before, I really don't want to wear one, but I will if she asks me to.

Lauren shakes her head. "I trust you."

If I wasn't already halfway in love with her before, I definitely am now.

Capturing her lips in a heated kiss, I line my cock up with her entrance and slowly ease in. A low growl leaves me at the feeling of her cunt clenching around me, sucking me further in. Tilting her hips, I rotate so I hit her clit at the same time.

"Fuck, that feels so good, Caleb," she moans. My skin glistens with sweat as I drive my cock deeper into her soaked pussy, the headboard banging against the wall, but all I can hear are her breathy gasps, telling me to go harder.

Her eyes flutter closed as her fingers dig into my back. "Caleb... I'm gonna come again."

"Come for me, sweetheart," I order as I take one of her nipples into my mouth and bite down.

"Fuck—yes. Caleb."

At the feel of Lauren coming, her walls tightening around me, I feel my own release hurtling its way through. "Lauren," I roar.

Collapsing on top of her, careful not to crush her, my muscles twitch as I try to get my breathing under control.

"I think I just saw stars," she laughs.

"Me too."

I slowly pull out of her, watching in fascination as my cum drips out of her.

*Fuck that's hot.*

I go to the bathroom, clean myself up, and grab a washcloth. Walking back into the bedroom I see Lauren still in the same place I left her. My lips curve into a small smile at the sight, and I think of how much of a lucky bastard I am. How right it feels her being here.

"That was—" Lauren begins but I cut her off.

"Incredible? Mind blowing? Out of this world?" I grin.

She laughs and I swear I could get addicted to the sound. "All of the above."

I clean her up before throwing the cloth in the laundry basket. "Good girl." I wink and she blushes.

Crawling into bed, I haul her to me, placing an arm around her as her head rests against my chest, her arm and leg thrown over my body. My fingers trace patterns on her skin as Lauren yawns, and I squeeze her tightly, giving myself one minute to think of this being our future before reality sets back in.

# Chapter Twenty-Nine

## *Lauren*

I wake up in a bedroom that's not my own and it takes me a minute for my sleep-addled brain to figure out where I am. I sit up and glance around. Caleb's room looks like any normal guys room—grays and whites, the odd sock left out, a laundry basket overflowing with clothes. There's not much in the way of furniture, a bed, wardrobe, chest of drawers and two bedside tables. It suits him though.

Slipping out of bed, I look for my clothes that were thrown around earlier but I can't find them. What I do find, though, is an old band T-shirt, so I put that on and go in search of Caleb.

I walk out of his room and come to a hallway with two doors on either side and a staircase down the middle. I go for the staircase and hope he's downstairs. When I get to the bottom I hear his voice so I follow the sound until I get to the kitchen.

*My god, it's like a wet dream in here.*

The kitchen's done in creams and blacks, giving it that high end cottage feel. State of the art kitchen appliances are everywhere and I have to wipe the drool away that's formed at the corner of my mouth. Caleb's sitting at the breakfast bar on his phone and he looks okay too, I guess. Who am I kidding, between him and the appliances I'm in heaven.

He's wearing sweatpants that hang low on his hips and no T-shirt, showing off the tattoos on his arms—tattoos that I really want to get up and personal with. Caleb's got his glasses on and my pussy flutters at the sight.

*What is it about him and those glasses?*

Caleb glances up, his eyes darkening with hunger as he takes me in. I blush, feeling self-conscious from the look he's giving me. He gestures to the coffee machine with a head tilt and I give him a grateful smile.

Once I've made my coffee, I pad over to the breakfast bar and sit down in the seat next to him, waiting for him to finish. I'm sipping on my coffee and gazing out of his kitchen window, which backs out onto a large backyard, when I feel a hand on my thigh. There's no funny business, it's like he's resting his hand there for comfort, like he can't bear not to have some part of his body touching me at all times.

Caleb finishes his call just as I'm draining the dregs of my coffee. In all honesty I have no clue who he was talking to or what it was about, I'd zoned out, my mind blank for once, as Caleb rubbed his thumb back and forth on my thigh.

"That was Brad. He's taking my classes for the rest of the day," he says as he runs a hand through his hair. "I, uh, told him I had a... sickness bug, which meant that I needed to go home."

"What about me? Does he know I'm missing?"

Caleb raises an eyebrow at me, and smirks. "No, I thought it would be better to not mention your name at all."

"That makes sense." I nod, feeling stupid. Of course he's not going to mention me to his TA.

"Are we going to talk about this?" Caleb asks as he takes his glasses off and cleans them on a towel.

"We probably should," I sigh. "I'm gonna need more coffee for this though." I get up and make another drink. Leaning against the counter I gesture for Caleb to start.

"I think we should date. In secret, I mean," he blurts out.

I nearly spit my coffee out but choke on it instead.

*Come again?*

"That's not where I thought you were going with this," I wheeze out around coughs. Caleb jumps up but I wave him off. "You just caught me off guard. Care to explain what you mean when you say 'date' and 'in secret.'"

Caleb looks a bit sheepish as he replies, "Look, we obviously have something here" —he gestures between us— "and I wanna know if there's anything here or if it's just lust that burns out in a couple of weeks. It's not ideal, I get that. There's gonna be a lot of sneaking around—" He stops and rakes a hand down his face. "Forget it, just—"

"Caleb," I interrupt. "I'm not too keen on the sneaking around thing but I get what you're saying." He comes to stand in front of me, placing both arms on either side of me, caging me in, his lips a hair's breadth away from mine.

"Okay, so we do this then? We figure out if there's something here. If there isn't, we go our separate ways, never to speak of it again. But... Well, we'll deal with the rest of it as and when." Caleb smiles at me and if I was wearing any panties, they'd be soaked.

"Okay," I breathe out. "We need ground rules though. You can't lose your job and I can't lose my scholarship," I point out. "Rule number one: No kissing, touching, or any kind of PDA in public."

"Got it," he agrees as he gives me a quick kiss. "Rule number two: No dates. I don't give a shit if it's the King of England. No. Other. Men."

"Agreed. But the same goes for you, as well." I raise an eyebrow at him.

"Done. I'm not really into men anyway," he says with a grin and another kiss.

Caleb!" I exclaim as I playfully swat his chest, before adding, "Rule number three: Calls and texts are to be kept to a minimum and contact names changed to something else."

"Good idea. Any preference over 'baby girl' or 'sweetheart?'" He grins.

I snort out a laugh and shake my head. "Caleb, be serious here."

"What? I am," he says with fake innocence.

"Baby girl will work just fine." I wink and his smile grows wider.

*God, I could stare at him all day when he's like this.*

Running my hands across his chest, I reach up and give him a kiss, but before it gets too heated I pull back. "Any more rules?" I ask.

"Not that I can think of right this second. I'll let you know after round two."

Frowning, I give him a confused look. "Round two?"

"Yup," is all he says as he lifts me up, flings me over his shoulder, and strides to the kitchen door.

"Oh, round two," I giggle. Caleb slaps my ass and I squeal.

I can't remember the last time I laughed as much as I do with Caleb or felt as safe as I do when I'm with him. But one things for certain, he's burrowing his way under my skin and I can't say I mind it.

Round two turned into round three and four—the man has some serious stamina. We're lying in his bed, my head on Caleb's chest as he runs his fingers through my hair. It's late and I'm tired but I don't want to waste any time that I have with him.

"Do your tattoos have any meaning?" I ask as I trail a particularly colorful koi fish.

"Yeah, each one is particular to a point in my life. They each tell a story. This one here" —he points to a smiley face in the middle of his left bicep— "that one was my first tattoo. Theo dared me to get it done one night so I did. We were eighteen at the time." He chuckles at the memory.

"And this one here was after Samantha and I broke up." Caleb points to a swallow bird that's intricately woven into the rest of the design. "It means hope, renewal or rebirth." He swallows before continuing, "We were together for so long that even though the feelings—for me—weren't there and I don't think they ever were, it was still the end of a long relationship. My longest really." Caleb smiles softly.

"I've never loved anyone before, I don't even think I'm capable of it," I whisper, putting it out into the universe, something that I've always been scared of—not being able to love someone and to receive that love in return. "My mom... she was never around. Always chasing the next bottle or the next man who was 'the one.'" I smile gently but I know it doesn't reach my eyes. "My best friend, Sydney, is the only one who can cope with my chaoticness, the one who, if I *can* love, would be her."

Caleb reaches for my chin and tilts my head up to face him. "You want to know what I think?" he says as he wipes a stray tear from the corner of my eye. "I think that you *can* love. You're just afraid to. You've been hurt by the one person who was supposed to protect you, and it closed you off to the possibility. But I know that with the right people, you'll flourish."

He kisses my forehead before leaning in to place his own against mine.

Being in Caleb's arms, speaking out loud something that I've never admitted to anyone, I'm starting to wonder if what he's saying is true, and I'm terrified he'll hurt me worse than anyone ever has.

# Chapter Thirty

## *Caleb*

Christmas is coming up in a few days and I haven't seen much of Lauren. We've called and texted as much as we could, already breaking one of the rules about keeping them to a minimum but between her work, studying, and my work, there hasn't been much time for us.

*Us.*

That's such a weird concept to think of, seeing as I've been on my own for a while now and even when I was with Samantha, I never thought of us as an... us. She was just always... there.

I'm sitting in my office wondering what to get Lauren for Christmas after deciding to spend it together. She normally goes to Sydney's parents but she made the excuse to stay on campus. I'm not exactly sure what she said but, apparently, Sydney brought it.

I've been staring at my computer screen for the last ten minutes trying to think of something when an idea hits me. I quickly type into

Google what I'm looking for and it comes up. I make my purchase and lean back in my chair, a self-satisfied grin on my face.

Let's hope she likes it.

The guys and I are meeting at Strokes tonight. I know, I know but I couldn't exactly say, *Hey boys, sorry, I can't go to the strip club, my girlfriend works there*, that'd go down like a lead balloon.

After a quick shower, I change into jeans, a white shirt, and my black sneakers. I mess around with my hair hoping it gives me the 'I just rolled out of bed' look, grab my jacket and head out the door. I get in my car and turn the engine on, *Mod Sun's Karma* blasting out the speakers.

*Damn, this is a good song.*

Once I get to Strokes, I park up and head in, finding the guys in their usual spot—for a bunch of old guys, they cause quite the stir.

I slap James on the back as I walk past him and wave down a waitress.

"Dude! Where the fuck have you been? I feel like we haven't seen your ass in weeks," James pipes up.

"I've been busy." I grin.

Theo fake pouts. "Too busy for us, fuckface? I see how it is, he gets some pussy and we're pushed to the side."

I flip him the bird. "A gentleman never tells."

"Fuck off are you a gentleman," Noah snorts.

I place my hands on my chest in fake shock. "Fuck me sideways, he speaks! Quick, someone call the doctor, something's wrong with Noah," I exclaim while laughing.

"Ha ha. This is why I don't say shit. You fuckers run your mouths plenty enough," Noah says as he takes a sip of his beer.

I sprawl back in my chair, marveling at how I got so lucky to have friends like these guys.

"Well, well, well. Who do we have here?" James says as he starts eyeing up someone behind me.

I roll my eyes. "Fuck sake, James. Keep it in your pants for once, yeah?"

"Not gonna lie... wow," Theo chimes in, eyes comically wide.

Both of them continue staring and I laugh as I turn around, needing to see what or who's got them so bent out of shape. As soon as I do, my laughter dies and my mouth goes dry.

*Mine.*

Those assholes are staring at Lauren.

To be fair, I'd probably be doing the same thing if I was in their shoes because tonight she looks absolutely fucking gorgeous. Don't get me wrong, she always looks gorgeous but tonight... I can't even put it into words. Lauren's wearing an emerald green two piece that barely covers anything. Her beautiful pale skin is a stark contrast to the dark green. Her hair's in messy waves that fall down past her shoulders, stopping just shy of her elbows and she's wearing skyscraper heels that are begging to be left on while I fuck her.

*Annnd that's my dick hard as a rock. Fuck my life.*

"I need a taste of that," Theo bursts out and I turn round and glare at him.

"Leave her alone, Theo. She doesn't need creeps going after her, I'm sure she gets that enough," I snap, my fists clenched at my sides, anger radiating off me. Lauren seems to bring the caveman out in me.

"She's a stripper, Caleb. She gets paid to have creeps after her," James points out with a raised brow.

*Cool it, Anderson. People are gonna start asking questions if you keep this up.*

"She's still a human being," I grumble.

"Yeah, and one I'd like to get my hands on," Theo quips and I see red.

"One more fucking word about my woman and we're gonna have a fucking problem," I bark.

You could hear a pin drop with how quiet it just got. Noah's head snaps up to look at me and I avert my eyes, looking over to Theo and James.

Fuck.

"I didn't mean *my* woman. I just meant woman in general," I utter, hoping they don't pick up on the lie.

"Uh huh." Theo squints at me like he's got no clue what's going on. For a lawyer he can be pretty dense at times.

James stands up, giving me a wicked grin, his eyes dancing with mirth as he says, "Well, seeing as she's not *your* woman... you won't mind me having a chat."

"Dude, she's like half your age. She won't touch you," I laugh, trying to make it look like I'm not dying inside.

"Never stopped me before." He winks as he walks off in Lauren's direction.

Coming here was a bad idea. I guzzle down my beer and stride towards the bar to get another one. I can't sit there and watch while James flirts with Lauren. I almost gave the game away as it is.

Someone comes and sits on the bar stool next to me, I glance over and see it's Noah. He gives me a knowing look and I just nod.

"Fuck. I thought we agreed you'd stay away, Caleb? You're playing a dangerous game here, man," he whisper yells.

"I'm well aware," I drawl, as I take a swig of my beer. "We've been... hanging out. Spending time together. I like her, man." I give him a pleading look, hoping he'll understand how hard this is for me.

Noah sighs. "I can't tell you what to do here, Caleb. I gave you my advice before and you clearly didn't listen. I just hope this doesn't come crashing down on you."

I run a hand through my hair and then down my face. "Yeah, man. I know. She's just... different. I don't know." I shrug, not sure how to explain it or if I even *want* to explain it. Noah's already made up his mind about the situation and I can't be mad at him for it. If it was the other way round I'd be the same.

He nods but doesn't say anything else. We grab our beers and head back to the table.

"You missed it. James here got the boot by another woman," Theo cackles, clutching his sides. "I swear this is becoming my new favorite place. That and the coffee shop. What was the name of the girl over there who kept turning you down? Rhiannon? Rhonda? Row—"

"Raven," James cuts in, giving Theo a glare that would have withered most men, but Theo just laughs harder.

"Funny you remember her name and not anyone else's. Something you wanna tell us, James?" Theo wiggles his eyebrows and James resorts to physical violence by punching him on the shoulder.

"She didn't keep turning me down, she's Andrew's daughter," he growls. "Act your fucking age. What are you? Twelve?"

I laugh because he's not wrong. We joke around but Theo will forever be known as the 'kid' of the group. We should really nickname him Peter, cause he'll never grow up. The guys continue ribbing each other and I glance around, catching Lauren's gaze. She smiles at me and I nod my head, her lust filled gaze causing my cock to harden again. It's been too long since I've physically been with her.

I pull out my phone and text her:

Caleb

I miss you. When can I see you again?

Knowing that she's working, I put my phone away and go back to what the guys are doing and try to keep my thoughts off a certain curvy blonde.

# Chapter Thirty-One

## *Lauren*

"Woman!" Sydney shouts from the living room, a mass of bangs and crashes following in her wake.

Wincing at the sound, I push myself up from my desk and go to see what she's hollering about. Poking my head around the corner of the door, I tease, "Is it safe to come out or have you destroyed everything in our dorm?"

Sydney whirls around from the counter with a pair of tongs in her hand. "Ha ha, hilarious." She rolls her eyes as she pinches the tongs together in an act of aggression towards me. "I've had it up to *here* with that fucking woman," she screeches.

Striding into the kitchen, I cautiously remove the tongs from Sydney's grasp before someone gets it. "Uh, Syd? What woman are we talking about here?" I enquire, earning me a death glare.

Hands on her hips, she retorts, "Hannah. The bane of my existence, the woman who loves to torture me on a daily basis. Shoving a dildo up my ass would be more fun than listening to her criticize me day in, day out." Sydney stomps around the kitchen, hands gesturing wildly. "I fucking quit," she huffs.

Wrapping my arms around her, I give her a tight squeeze. "No you're not, Syd. And you know why?" I ask as I raise an eyebrow at her.

Sydney peers up at me from beneath her eyelashes, a pout on her lips. "Why?"

"Because you're motherfucking Sydney Johnson, that's why. When have you ever let someone come in and tell you, you are anything other than the absolute fucking best?" I take her face in my hands, my tone softening. "Don't listen to her, Syd. You are one of the most talented people I've met, anyone who doesn't agree can kiss my hairy ass."

A burst of laughter comes from Sydney. "Too much info, babe."

"Shut up," I giggle as I shove her slightly. Sydney's meltdown comes to an end as she gently shoves me back before going to put the coffee machine on.

"Right, so what's the plan for Christmas? What time are we leaving?" she asks.

Panic surges through me and I lose my words for a moment, my mind going momentarily blank as I try to think of what to say to her. Since the moment Caleb suggested spending Christmas break together, I've been excited yet terrified. Excited because—even though we can't go out anywhere together—we get to spend two uninterrupted weeks together. Terrified because I spend all the holidays with Sydney, whether it's with her family or not, so having to tell her that I'm sitting this one out is causing my chest to tighten with anxiety.

Wringing my hands together in front of me, and hoping she isn't going to hate me, I mumble, "Erm, I'm not coming for Christmas this year."

Sydney pauses what she's doing and turns to face me. "Beg pardon? Care to tell me why?" Those hands go back on her hips and I know she means business. "We always spend Christmas together." She squints and points a finger in my direction. "What are you up to, missy?"

I put my hands up in surrender. "Nothing. I just have a ton of schoolwork to catch up on and one of the girls has gone sick at Strokes, so I've picked up some more shifts to help out." Throwing the final bone that I have to throw her off the scent, I say, "You know I'm trying to save for my house fund."

Sydney's face is a mask of worry and concern. "Are you sure? I hate the thought of you being here all by yourself over Christmas."

I scoff. "Wouldn't be the first time."

Sydney purses her lips, clearly upset by what I've just said but it's the truth. She searches my eyes before nodding her head in acceptance. "I want to put this on record that I am not happy about this... at all."

Beaming a smile at her, I give her a quick hug and rush to get ready for work.

---

My shift at Strokes started a couple hours ago. I've been on stage but with the lack of people in here tonight, I came off early and have been milling around the bar area catching up with the girls ever since. Even though we're dancers, on the odd occasion, we'll go out front and help serve drinks.

I'm wearing something a little more daring tonight. When I saw the emerald two piece, while out shopping with Sydney, I had to have it. The thought of Caleb's reaction immediately entered my head and I knew it was the perfect choice. My choice in shoes is to be desired, though. They feel like hell but they were cute so I had to have them. Hashtag girl problems.

I'm talking to Izzy, one of the waitresses, when a guy approaches. He's good looking in the older, pretty boy sense, but I've only got eyes for a certain silver fox. I smile as he stands there looking at me.

"What's a pretty little thing like you doing in a place like this?" he asks.

I start laughing, before replying, "Does that line usually work for you?"

He grins. "Usually yeah." He places his hand out. "I'm James."

"Lauren," I admit, as I place my hand in his.

"Well Lauren, you're stunning and I'd love to take you out some time."

"Thanks, but I'm not interested." The poor man's face falls, clearly not used to rejection. I pat him on his chest and lean into whisper, "You're not my type." I give him a wink and walk off.

Glancing around the bar, I notice a familiar pair of blue eyes and my heart flutters.

*There's my guy.*

I should probably stop being so sappy but Caleb does things to me that no man ever has and if it wasn't for the fact that he's my professor and I'm his student, I'd be shouting it from the rooftops.

Caleb nods at me and I smile gently, not wanting to draw any attention to us so I keep walking to the bar to see if I'm needed.

I'm due a break so I go back to the lockers, grabbing my phone before sitting down on one of the benches, and slipping my heels from my feet with an audible groan. I rub the balls of my aching feet as I open the message from Caleb, a grin plastered to my face.

> Caleb
>
> I miss you. When can I see you again?

I type my reply quickly:

> Me
>
> I get off in an hour. Take me back to yours?

His reply comes instantly:

> Caleb
>
> I'll wait for you at the front door.

Caleb and I have barely had any time together since we decided to 'date' so I'm excited to see him. I message back to say, "Okay" then shove my phone in my locker and head back to the bar.

---

After my shift finishes, I quickly change into my comforts, grab my bag and race to the main entrance.

"Night Steve," I holler as I push through the doors and into the fresh night air.

I look around and my eyes land on Caleb. He's leaning against the wall, arms crossed and one leg bent back. He sees me and pushes away from the wall, smirking at me.

"Professor," I purr quietly.

Caleb nods in greeting before saying, "My cars parked around the corner, I'll follow behind you. It's unlocked."

Walking quickly to the car, I feel like someone's watching me and I don't mean Caleb. I shiver and quicken my steps, almost jogging to get to the car. I open the passenger side door and get in. Luckily there's not much lighting around here so we shouldn't have been spotted, it's just me and my overactive imagination... right?

# Chapter Thirty-Two

## *Unknown*

I watch as she basically skips out of the club and starts talking to him. *What's he doing here?* Rage surges within me and I clench my fists, my teeth grinding.

She's *mine*.

I stay out of view, watching with an intensity as I follow her, she doesn't know I'm here. She doesn't know that I'm *always* watching her.

She gets into the car and *he* looks around, checking to see if anyone's seen them.

I have. And I'm just biding my time until I can crush him and take her for myself. I won't let him keep her from me.

"Soon, my love. Soon."

# Chapter Thirty-Three

## Lauren

Caleb gets in the car and looks over at me smiling. "Hi, baby girl."

I preen at the name. Why is that nickname so hot? My core clenches and my panties dampen with my arousal.

God, I need him like I need my next breath.

A knowing smirk graces Caleb's handsome face and I know I've been caught. "You need something, sweetheart?"

"Uh huh." I nod as I lean into him, smelling his fresh cinnamon and leather smell.

He cups my cheek and tilts my head as he leans in and devours my lips in a heated kiss. I wrap my arms around his neck and kiss him back, my tongue slipping into his mouth, both of us fighting for dominance—he wins. Using my arms as leverage, I move my body so I'm straddling him in the driver's seat. I start gyrating my hips against his cock to give me the friction I need. I moan into his mouth at the feel of him, my desire for him growing with every passing minute.

Caleb's hands come down to cup my ass cheeks, moving me faster against him as I chase my orgasm. Removing my hands from around his neck, I move them to his belt buckle, undoing his jeans and—awkwardly—reaching in to grab his cock, pumping him a few times.

Caleb groans and trails kisses down my neck, putting his hands under my hoodie to cup my breasts. "Fuck me," he growls as he realizes I'm not wearing a bra.

"I'm trying to," I half laugh and half moan as he gently pinches my nipple.

I reluctantly let go of Caleb's cock and shuffle my sweats down, conscious not to hit the steering wheel.

"Whoever thought having sex in a car was a good idea…" I trail off as I smack my head on the mirror trying to shimmy down my sweats. Caleb chuckles and helps me the rest of the way.

Once I've removed the offending sweatpants, Caleb works on getting his jeans down far enough as I slowly work my hand up and down his cock. If there was room to move in this car, I would've had him in my mouth, but alas my hand will have to do. I watch in awe at his facial expressions, his eyes are closed and his head rests against the seat. My free hand snakes its way under his shirt as it glides along the silky, soft skin beneath, his muscles contracting as I continue my exploration.

He grunts at my pace, shifting his hips up with my movements. Caleb suddenly grabs my hips and—as much as he can—lifts me to straddle him, lining his cock up with my entrance. I slowly lower onto him, my pussy walls clenching around him, not moving as I enjoy the feel of him filling me up. Of his cock inside me, of being this close to him and feeling the warmth of his body pressed against mine.

Lifting his head, Caleb's eyes search mine, a warmth to his gaze that sends a thrill through me. "Baby girl, I'm gonna need you to move now," he grunts out.

*Don't need to tell me twice.*

Placing my hands on Caleb's shoulders, I start moving my hips, the angle perfect as I gyrate faster, whimpering at the impending orgasm that's so close I can taste it.

"Fuck, Caleb," I moan as his fingers dig into my hips, the bite of pain only adding to the intense pleasure as he drives his hips up, matching me in rhythm.

"That's right, baby girl. The only name that should ever come from these pretty lips is mine," he growls as he nips at my bottom lip.

Caleb brings his hand to his mouth, sucking on his middle finger and getting it wet. Not paying much attention, I yelp when his finger swipes across my ass. Leaning back, I give him a 'what the fuck' look. Caleb, clearly not fussed, just gives me a smirk before circling my clit with his other hand. Relaxing into Caleb, who is working my body like the pro he is, I don't yelp this time when he gently presses a finger into me. The slight burn only lasting for a second before I'm overwhelmed with pleasure.

"Jesus fucking Christ," I exclaim, the feeling foreign to me but not altogether unwanted. It takes me a moment to adjust before he starts fucking up into me, finger in my ass and one on my clit. The sounds I'm making are completely obscene, a cross between a whimper, a moan and some profanity mixed in. "Caleb..."

"Look at how well you take my cock, Lauren. Like you were made for me," he pants out, watching me as I move back and forth.

The windows steam up and I feel like Rose from Titanic as I throw my head back and slap one hand on the window as I come so hard I black out for a second, coming to as Caleb roars his release. He places his head in the crook of my neck as both of us breathe heavily.

"We should do this more often," he grumbles and I snort.

"I can't feel my legs."

"They feel pretty good to me," he quips as he runs a hand up my thigh, giving them a squeeze. I can feel him grinning against my neck.

Caleb slowly draws back, his lips brushing mine in a tender kiss, before sweeping a stray hair out of my face and gently rubbing his thumb across my puffy lips. An emotion I don't quite catch flashes in his eyes before it's gone.

"We better get going," he says with a shit-eating grin but makes no attempt to move.

My legs have officially gone numb but I'm too content where I am, not wanting to break the moment between us. "I should probably try and get up," I chuckle as I move my legs, but with how long I've been in this position for, it isn't an easy task. We get cleaned up, luckily Caleb had some tissues hidden in the glove box, and I sit back in the passenger seat.

"You ready to go home, baby girl?"

*Home.*

"Yeah," I say as Caleb smiles, places a hand on my thigh and begins to drive.

# Chapter Thirty-Four

## *Lauren*

"Wake up, sweetheart," I hear as kisses are trailed down my spine, the deep timbre of his voice causing goosebumps to appear on my skin.

"Hmm."

I'm still half asleep as a hand brushes a lock of hair from my face. I pry my eyes open to see a beautiful pair of blue ones looking at me. I smile sleepily and lean into Caleb's hand.

"Merry Christmas, Lauren," he says with a smile and kisses me gently.

I pull back and cover my mouth. "Caleb, no. Ew. I have morning breath."

Caleb laughs and moves my hand, bending down for another kiss. "Yeah, you're right." He wrinkles his nose and winks. "You do stink. I think you need a shower."

"Shower? It's my breath that smells, Caleb, not my body." After a second, I sniff myself just to make sure. Yup, definitely smell like sex and Caleb, not a bad combination at all.

He swats my ass as he gets up out of bed, calling over his shoulder that coffee is ready.

*Great, another morning person.*

But he did say coffee was ready, so after throwing one of Caleb's T-shirts on, brushing my teeth because ew, and throwing my hair up into a messy bun, I head downstairs to find my morning fuel.

Padding into the kitchen, the tiles cold under my feet, I see Caleb standing in front of the kitchen window, coffee in hand, watching—I don't even know what, as it's just a backyard.

I'm not gonna lie, my mouth waters at the sight of him. No shirt and gray sweats will do that to a girl. His tattoos on full display and the muscles shifting in his back as he inhales and exhales. All I can think about is running my hands over them, so that's what I do... coffee can wait.

*Coffee can wait? Who am I?*

I walk up behind Caleb, running my hands over his back and down his arms before bringing them round to his stomach. Is this normally a guy move? Yeah, but we're in the 21$^{st}$ century here, a girl can do what she wants. He softens his stance as if he's melting at my touch.

*Glad to know I have the same effect on you, as well.*

Caleb leans down and I raise up onto my toes to give him a kiss. I reach round, sneakily grabbing his coffee cup and taking it from him, sipping the heavenly goodness before he's even realized what I've done.

"Menace," he cries in faux outrage. "That was mine."

I smirk. "'Was' being the operative word here, Professor," adding in a wink for good measure.

He grins as he goes to grab another cup, calling over his shoulder, "Tease."

"Merry Christmas," I mumble around my coffee cup, remembering he'd said it and I never replied.

Caleb smiles at me. He knows how I feel about the holidays, it was one of those 'get to know you' conversations that we had last night. I'm not one for Christmas, it's not a holiday I've ever really enjoyed or celebrated. Kinda hard to do when you grew up the way I did. I've always tried to make an effort for Sydney's parents, but it's still just another day—might as well nickname me the Grinch.

"I got you something," he says sheepishly as a blush covers his cheeks.

I furrow my brow in confusion as I place my cup on the counter. "Huh? When? I didn't get you anything. Were we supposed to get each other something?"

*Shit. World's Worst Girlfriend award goes to...*

"No, baby girl, we weren't. I just wanted to get you something." He shrugs. "It's not much and you'll probably hate it." Caleb dips his head as if embarrassed, so I hastily walk over to him, placing my hands on his face to make him look at me.

"I know, no matter what it is, I'm gonna love it. Thank you." I can feel the blush creeping up my own face from how intently Caleb's gazing at me. I brush his cheeks with my thumbs before removing my hands and putting them in front of me. "Gimme."

Caleb laughs and gestures with his head toward the living room. "Go grab a seat and I'll get us a refill." He kisses me before smacking my ass and sending me on my way. I giggle at his playfulness, which only warms my heart.

Making my way into the living room, I marvel at how beautiful it looks. We decorated the tree last night, and it stands in all its silver and black glory in the far corner. It was my first time decorating a tree and the fact that it was with Caleb was just icing on the cake.

Caleb walks in behind me and I sit on the sofa, pulling my feet up under me as he passes me my coffee before moving toward the tree.

"Caleb, I still feel really bad I haven't got you anything," I complain.

He looks up at me from his crouched position, smirking. "I have everything I need, sweetheart." Caleb doesn't say anymore as he starts rummaging around.

"Erm, handsome..." I trail off as Caleb whips his head around to face me, his eyes wide. "What?" I ask.

"Say that again," he demands, his blue eyes sparkling.

I'm totally lost right now. "Erm?" I question.

"No, the other word."

"Handsome?" Just as I say this, a huge shit-eating grin develops on his face. "Oooh, I take it we're a fan of the nickname," I laugh, warmth spreading through me as I gaze at his happy expression.

"You know when I call you baby girl?" I clench my thighs and his gaze darkens, the desire plain to see. "Yeah, that's what you do to me, too."

I nod in understanding. Looks like I'm now giving him a pet name. "Okay, going back to what I was saying... What's with all the presents? You don't have any family... Do you? Oh god! We haven't had the family talk yet," I exclaim, nearly dropping my coffee.

"Woah, woah, woah. Lauren calm down," he laughs as he comes and sits down next to me, taking my cup, luckily, I'd just finished, or he'd have a fight on his hands. He picks me up and sits me on his lap, pulling me close. "I don't talk to my family," he whispers into my hair.

My heart breaks just that little bit more for him, knowing exactly how that feels.

"I grew up in a trailer park, no rich mom or dad. The guys were all I had."

Giving him a small smile, I reply, "You grew up the same as me."

"I did, yeah." Caleb blows out a breath before continuing, "Mine probably wasn't as bad as yours. My parents did the best they could, they got saddled with a kid at sixteen. One they didn't want." He shrugs. "I just got ignored for the most part, spending time anywhere else but at home. As soon as I was old enough, I got out of there. Noah, Theo and James followed shortly after, and I never looked back." Caleb wipes a stray tear from my eye. When did I get so emotional? "Hey, there'll be no sad faces on Christmas," he jokes.

"Did you just quote the Grinch?" I laugh.

"Of course I did, best Christmas movie ever made."

"I agree." Turning around to straddle him, my hands placed on his shoulder, I say, "Question."

"Shoot," he replies, chuckling, settling himself back like he's getting comfortable.

"Now go careful with this one. Your answer will be the deciding factor as to how our relationship progresses."

He tilts his head to the side, eyebrow raised and a smile quirking at his lips. "No pressure here, sweetheart."

I roll my eyes at him. "Is Die Hard a Christmas movie?" I hold my breath waiting for his reply, his face a mask of contemplation. I'm slowly going out of my mind waiting for him to answer when he finally comes to a decision.

"One hundred percent... a Christmas movie." I squeal as I throw my hands around his neck, peppering his face with kisses.

"Oh, thank fuck. Why must you be so perfect?"

Caleb gives a hearty laugh. "Sweetheart, I am far from perfect but I'm glad you think so. But to finish answering your other question...

those presents are for the guys. We didn't have much growing up, so we always make a big deal out of birthdays and Christmases. I'm not talking about the most expensive gadgets, though, I'm talking about presents that make you smile. Silly little token presents that mean something to us. Like James, he spends so much time in the new coffee shop on campus, I brought him a gift card to feed his habit. Noah, I brought an 'I smile' T-shirt, because honestly, he's a grumpy asshole." He chuckles.

"I love that. I do something similar with Sydney, but it's usually stuff we love and want." I move to sit next to Caleb, bringing my legs up under me and placing my hand under my chin. "You seem close with your friends," I remark.

Caleb moves so he's mirroring my position. "Yeah we are. I've known those guys my whole life. There isn't a part of anything I've done that they haven't been involved with—good or bad." He chuckles before adding, "Some of the stories I could tell you…" He trails off and I can't help but love the fact he's opening up to me, that I get to see another side to him.

I mean, don't get me wrong… Professor Caleb and the Caleb that fucks me seven ways from Sunday are completely perfect, but this… vulnerable side to him, endears him to me. Butterflies take flight in my stomach as I gaze at him, my heart pounding as I try and hide the emotions that are beginning to unfurl in my chest

Sensing the sudden tension that's gripped us, Caleb reaches behind him and pulls out a small box and hands it to me.

"What is it?" I ask, staring at it.

Laughing, he says, "Open it and find out."

I slowly open the lid, feeling like Pandora when she opened the box. I move tissue paper to the side to find nestled inside is a silver pendant with a tiny swallow bird attached.

"Caleb," I gasp, picking it up and holding it to the light.

"I told you that it means hope, rebirth and renewal." He tilts my chin to look at him, emotion pooling in his blue eyes. "I feel like you're my hope."

The blood rushes to my ears as tears begin to fill my eyes. I feel like I'm having an out of body experience because no one has ever said these kinds of words to me before. I open and close my mouth to say something... anything, but nothing comes. What can I say back to that?

"Here, let me put it on."

I turn around and lift my hair as he places the necklace around my neck and does the clasp up. Once he's done, he leans down to kiss my neck, goosebumps breaking out across my skin. Caleb puts his arms around me, and I rest my back against his chest, breathing in the scent of him and trying to calm my riot of emotions.

I can't be falling for him... can I?

# Chapter Thirty-Five

## *Caleb*

I don't know if it was a good idea to give Lauren the necklace or not. Ever since I gave it to her, she's been quiet... too quiet. Did I speak too soon? I'm not declaring my love for her or anything... yet. What I do know for certain though is she brings color to my life, she makes the mundane exciting, and I don't want to lose this feeling.

The moment I laid eyes on her she stirred something inside me, she called to me like a beacon in the dark. That obsession hasn't lessened in the time I've known her, if anything it's just gotten worse, that all-consuming need to be around her, in her presence at all times. Lauren just has this intoxicating mix of soft and hard that calls to me, soothes my dark edges, and makes me feel like I've found the one person who completes me.

*Fuck me. The boys would have a field day with me right now.*

We spend the rest of Christmas Day cooking, laughing, and getting to know each other more. I tell her stories about me and the guys when we were younger and she tells me stories of her and Sydney. We don't delve too deep into our past home lives, I guess that will come later or not at all. It's the best Christmas I've ever had, and that includes the turkey that we burnt because I was too busy eating Lauren's cunt to care about anything else.

There's a couple weeks left to go before school starts again so Lauren's staying here until Sydney gets back. Lauren still goes to work and as much as it kills me watching her getting into an Uber each time, when it should be me taking her, we have to be careful.

But I'm finding that this woman is quickly becoming a risk I'm willing to take.

# Chapter Thirty-Six

## *Lauren*

I just got off the phone with Sydney—god I miss her. She's been with her parents for nearly two weeks now, but we've spoken every day. Christmas break's coming to an end, which means she'll be home soon, and I'll have to go back to the dorms, which in all honesty I don't mind. I've loved spending time with Caleb but the emotions he's bringing out in me are starting to make me panic slightly. And what do I do when I panic? I run.

Things with Caleb have been going well—too well. We've developed a domestic routine which I absolutely love and yet at the same time hate because we all know something's bound to go wrong. This isn't my life. I don't get the guy at the end of it. We're deluding ourselves into thinking this could actually work. The man is a literal walking pornographic sex god and I'm… just me. Caleb could have his pick of any woman, why would he want me long term, especially seeing as I'm not sure I want kids. Surely that's something he wants seeing as he's older than me? Shit, I really need to have that conversation with him. Maybe it'll do me a favor and he'll dump me on my ass before I get too far into this?

I'm also in a constant state of 'will we, won't we'—will we get caught, will this last? I'm trying to live in the moment but it's hard. The guilt over lying to my best friend, who still thinks I'm staying in our dorm room, by the way, and the fact I could lose my scholarship. The scholarship that means everything to me. I make decent money as a stripper but it doesn't cover everything.

I'm having a complete meltdown, so thank god I'm working tonight, otherwise I think I'd be making an excuse to get out, anyway.

*Breathe Lauren, breathe.*

Pushing my impending meltdown to the back of my mind, I concentrate on the lights flashing past me as the Uber driver takes me to Strokes. It's gonna be slammed tonight, it's a Saturday after all, but it should keep me busy enough.

Walking through the back entrance, I walk into the dressing room and get bombarded before my foot's even fully through the threshold.

"Look what the cat dragged in," Zoey drawls, eyeing me up and down.

"Fuck off, Zo, I was here two nights ago," I retort. The girl has a memory like a fish.

"I know, I'm just trying out something different," she says with a wink.

Cringing, I reply, "I'm not sure I want to know."

As usual, Destiny pipes up from behind her mirror, "Zoey here decided that she wants to try out being a Madam, so she's been practicing her 'act.'"

"Wow, and I thought I'd heard and seen it all. Good for you girl!" I applaud. If anyone's gonna be able to do it, it's Zoey.

I start getting ready for the night, changing into my outfit—a turquoise all in one. It doesn't leave much to the imagination but it made me feel sexy, so I'll take it as a win. My hair's up tonight, I normally wear it down when I'm working, as it helps hide my face more, gives me that shy look that the customers love. But tonight, I'm switching it up a bit, maybe it's because I'm feeling feisty, or maybe it's because I need to claw back some of my independence, I don't know.

I'm feeling out of control, like my body, my thoughts, and my feelings aren't my own. Like someone's come in and stolen them from me. I've been on my own for so long, never having to depend on anyone, that now Caleb's around, I'm feeling dependent on him. Worrying about how he's feeling, what he's thinking. These are completely alien thoughts to me and it's not a feeling I like... at all. I need to figure out how to be *me* but also to be a part of this relationship.

Sapphire calls out, just as I'm finishing up with the last of my makeup, "Lauren girl, you're up." I wave in acknowledgment and head toward the stage.

I chose a different song to work with tonight, so when the notes of *I Don't Need A Man* by *The Pussycat Dolls* starts playing, I roll back my shoulders and put on a show.

---

Once my set's finished, I wander around the bar area, helping the girls who are rushed off their feet. I've felt eyes on me all night, and no, I don't mean the regular customers, I'm talking weird, creepy eyes. I definitely know it's not Caleb, he messaged me a while ago saying he was at home grading papers, but I just can't shake that unsettling feeling.

Glancing around I catch sight of a figure sitting in one of the booths. He raises two fingers in the air at me, nodding, I swing my hips in a seductive manner and make my way over. The lighting in the back of the booths is darker, giving the space an almost eerie feeling to it. The music isn't as loud either, meaning that you don't have to raise your voice in order to be heard.

Stopping in front of the table I paste on my best smile and ask, "What can I get you?"

The stranger doesn't reply at first, but I can feel their eyes on me—assessing me, judging me. Don't ask me how I know this, I just do. The spine-chilling feeling I get from it sends a shiver through me.

"Whiskey, neat," the voice says, one that sounds vaguely familiar.

"Do I know you?" I ask, squinting into the dark but I'm met with silence. "I'll just grab that for you." I quickly leave and walk to the bar, putting in the order and asking another one of the other waitresses to take the drink.

*Fuck that am I going back.*

The rest of my shift is uneventful, though I still feel those lingering eyes watching me everywhere I go. After I've changed and grabbed my stuff I head to the entrance where I know Steve will be.

"Hey, Steve. Any chance I can wait here until my Uber arrives?" I ask.

He instantly perks up, standing from his seat and coming over to me, concern clear on his face. "What's going on?"

"I'm okay, honestly." I smile, though it doesn't reach my eyes. "You know how the customers get, one just creeped me out more than usual and I don't want to be on my own." I shrug, hoping that I'm giving an 'I'm not bothered' attitude when, in fact, I *am* bothered by it.

"Who?"

I should have known this was coming and suppress an eye roll. Steve's incredibly protective of us and if there's anyone who even so much as looks at us the wrong way, they're out on their asses. He crosses his arms over his chest waiting for me to tell him.

"I don't know." Steve gives me a look that says he doesn't believe me. "Honestly, I have no clue. I didn't see their face. They were in one of the back booths, ordered a whiskey, but I got one of the other girls to send it back to him. I just didn't get a good vibe is all."

Steve tilts his chin up, assessing to see if I'm telling him the truth—the whole truth. He must see something in my eyes because he nods his head and says, "Okay. How far out is it?"

"Should be here any minute." I look out the doors and sure enough the Uber's there. I go to leave but Steve stops me.

"I'm walking you out."

I don't have the energy to argue with him, my mind and body still tense from the stranger so I nod and let him lead me outside to the waiting car.

Once I'm settled inside, Steve leans his head in slightly. "Get home safe. Any problems, you have my number."

"Thank you," I say as exhaustion finally catches up with me and I lean my head back against the seat.

My thoughts drift back to the stranger at the club. Why did his voice sound so familiar? Where had I heard it before? My mind replays the interaction over and over, but by the time I pull up outside Caleb's house I still can't place it.

*I'm going mad.*

Walking up to Caleb's front door, I knock. We haven't had the 'key' talk yet, he hasn't offered one and I haven't asked. He's always up whenever I get home though, sometimes he'll have been in bed and my text to say I'm on my way back wakes him, other times he stays up grading papers, hanging with his friends, or just sits watching a movie.

After being at work, I feel slightly calmer, the anxiety, panic, and loss of control I was feeling earlier still there, but it's dulled to a whine in the back of my head instead of the roaring tornado it was earlier.

Caleb opens the door wearing his glasses—*swoon*—a black T-shirt and gray sweatpants. I start drooling at the sight of him and that's just my pussy. The need and want for this man never seems to disappear, it's like he's my own brand of heroin—the more I have, the more I crave. Even after being rushed off my feet all night, exhausted and tense, I still want this man with a passion. What has he done to me?

He runs his hand through his hair and leans on the door frame, crossing his arms over his chest, the veins in his forearms popping out.

*I think I've just died and gone to heaven.*

"Take a picture, it might last longer." He smirks.

"I just might do that." I wink as he moves to the side and lets me in.

I place my bag on the side and walk into the kitchen, grabbing a glass of water. Sipping it, I notice Caleb looking at me.

"Take a picture, it might last longer," I snark.

"What's wrong?"

How does he do that? Not wanting to get into it I play dumb.

"Nothing. Why?" I rinse the glass out in the sink and place it in the dishwasher, trying to keep myself busy in the hopes that he can't see my lie.

"You're tense. Did something happen?" he questions, brows furrowed.

I sigh. Guess we're doing this then. "It was a long night and there was a guy that gave me the creeps." Caleb is just about to interject but I hold my hand up to stop him. "Before you say anything, nothing happened. He was just giving off major weirdo vibes. Steve walked me out at the end of my shift. I'm fine."

Caleb comes over to me, placing his hands on my face and running his thumbs over my cheeks. "I don't like it, Lauren. Can you not find another job?"

"No, Caleb. I like my job, the money's good, and it works around school. You know I'm not going to be doing this forever."

"I can give you the money."

I stare at him, mouth agape. *No, he didn't.* "I'm going to pretend you never said that." I pull back from his touch, needing space, anger coursing through me at the audacity of him. The feeling of not being in control coming back with a vengeance and my stubborn streak comes out to play.

"Why? What's so wrong with me wanting to look after you? Lauren, you work so hard, both in school and out. I just want to help," Caleb exclaims, throwing his arms up in the air in exasperation.

"Because I'm not a woman to be kept, Caleb. I do things by myself. I don't need your charity or handouts. I'm not some damsel that needs saving," I shout back. I pinch the bridge of my nose, inhaling and exhaling. I'm so done with this conversation. "If you can't already see that, then you obviously don't know me at all." I march past him, heading for the stairs. "I'm going for a shower."

I quickly shower and change into my pjs, I'm so angry and wound up that I go into his spare bedroom, pulling back the covers and climbing in. I don't want to be around him right now, so I bunch the covers up round my head and fall into a fitful sleep.

# Chapter Thirty-Seven

## *Caleb*

*F**uck! Did we just have our first fight?*

I lean my forearms against the kitchen counter and place my head in my hands. What the fuck just happened? I only want to look after her, why's that so wrong? I know Lauren's independent and I know she wants to do it by herself but if I have the means to help her… why can't she accept it?

The inner voice of reason decides to pipe up, *Would you accept it?* Fuck no I wouldn't, but this isn't about me, it's about her. Surely, she can see what I mean, right?

I look over at the clock and see it's 3 a.m., so I drag my ass up to bed—I'm not as young as I used to be, and these late nights are playing havoc with me. I open the door to my bedroom and pause. *Where's Lauren?* I glance around and see that the bedroom and bathroom are empty. I quietly walk down the hall to the spare room and push the door open gently, where I see Lauren curled up on her side under the duvet, fast asleep.

I pad over to her quietly, careful not to disturb her and crouch down by the side of the bed, watching as her chest rises and falls gently as she sleeps, her pale eyelashes resting on her cheeks. I gently tuck a stray hair behind her ear and kiss her forehead.

Getting undressed, I climb in behind her, wrapping my arm around her waist and pulling her into me so her back is flush with my front. Lauren can be as mad at me as she wants but she sleeps in *my* bed with me.

As I lie in the dark, I replay our conversation in my head, wondering where I went wrong and why she's so upset with me. I eventually fall asleep, still none the wiser.

# Chapter Thirty-Eight

## *Caleb*

"You said what now? Are you asking for an ass whooping?" Theo laughs. "Man, are you really that stupid? Come on, out of all of us, you're the one who's been in a stable relationship." Theo touches his finger to his chin as if to contemplate an idea and I'm contemplating punching him in the face. "Hmm, maybe that's where you went wrong?"

"I mean, he's not wrong, Caleb," James pipes up. "You don't tell a woman you've been dating for all of five minutes that you'll take care of her—"

"Unless she's only out for your money, then she'll bite your hand off," Theo interrupts.

James gives Theo a dark look but continues, "Lauren sounds like a woman who can take care of herself. She's not looking for a 'daddy' to support her. You fucked up, man." He gives me a knowing look and leans back in his chair, tipping his beer toward me in a salute.

I woke up this morning and Lauren was gone. She hasn't replied to any of my messages or calls, so I had to call in Tweedle dumb and Tweedle dumber for crisis intervention at Bucky's. I would have gone to Noah, seeing as he's usually the voice of reason but considering he knows all about Lauren and the fact she's my student, we don't exactly see eye to eye on the subject.

I run a hand through my hair before asking, "So what do I do?"

They both look at each other and reply in unison, "Grovel."

I choke out a laugh. "That easy, huh?"

"If you want to make it right, then yeah, it's that easy." James shrugs.

I eye them both, an eyebrow raised. "When did you two get so smart on relationships?"

Theo pipes up, a shit-eating grin on his face, "Oh, we didn't. We just know how to fuck up."

I sit back in my chair, scared that the two biggest fuck boys I know called me out on my shit. The realization that I fucked up suddenly hits me and I sit bolt upright.

"There it is." Theo points at me and laughs. "Dipshit figured it out."

"I gotta go." I grab my jacket from the back of my chair, Theo and James' laughter echoing around me as I race out of the bar, and to my car.

The drive home is quick. I get to the front door, unlocking it as I call out, "Lauren, you here?" I dash around the house like my ass is on fire, checking every room. "Lauren," I call out again, but I'm only met with silence.

I know she's not working tonight so where can she be? I head into my bedroom and stop, noticing all her things have gone—the toothbrush that was next to mine in the cup, gone. Her makeup and hairbrush on the sink, gone. I frantically run into the guest room hoping she's just moved all of her stuff in there but it's empty.

I pull my phone out of my pocket and dial her number. "Come on baby, pick up." I pace around the room waiting for her to answer but it goes to voicemail. I try again, this time it doesn't even ring. I sit down on the bed with my head in my hands.

"Fuck."

## Chapter Thirty-Nine

## *Lauren*

Getting back to my dorm room, I open the door and put my keys and bag on the side. Taking a deep breath, I head to the kitchen to make a coffee. While it's brewing, I put my stuff away, suddenly glad to be back. Sydney's at her parents until tomorrow, so I have the day to myself.

I take my coffee and sit on the sofa, turning the TV on for background noise as I sip my liquid gold.

I left Caleb's this morning before he woke up. After a restless sleep, I couldn't be there anymore. When I turned over and saw him sleeping peacefully next to me, I knew I had to get away. My feelings for Caleb are clawing at me, threatening to drown me. The overstimulation of caring for him and the anger over last night warring with each other in my head.

Did I overreact? I know he was trying to help but did the lack of sleep and overstimulation turn me into a crazy person?

Turning on my phone, I see a missed call and text from Caleb:

>   Caleb
>
> Where'd you go?

I don't reply, I close my messages and throw the phone down next to me. Suddenly feeling like I'm suffocating, and the walls are closing in on me, I get up and grab my shoes and jacket.

*I need to get out of here.*

Taking a slow stroll through campus I end up at the Honey Pot. Seeing as it's still early on a Sunday morning, it's pretty dead. Opening the door, I see Raven standing behind the counter.

"Hi, Raven," I call out. "Do you ever have a day off?"

She turns around and smiles when she sees me. "Lauren, hi. How are you? And yes, I have the odd day off... sometimes," she chuckles before adding, "The usual?"

"Yes, please."

"Go take a seat, I'll bring it over for you."

I nod and take a seat in the window. Raven comes over, sitting down with her own coffee.

"We haven't had much time to catch up and seeing as it's so quiet, I thought I'd come sit with you, keep you company?" She blushes.

"Of course, I feel so in my head at the moment that it's nice to think about something else. How's everything going for you?" I ask as I take a sip of my coffee.

Raven shrugs. "Can't complain, only a few months left, and I'll be done here which is a scary thought." She pauses before giving me a knowing look. "What about you?"

Chuckling, I reply, "I'm that easy to read, huh?"

"Sweetie, your shoulders are up round your ears," she retorts with a smile.

I guess it wouldn't hurt to get another person's perspective, right? I haven't been able to talk to Sydney, quick texts or calls don't give you time to fully get into the ins and outs of one's life.

I sigh and tell Raven, omitting certain details—who Caleb really is. She sits and listens to me ramble on, I even tell her about the weird vibes I've been getting recently. Once I've finished purging my soul, I feel better. Like a weight's been lifted off my shoulders... guess I'm no longer tense.

"Okay, first off, the boyfriend was wrong to say that, but it sounds like it came from a good place, and I'm sure it wasn't meant to upset you. Second, the weird guy? What's that all about? I'm getting freaked out just by you talking about it." Raven shudders.

I may have slightly overreacted with Caleb. I can't be the only person to feel like when you're backed into a corner, sometimes the only way out is to be defensive, to attack the other person? After spending so much time with him over Christmas, I guess my fight or flight mode kicked in? Resulting in me throwing a tantrum instead of having an adult conversation with him.

The shop door opens, distracting me from having to reply. I glance up to see a gorgeous man enter, he's no Caleb but he's got that George Clooney vibe going on—tailored suit, hair styled to perfection, and a smile so white you can see it on the other side of the world. I'm pretty sure he tried chatting me up at Strokes a while back, but being the professional I am, I hide in my seat keeping my face from view.

Raven visibly stiffens and her face pales. "You okay," I ask, reaching across the table to touch her arm.

"Uh, yeah, fine. Excuse me for a minute."

She strides over to the counter where, what looks like, a heated discussion is starting to take place. I can't hear what they're saying but I keep an eye on them to make sure Raven's safe. After a few minutes the guy walks out of the shop, slamming the door behind him. A glance at Raven shows she's on the verge of tears.

Standing up, I rush over to her. "Raven? You okay?"

She sniffles and wipes her eyes, looking up at me. She plasters on a fake smile and says, "Yeah, I'm good. James is a, uh, friend of my dad's."

"Are you sure? That looked a bit heated." The concern is evident in my voice.

"That was nothing, I've known James my whole life. He always thinks he knows best, when he really doesn't. I just don't do well with confrontation. I get so angry I end up crying." Raven starts laughing. "Stupid, I know."

I'm not a hugger but I feel like Raven's in need of one, so I lean in. I'm a bit awkward but we make it work. "Oh hun, it's not stupid at all. Just as long as you're okay?" I whisper in her ear.

Raven pulls back, nodding her head. "I'm good. How much did it pain you to give me that hug?"

"So much you wouldn't believe." I roll my eyes and chuckle. "I'm gonna grab another coffee then head over to the library to study. Text me and we'll get together."

Raven agrees and goes to make my drink. We say our goodbyes and I head toward the library, wondering what her story is with James.

---

After I finished at the library I went back to the dorm, Sydney texted me just after I'd got there to say she was on her way home so we're planning an evening together.

Caleb's sent the odd message throughout the day and has tried calling but I can't deal with him right now. I need to figure out in my own head what's going on before I can sit down and talk it out with him.

I'm sitting on the couch when Sydney comes barreling through the door. "Honey, I'm home," she calls out as she lugs her bag behind her.

I get up and run to her, nearly knocking her over in my excitement to get to her.

"I missed you too, Lo," she laughs as she hugs me back. "Now, we're cracking open the good stuff while you catch me up on everything that's been going on."

We spend the night catching up—minus Caleb. Even though I told Raven about him, in not so many words, I can't bring myself to tell Sydney. I'm already lying to her as it is, if she finds out I have a 'boyfriend' all of a sudden I don't think I'll be able to stop the flood gates from opening and telling her *everything*.

"How're classes going?" I ask after my second glass, the wine really going to my head and making me fuzzy.

Sydney rolls her eyes. "Ugh, Hannah is still riding my ass. Everything I do is wrong." She takes a sip of her drink before adding, "Like, I know I'm not the greatest—"

"I'm gonna stop you there," I interrupt. "We've had this conversation a million times... You know you're amazing. Don't downplay your talents, Syd. I won't allow it." I raise my eyebrow, challenging her to fight me on it.

"Fine. I'm the best dancer she has but that witch makes me feel like banging my head against a brick wall. I don't care how hot she is," she exclaims.

I smirk. "Hot for teacher are we, Syd?"

*Yeah, yeah, pot, kettle.*

Sydney blushes and I sit up from my slouched position. "Sydney Johnson are you blushing right now?" I tease.

"Hannah is hot, yeah, but like I said, she's a witch. Woman needs to get laid," she huffs, blowing her freshly cut bangs out of her face.

I smile around my wine glass. "By you, yeah?"

Sydney throws a pillow at me as she says, "Shut up. I don't know why I tell you anything."

"Because you love me, that's why."

Sydney puts on a film and we huddle under the blanket, wine glasses in hand, but my mind keeps drifting. I hate lying to Sydney, she doesn't deserve it. We've only ever been open and honest with each other, so keeping this from her causes an ache to settle in my chest.

To be honest, I'm not sure how she'll react to the news. She might cuss me out, she might kiss me and say, "Atta girl"—the jury's still out. All I know is that I can't keep lying to her, I'm either gonna have to come clean soon or end it with Caleb.

I'm just not sure which one sends a wave of anxiety through me more.

# Chapter Forty

## *Caleb*

After not being able to find Lauren or contact her last night, I barely slept. Worry over where she was and if she was okay at the forefront of my mind. Unlike other protective boyfriends I couldn't exactly go raising hell trying to find her. I'm just fucking glad it's the first day back after Christmas break so I know she'll be in class.

I shower quickly and get dressed—white shirt, black slacks, and black sneakers. I grab a coffee and head out to my car. *Make It Make Sense* by *A Day To Remember* plays to match my mood. I need to apologize to Lauren, and I need to do it soon. I'm just not sure how.

I could buy her flowers? Too obvious.

I could take her to dinner? We can't be seen out together.

I could buy her chocolate? No, she hates chocolate.

Think, dammit! What can I do to make Lauren forgive me?

Pulling up on campus I park my car and head into the English building, weaving between students catching up after the holidays. I head to my office and see Brad waiting outside.

*Breathe.*

Pasting on a fake smile, I greet him. "Brad. You looking for me?" I unlock the door and head in without waiting for his reply. Rounding my desk, I throw my satchel on the desk with a *thump*.

Brad hastily follows me in, saying, "Yeah, I just wanted to catch you up on Lauren Taylor."

Hearing her name is like a punch to the gut. I swallow thickly as I ask, "How's she doing?" I try to play it cool, my face devoid of any emotion but every muscle in my body tenses. Has he heard from her?

He takes a seat in the chair opposite my desk as he says, "Good. She's caught up with all her assignments. I've marked them and she's straight A's. That brain of hers is incredible," he chuckles.

I can't hit a student, right?

I hum in acknowledgment, but he carries on.

"The dean keeps wanting to see her. At first I thought he was just keeping tabs, but he asked me if she has a boyfriend. I told him I didn't know..."

Brad's still talking but I've zoned out, lost in thought. I get that he's a creep but why is Dean Williams so interested in Lauren? What's his endgame here?

"... so that's you all up to date," Brad finishes.

I wave my hand to dismiss him, I'm being a dick I know but I've got a lot on my plate, plus Brad's still on my shit list for taking Lauren on a date. He leaves and I focus on work.

Walking into the auditorium, I desperately quell the urge to look for Lauren, instead, walking to the desk, I brace my arms against the corner, taking a deep breath and practicing my fake smile as students filter in behind me. Once I've practiced enough, I stand to my full height and turn around, starting with the opposite side of the room where I know Lauren is.

Sweeping my gaze around slowly, I'm finally met with the green eyes I've been searching for.

A breath I didn't know I'd been holding releases from me knowing that she's safe. Lauren holds my gaze, her emotions for once closed off, and I've never been so pissed. Pissed because all I want to do is vault over the chairs and claim her in front of everyone. To tell the world that this girl belongs to *me*.

I convey with my eyes—as much as I can—how sorry I am. If she notices, she doesn't acknowledge it.

Averting my eyes and clearing my throat, I start the lecture, keeping my eyes trained on anything and anyone that isn't Lauren.

Just before the bell rings, I hand out the recently graded papers, leaving Lauren's until last on purpose. Sliding her paper in front of her, she peers up at me, her eyes shining with a multitude of different emotions—anger, lust, frustration, and my personal favorite, sadness.

"Can you stay after class?" I ask quietly. My heart thumping wildly at the thought she might tell me to get fucked, and not in a good way.

She doesn't say anything, just inclines her head once. I'll take it. At least she's giving me the chance to—hopefully—fix this clusterfuck I've made.

I wait until everyone's left before locking the door. Lauren's still sitting where I left her, so I stride over, my long legs eating up the distance in seconds.

Sitting down next to her, elbows on my knees, I whisper, "I fucked up, sweetheart."

When Lauren doesn't reply, I glance up at her so she can see the sincerity in my eyes, that if I could take it back, I would.

"I was wrong. In my head I was trying to help, but instead I made you feel like I was trying to control you. I'm sorry."

Lauren sighs, mirroring my posture. "You're right, Caleb. You *did* make me feel like you were trying to control me, but you also made me feel like what I do doesn't matter. Yes, being a stripper isn't exactly the world's greatest vocation, but I love it. Any job I do *matters* to me."

Sitting back up, I can see the tears forming in her eyes, and I feel like she's punched me in the gut, *again*.

"It sent me into a spiral, Caleb, and that is *not okay*. Yes, it was partly my fault for allowing it, but I felt like all my control had vanished. I couldn't *breathe*."

Lauren pauses, wiping the unfallen tears on her sleeve, before continuing, "I don't want to end up like my mom, Caleb. She relied on men to make her feel good, to feed her addiction, to keep a roof over her head. I don't want that. I want a partner, someone who sees me as their equal no matter the job I'm doing."

If this woman could rip my heart out and feed it to me, she just did. Phantom pain races through my veins at the hurt I've caused her. Not realizing what a few little words—inconsequential to me but massively triggering for her—could do. I'm desperate to wrap her up in my arms and protect her from the world, but I can't so I clench my hands, to keep from reaching for her.

"I have some serious making up to do, sweetheart," I choke out, emotion pooling in my eyes.

Lauren's smile is small but it's there. "Yeah, you kinda do."

"Come over tonight? I'll grovel anyway you see fit," I plead, sitting up straighter, hope blooming in my chest that I haven't fucked this up completely. "I'm working late tonight, I have a meeting, but let me get you a key and you can let yourself in." I guess it was the right thing to say because Lauren's eyes light up like the Fourth of July and I get a wide, toothy grin.

"Oh, handsome. You're going to wish you never said that," she purrs.

My cock goes instantly hard in my slacks from her sultry tone, and I groan. "Fuck. Why is that so hot?"

I adjust myself as I stand up and walk to my desk, anticipation for tonight causing goosebumps to raise on my arms. Removing the keys from my bag, I take my house key and hold it out to her.

Lauren grabs her bag and stands up, swinging her hips as she walks toward me, a wicked grin—one full of promise—on her gorgeous face. She takes the key and heads for the door. As she unlocks it, she turns around, giving me a wink before slipping out into the hallway.

*Yup, I'm fucked for this girl.*

# Chapter Forty-One

## *Lauren*

After Caleb apologized, I decided to take things into my own hands. He wants to grovel. Then grovel he will. A wicked grin graces my lips as I think about what he's in for when he gets home.

I'd had some time to think and to get my emotions back in check after our 'fight.' It wasn't all Caleb's fault—I'm damaged goods so I'm going to react in a defensive manner whenever I think someone's attacking me. It's not right and it's not okay, it's just how I'm wired. He hit a nerve when he offered to pay for me, so my mouth did all the talking.

I'm still mad as hell at him, but after what I have in mind for tonight, let's hope he thinks twice in future. An evil super villain chuckle chimes in my head as I rub my hands together at the thought.

Unlocking his front door, I make my way inside, putting my bag on the kitchen counter, and heading over to his sound system where I plug my phone in, swaying my hips as *Taste* by *Sabrina Carpenter* starts playing.

I finished classes early, so I had plenty of time to think of ways to exact my revenge on Caleb, to show him that he doesn't always get to call the shots in this relationship.

I had just enough time to shower and put on a sexy little number, one I've never had the courage to wear but felt appropriate for the situation. It's a two piece in my usual black, the bra in a cross like pattern across my breasts with a bow strategically placed on my nipples. The pants cut high on my waist with a small patch of fabric covering the barest amount of my pussy. They're crotchless, so easy access. I finish the outfit off with my matte black spiked Louboutin heels.

I didn't bother dressing after I'd put my little number on, I just grabbed a coat long enough to hide the important bits. What can I say? I love a cliché.

Caleb should be back any minute—the garage door opens. I smile to myself, *Right on time.*

Walking over to the single chair in the living room, I lean against it with my arms crossed, waiting.

"Lauren?" I hear him call.

"In the living room."

I hear Caleb putting stuff away in the kitchen as he starts talking. "Look, I know I've already said it but I'm willing to—" He cuts off as he walks in, seeing me standing there. "Everything okay?" He swallows.

I push myself away from the chair. "This is the part where you grovel, Professor," I purr as I start undoing my coat before shrugging it off my shoulders to land in a heap at my feet.

Caleb's mouth gapes open at the sight, lust filling his gaze as he clenches his hands at his sides. "This is my punishment?" he chokes out, breathing heavily and a small smirk playing at the corner of his lips. "This doesn't seem like much of a punishment from where I'm standing, sweetheart."

Giving a small smirk of my own, I strut over to him, almost like a model on the runway. As I get to him, I trail a finger down his chest before grabbing his cock through his slacks. Caleb hisses as I reach up to lean in his ear. "Just you wait, handsome." Giving him a quick peck on the cheek, I gesture to the seat. "Sit."

Eyeing me up like he's enjoying every minute of this, he goes over to the chair and sprawls out. He cocks his eyebrow at me as if to say, "What now."

Trying to hide the smile that wants to come out, I turn my back on him and walk to my phone, changing the song for something a little bit more... interesting. I peer over my shoulder at Caleb, his gaze firmly on my ass, but his eyes snap to mine when the sultry, country voice of *Dixon Dallas' Something To Feel* starts playing—don't judge me, he's a guilty pleasure.

The twinkle in his eyes, gives away that he's enjoying this... for now.

Running a hand up my body and into my hair, I lift it up as I start swinging my hips to the song. Slowly and deliberately, I drop to the floor coming into a crouched position with my knees wide so he gets an eye full of my crotchless panties. Caleb's hands grip the arms of the chair and his breathing starts to pick up, the desire evident in his eyes as he watches my every movement.

Continuing my floor show, I tease him with moves I've perfected over the years—slut drops with my ass out, crawling toward him, shaking my ass, palming my boobs—the knuckle biting and sweat beading on Caleb's forehead shows me that it's working.

Bringing myself into a standing position, I point my finger in a 'come here' motion and I've never seen anyone move so fast, Caleb practically launches himself out of his seat to get to me. Just before he can touch me, I put up a hand to stop him.

He groans at me. "Please," he begs and I give him a wide smile, pleased that my punishment is finally working.

"Stay," I order, as I strut over to the chair Caleb just vacated, and run my fingertip across the arm of the couch before sitting down. I lean back, placing my arms on the side of the chair and spreading my legs wide, wide enough that he gets an eye full of my pussy.

Caleb groans again. "Baby girl, you're killing me here."

"Good," I purr. "Maybe you'll think twice before you try and tell me what to do." I raise an eyebrow in question.

"Uh huh." Caleb clenches his jaw and nods his head, a pained expression on his face.

"Get on your knees, Professor," I demand.

Caleb smirks. "So that's how we're playing it, sweetheart?"

"Turnabout's fair play and all that." I wave a hand in dismissal. "Let's see how well you do when the control is taken out of *your* hands, handsome."

He looks at me and for a second I think he's going to refuse but his gaze locks with mine and he lowers, ever so slowly, to the ground. My heart is thumping in my chest at the sight, my core pulsing to match. I swear if I was to touch myself right now, one swipe would be all it took to come.

Seeing Caleb on his knees in front of me gives me a feeling of power I love. It makes me feel sexy, wanted, *craved*. That this man would do anything I asked just to make me happy.

"What now, baby girl? You've got me worshipping you on my knees."

"You'll be worshipping me in a minute, handsome. But first... crawl to me. Let me see what it looks like when you're at *my* mercy instead."

His breathing picks up, his desire plain on his face, as he crawls slowly towards me. He's stilted and jerky in his movements but he's making it work... kind of. Just as he gets to me...

"Stop," I command. Caleb stops immediately and sits back on his legs in a submissive pose, a look of confusion passing across his face. "You're going to sit and watch now, handsome. Don't move."

"Lauren." He drags the word out like he's in pain. I mean, he probably is, but it serves him right.

I grin as I trail a finger down in between my breasts, moving back up to cup one. I lean my head back against the chair and whimper. Needing more, I expose one of my breasts, my nipple erect from the cool air touching it, as I roll it around between my fingers, pinching every so often.

I bring my head up as I hear Caleb's breathing pick up. His eyes never leave my wandering hands.

"Baby, please," he grunts.

"Please what, handsome?" I taunt as I move my hand down to my panties and gently rub my clit.

"I need to touch you," he grinds out.

Caleb watches with greedy eyes as I bring my other hand down to my pussy, pushing one finger inside. I gasp at the sensation, not only of me touching myself but of Caleb watching me. This isn't something I've ever done before so I'm winging every moment.

I'm soaking wet, making it easier to circle my clit and pump a finger in and out, getting faster with my movements as I get closer and closer to my climax. Just as I'm about to come I peer at Caleb through hooded eyes, his blue ones boring into mine as my orgasm hits me. I cry out his name as I ride the waves, shuddering with aftershocks as my clit becomes sensitive to touch.

"Fuck, baby girl. I think that has got to be the hottest thing I've ever witnessed," he breathes out.

I smile as I remove my fingers from my sopping cunt and hold them out to him. "Suck."

Caleb damn near pounces on me to get at my fingers, licking and sucking my release from me. He groans around my fingers as I give him a wicked grin and say, "Good boy." I stroke his face, watching the emotions swirling around in his eyes, and he leans into my hand.

He lets go of my fingers with a pop. "Does this mean I'm forgiven now," he asks as he starts removing his shirt.

*Fuck, his body's hot.*

"Yeah, handsome. You're forgiven," I laugh.

"Thank fuck for that," he exclaims. "My turn."

# CHAPTER FORTY-TWO

## *Caleb*

Walking into my home and seeing Lauren standing by my chair nearly caused me to have a heart attack. Her hair hung in loose waves down to her breasts covered by what can only be described as a short trench coat. She had 'fuck me' heels on and I swear my soul nearly left my body when she dropped the coat to the floor. The barely-there bra pushing her tits up made me want to shove my face into them, my cock agreeing as it pushed painfully against the confines of my slacks.

I know I'm meant to grovel but this didn't seem like any kind of punishment to me, though, I understand where she's going with it. I'll allow her this, but after that, the bedroom is *my* domain, not hers.

Watching her dance for me was its own painful torture, not being able to touch her nearly drove me out of my mind. I wanted to take her, to control her—the irony isn't lost on me with what she's trying to achieve and dear god, she did. The way her body moved to the music... fuck me sideways. She literally killed me and brought me back to life with that little stunt. And crawling to her? Jesus wept. Never in my life did I think I'd be doing *that*, but a guys gotta do what a guys gotta do to get out of the shit.

When Lauren told me to stop and started playing with that pretty little pussy of hers, I'm man enough to admit I nearly came in my pants. Watching her come undone by her own hand was a sight to behold—her breathy moans, and the way her hips moved in time with the thrusts of her fingers.

Fuck!

And when she told me to suck, I'd never moved so fast in my life. I would have done just about anything to get my hands on her. I groaned at her sweet, musky smell, and I'm pretty sure my eyes rolled to the back of my head in ecstasy. I'd eat this woman morning, noon, and night if I could.

*Hmm... weekend plans?*

Now that I'm forgiven, all bets are off and I smirk at the thought. I grab Lauren's hips and slide her to the edge of the chair, her bare ass squeaking on the leather as she moves. Without giving her any warning, I dive in, the crotchless panties she's wearing giving me the perfect access to her cunt.

"Caleb," she moans as she grabs my hair, pulling me closer.

I don't stop. I don't say anything. I just keep licking and sucking, bringing my hand up and inserting two fingers into her eager cunt. I'm like a man possessed at this point, wild horses couldn't drag me away. I'm pretty sure my stubble is gonna to leave behind a red mark and the possessive asshole that I am feels proud of that, that it's me who's left those marks on her delectable thighs. My fingers slide in where she's so wet and I tilt one of my fingers up, massaging her G-spot.

"Yes, fuck! Right there, don't stop. Please don't stop, Caleb," she cries as her arousal coats my hand. "I'm gonna come."

Lauren's hips shift up further as she grinds against me, riding my hand and face. I glance up and see her head thrown back, one hand pinching her nipple while the other is still tangled in my hair.

I suck on her clit, and she comes, clenching around my fingers. I ease my fingers out of her while still attached to her clit and palm myself, desperate for my own release. Lauren starts pulling at my hair trying to get away from me, so I slowly move back and wipe my mouth, before sucking my fingers.

Grabbing her hips, I flip her over, so she lands on all fours, her face on the chair.

"You seem to like this position, Professor," she laughs as I gather her hair in my hand and pull her head towards me, leaning in for a kiss. It's sloppy and wet, our tongues tangling together.

I break the kiss, leaning into her ear to whisper, "Any variation of you on your hands and knees is my favorite, baby girl." Her sharp intake of breath tells me that she likes that, and I smirk.

As eager as I am to sink my cock into her soaking cunt, I grab hold of her ass cheeks, spreading them wide, licking my lips at her glistening pussy, my thumb gliding along the seam, teasing. I'm breathing heavily at this point, caught between wanting to give her another orgasm and just rutting into her like the animal she's made me.

Letting go of her ass, I unbuckle my belt and pull my aching cock out, giving it a couple of tugs before wiping the pre-cum with my thumb and placing it on her clit, circling it a few times as I line myself up with her entrance.

I slowly enter her, wanting to savor the feeling of her walls clenching around me. I groan at the feel of it.

Grabbing Lauren's hips, I start moving, my hips snapping and my balls hitting her clit. I wind her hair into my fist and lean back, pulling her with me so we're upright, her back to my chest. I reach round and play with her nipple, pinching and rolling it with my free hand. Whimpers, groans, and grunts fill the air around us, and our sweat soaked bodies writhe together. She pushes back against me, chasing her own high.

"Say my name," I demand.

Thrust.

"Say it, Lauren."

Thrust.

"I'm not going to ask again, baby girl. Say. My. Name."

Thrust.

"Caleb," she screams as she comes on my cock.

*God I will never get tired of hearing my name from her luscious lips.*

Two more hard thrusts and I'm following her over the edge, my release coating her insides. My heart's pounding as I lift her off my softening cock and sit her on my lap, my arms reaching around her and my head resting on her shoulder. Lauren relaxes against me, sated, and half asleep.

I breath in her vanilla and strawberry scent knowing I might have to fuck up again if this is my punishment. A man could get used to this.

My legs start going numb so I hook my arms under Lauren's legs and lift her up, rising to my full height and carrying her bridal style to my bedroom.

"Shower, sweetheart?" I ask, even though I already know the answer.

"No, too tired," she mumbles.

I chuckle and kiss her forehead. Lauren nestles further into my chest as I carry her up the stairs and gently kick open my door, striding over to the bed, and placing her on her side.

*Shit! When did I start thinking of it as 'her' side of the bed?*

Wrapping the blanket around her, I place a gentle kiss to her lips but she's already fast asleep. I'm wide awake so I go back downstairs and start tidying up wondering how I can have this as my life permanently.

# Chapter Forty-Three

## *Lauren*

I wake up too hot, the furnace wrapped around my body causing me to sweat profusely. Needing to use the bathroom, I get up slowly, careful not to wake Caleb. I turn around and gaze at him—he looks so young in his sleep, like the weight of the world isn't on his shoulders.

Throwing on one of Caleb's discarded T-shirts, I pad to the kitchen and start making coffee. While it's brewing, I hunt around for my phone knowing I didn't take it to bed with me. I rifle through my bag but it's not in there. I go to the living room and see it's on the side where I left it last night. A small smile tugs at my lips as I remember Caleb's punishment.

I've got a couple of messages from Sydney asking where I am, a message from Sapphire asking if I'll swap my shift on Friday night, and an email from Dean Williams. I reply to Sydney first:

Me

> I'm alive. I stayed at Esme's last night as we got out late and didn't want to disturb you. I'll be back later today after class.

*What's another lie to add to the pile?*

I text Sapphire saying yes to the shift swap and then I open the email from the dean.

---

From: DeanWilliams@abingdonuniversity.com

To: LaurenTaylor@abingdonuniversity.com

Dear Miss Taylor,

I've heard excellent news in regard to your progress and would like to invite you to a gathering at my house this Saturday at 8 p.m. sharp. The dress code is formal.

Please RSVP

Best wishes,

Dean Williams

---

After our last exchange of words, I'd rather not be anywhere near the dean, sticking pins into my eyes springs to mind, but can I refuse? Is anyone else going? I close down my emails and make a mental note to ask Caleb about it when he wakes up.

I make a coffee and sit at the breakfast bar when I hear, "Morning, sweetheart." Caleb comes up behind me and kisses the side of my neck before going and making his own coffee.

"Hey, handsome."

"You sleep okay?" he asks after adding cream and sugar to his drink. Ew.

"I did, yeah. I got a weird email this morning."

Caleb raises an eyebrow as he leans back against the kitchen counter. "What about?"

"It was from Dean Williams. Something about a 'gathering' at his house this weekend. You know anything about it?"

*Please say yes, please say yes.*

He nods. "Yeah, I heard he was putting together something for his 'promising students' but I didn't know when. Hang on, let me check my phone real quick." Caleb walks out and comes back in a couple of minutes later with his phone in his hand. "I got an invite as well."

*Oh, thank god.*

"Okay, the fact you got one makes me feel better. After my run-in with him I thought he might have made it up to get me to go to his house. I need to stop reading so many dark romance books," I laugh.

"Dark romance? Do tell. I may be an English professor but apparently I've been living under a rock." Caleb grins and he stands in front of me, waiting on my answer.

"Oh, you know, morally gray masked men, kidnappers, 'touch her and die' vibes." I smirk at the look on Caleb's face. Pointing a finger at him, I say, "Don't yuck someone's yum, handsome."

A wicked grin graces Caleb's mouth. "Oh, baby girl, I wasn't yuking anything, that was my thinking face."

I stop mid drink and slowly turn my head towards him. "Thinking face? What ya thinking, handsome?" I choke out.

He winks and goes to walk out of the kitchen, calling out behind him, "That's for me to know and you to find out."

*"That's for me to know and you to find out."* I roll the words around in my head and then say them out loud before they sink in. My eyes go wide, and I run after him. "Caleb!"

I hear his laughter echoing upstairs. "Come on, baby girl. You need a shower and to get you to class. I heard your professor likes to spank you, if you misbehave."

*Dead. Gone. Deceased. RIP my panties, if I was wearing any that is.*

I race up the stairs and join Caleb in the shower.

---

Getting ready for this 'gathering' tonight is nerve wracking to say the least. According to Caleb, all of the faculty members and some of the university's most prestigious students will be there. I'm just putting the final touches to my makeup when Sydney pokes her head round the door.

"How you doing, girl?" she asks as she props herself up against the doorframe.

I sigh as I place my earrings in my ears, looking at her in the mirror. "Nervous. You know I hate this sort of thing."

"That's why I wanted to check on you. You know all you have to do is send me an SOS and I'll make up an excuse to get you out of there."

"What would I ever do without you?" I smile as I turn round in my chair to face her.

Sydney winks. "Let's hope you never have to find out." She suddenly stands up straight and announces, "Oh, I forgot—"

I stare after her, trying to look around the door. "Forgot what, Syd?" I shout to her retreating form.

She comes in a few minutes later. "This." She holds out a garment bag. "*Voila.*"

I'm confused but I take the bag from her anyway, opening it up tentatively as if expecting something to jump out at me. I gasp when I finish opening the bag—sitting inside is the most stunning black dress I've ever seen. The sequins bounce off the light in my room, making it almost twinkle.

"Syd. What? How?" I'm at a loss for words with how beautiful it looks.

"Call it a power play. Something to make you feel like the goddess you are." She grabs the dress from me and says, "Come on, I need to see it on you."

I get out of my pajamas and let Sydney help me with it. The bodice is low cut and fitting, giving me a slight hint of cleavage, allowing the swallow necklace Caleb got me for Christmas to sit perfectly on my neck. The dress flares out at my hips with a thigh high slit up one side.

*I'm so glad I shaved my legs.*

Walking to the long mirror hanging on my wall, I take a look, gasping. The reflection staring back at me doesn't look like me—I'm a stripper, so I'm not unused to hair and makeup. I went for an understated makeup choice making it look like I'm not wearing any at all. My hair is pulled back in an elegant chignon with a silver butterfly clasp holding it together.

"You look stunning, babe," Sydney gushes from behind me, her hands covering her mouth in her excitement.

I move over to Sydney and hug her. "Thank you."

"Right, leave before you ruin my makeup. You know we don't do this mushy stuff." She laughs and pushes a stray hair out of my face. "You deserve to be there tonight, Lo. Don't let anyone tell you any differently," she says softly.

"Quick, call me a bitch or something, you're gonna make me cry," I exclaim.

Sydney gently shoves me and laughs. "Bitch, get out of here. I need to go and get ready for a hot date." She winks and leaves the room.

I grab my bag and head for the door. "Love you," I call out.

"Love you more," I hear shouted back.

Brad was invited tonight, so we arranged for him to pick me up. I would've gone with Caleb but for obvious reasons that wasn't going to happen. I didn't feel comfortable with Brad coming up to the dorm so I told him to message me when he was downstairs, and I'd meet him there.

I push open the door and instantly see him standing next to his truck. His black suit and gelled hair making him look less nerdy and more mature. I wave and smile as I walk over.

"Hey, Brad."

"Hey. You ready for the most awkward night of your life?" he chuckles.

I groan at the thought. "Absolutely."

Brad helps me get into the passenger seat before getting in. He starts up the engine and we make the twenty minute drive to the dean's house. We make small talk on the way—how we've been, upcoming assignments and exams. We finally pull up to a gated estate where houses are few and far between and the trees line up perfectly along the sidewalk.

*Oh, how the other half lives.*

Brad parks his truck in a free spot and comes round to open the door for me. I place my hand in his as he helps me down. As we walk closer to the house, the sound of chatter and clinking glasses fills the air.

Brad places a hand on my lower back, and I try not to flinch at his touch. I know he's only trying to be a gentleman but if it's not Caleb touching me, I don't want *anyone* touching me.

We walk in through the front door and a waiter offers us a tray of drinks. I grab a glass of champagne, needing the bubbles for liquid courage. I take a sip and shudder at the awful taste.

"Not a fan?" a voice says from behind me, causing me to shudder for other reasons.

I choke on my drink, before spinning around and coming face to face with Dean Williams. An attractive older woman, in a long floor length gold dress—that shows way too much boob for an academic gathering—a face caked in makeup, her badly dyed blonde hair down in loose waves, stands next to him with her hand on his arm.

"Erm, no. It's a little too... expensive for my tastes."

The dean laughs and I try to work out what's so funny.

"My dear, this is Lauren Taylor and Brad Moore," he introduces us. "Miss Taylor, Mr. Moore, this is my wife, April."

"Nice to meet you," I say with a forced smile, the dirty look I'm getting from her causes my hackles to rise.

Brad removes the hand that's on my back and holds it out to the dean. "Thank you for having us." Dean Williams grabs his hand and from the wince on Brad's face, I'd say the grip is pretty hard.

The dean's wife gives her own forced smile to Brad and looks me up and down with what looks like a sneer, before leaning to whisper into her husband's ear and walking off.

"She seems... lovely," I remark. Lovely not being the right word. Bitch would be more appropriate.

"Indeed." The dean stares at me, an eerie grin firmly in place, my skin heats uncomfortably under his watchful gaze. No one says a word, the air is so thick with tension, you could cut it with a knife.

"Well, uh, I guess I'd better go and mingle," I say, taking a step away from both the dean and Brad.

Dean Williams just nods his head. I turn and make my way to the gardens, needing some fresh air, feeling his eyes boring into my back the entire time.

Brad catches up to me, grabbing my arm gently before saying, "Lauren, I've just seen someone from my econ class, I'm gonna go and say hi."

"Oh sure, I'll catch you in a bit." A breath I didn't know I was holding releases, and I feel the tension leaving me, glad to be on my own for two minutes. Between Brad's touches and the dean's disturbing looks, I'm about to hightail it out of here, consequences be damned.

Getting to the balcony, I wrap my arms around myself, the evening breeze turning slightly colder, my champagne glass finished and put on a waitress's tray on the way out.

"Good evening, Miss Taylor."

I whirl around at the sound of the voice behind me, my heart pounding in my chest at the deep tone, smiling as I say, "Good evening, Professor Anderson."

The urge to jump this man and rub myself all over him is strong. His dark hair has been cut, the sides shorter and the usual mop of hair on top—that I love to run my hands through—has been styled in a way I just want to mess up. His all-black tailored suit fits him like a glove and every part of my body flutters at the sight of him.

*Henry Cavill eat your heart out.*

Caleb smirks as he watches me basically eye fucking him. My core pulses in time with the beating of my heart as my nipples pebble, which he notices, if his eyes growing darker with desire is anything to go by.

He takes a step closer, and my heart feels like it's about to burst from my chest. Emotions threatening to spill over as I take in the glorious sight before me. The world outside of us ceases to exist as we continue gazing at one another.

Caleb speaks, his tone low enough that only we can hear. "You look absolutely breath-taking, baby girl."

I blush. "Thank you. You don't look too bad yourself, handsome."

"What I wouldn't give to kiss you right now." He clenches his fists at his side, almost as if he's fighting with himself to not reach out and touch me.

My body instinctively wants to lean into him. To have him hold me and wrap me in his delicious scent.

A glass shatters along with a chorus of shouts, brings the world around us back into focus. I'd somehow managed to move closer to him without realizing so I take a step back, trying to get my heart rate to calm.

"I hate this, Lauren," he grinds out as he goes to run a hand through his hair and thinks better of it at the last minute.

"I know. I finish in a few months and—"

I'm interrupted by a voice calling my name.

Caleb puts his hands in his trouser pockets and nods towards the house. "You better go in, sweetheart."

"I'll see you later?"

"Yeah, I'll be around."

I nod and walk back into the house, searching for the voice that called my name.

# Chapter Forty-Four

## *Caleb*

I hate suits. The itchy collars. The uncomfortable jackets. Pure torture. The only reason why I didn't make my excuses for tonight and stay at home balls deep in Lauren is because she's here. And anywhere that Lauren is, you bet your ass I'm gonna be.

I've been here for about an hour, watching the door, hoping that every person that walks through is her. I had a glass of whiskey when I arrived but I've stuck to water since, wanting to keep a level head. Sober me can barely keep my hands off Lauren… drunk me? *Houston we have a problem.*

I get roped into conversation with a couple of faculty members, trying not to glaze over at how boring and stuck up these people are. Most of these professors have grown up with a silver spoon in their mouths, having everything handed to them. They'll never know the struggles of having to work your ass off to get everything you dreamed of. To not worry about the roof over your head or where your next meal is coming from. Needless to say, I have nothing in common with these people.

I notice a figure out of the corner of my eye, turning my head slightly, I see Brad walk through with Lauren next to him. If it wasn't for the fact I'm too busy drooling at how stunning my woman is, I'd be punching Brad for touching my woman.

*Goddammit, I'm one lucky son of a bitch.*

Lauren's got her hair up tonight showcasing her beautiful slender neck that fits perfectly in the palm of my hand. She's got my necklace on, and I can't help but puff out my chest at the pride swelling within.

Her dress fits to her curves like a second glove and all I can think about is that I know what she looks like underneath. The way her skin feels under my hands. How her body flushes after she comes. Turning toward the bar, I discreetly adjust myself, my gaze never leaving Lauren.

This woman.

*My woman.*

Dean Williams and his wife glide over and I see Lauren's body tense. Every bone in my body tells me to go over there, to protect her but I can't, so I grit my teeth and watch the encounter unfold. They don't talk for long, Lauren looking more uncomfortable and awkward the longer the dean is with her.

Finally, she makes her excuses and heads toward the doors leading to the balcony. I quickly make my own excuses and follow her.

Lauren looks ethereal standing under the lights, her blonde hair looking like a halo compared to the dark night. I move slowly towards her, basking in the glow that is Lauren Taylor.

"Good evening, Miss Taylor," I say quietly, not wanting to scare her.

She twirls around at the sound of my voice. A smile gracing her beautiful features and my heart stops in my chest at the way she's looking at me—lust mixed with something else.

"Good evening, Professor Anderson," she purrs. I swear to god I could listen to her recite a grocery list and still get hard at the sound of her voice.

I lower my voice knowing there are people around. "You look absolutely breath-taking, baby girl."

Her eyes light up at my praise as she replies, "You don't look too bad yourself, handsome."

*Handsome*. Never in my life have I used a pet name before Lauren, and never have I had one used for me, but it all just feels right. The way she calls me 'handsome' causes my lungs to constrict with the emotion it brings me.

I clench my fists, the need and want to reach out and claim her in front of everyone nearly overtaking all common sense. Lauren starts to lean in towards me, like she doesn't know she's doing it. Like it's instinct.

A glass shatters and she shakes her head, taking a step back.

I gaze at her—the situation making me frustrated beyond belief—when someone calls her name and she leaves. I swear I'm destined to keep watching her walk away until we either stop *this*, or she finishes school.

But one day... one day she'll never walk away from me again. Why? Because I'm never letting Lauren Taylor go.

## Chapter Forty-Five

## *Lauren*

Walking away from Caleb is getting harder and harder to do. The more my feelings for him progress, and progress they are, the more time I want to spend with him. He makes me feel safe and cared for, and considering I've spent my life in a constant fight or flight motion, I don't want to lose the feelings he inspires within me—even if I do freak out at times.

After looking for the voice that called my name with no luck, I head towards the ladies' room. I get about halfway down before...

"Ah, there you are, my dear."

*Shit.*

I stop and turn towards the voice. "Dean Williams. How can I help you?" If my voice got any more saccharine I'd need to see a dentist.

He apparently doesn't get my distaste for him as he smiles before saying, "I'd like to talk to you... in my office."

"You can't talk to me here?" I look around hoping that someone will see us and intervene, but they don't, the hallway is deserted.

"It's a... private matter. One that would be best discussed in my office. I'm sure you appreciate that." A sinister grin creeps over his face and his dark eyes gleam in the light causing a shiver to race down my spine.

I've never had an interaction with this man and come away feeling good about myself after. The way he looks at me, as if he's undressing me with his eyes, is something I *do not* like.

The dean stalks closer to me, his musky cologne overpowering my senses and making me want to sneeze. He takes my arm in a grip that isn't altogether soft, my protests dying on my lips when he grabs me harder and offers me a cold glare.

"I would suggest coming quickly and quietly, Miss Taylor."

Terrified as to what his un-worded threat could be, I allow him to pull me along, looking back down the corridor and hoping that Caleb will do what he's always done after I've walked away—follow me.

The dean leads me to his home office after marching us down several different corridors. If I was to try and leave here, I wouldn't know the way back. I hadn't realized I was shaking until he stood at his door, unlocking it and not so gently pushing me in. I nearly trip over the rug on the floor in my haste to get away from him. The terror I'm feeling is starting to claw its way up my throat, and it's the only thing that's stopping me from screaming.

"Have a seat, Miss Taylor." He smiles, almost shark-like, showing off his perfectly white teeth.

I don't move. I can't. I'm rooted to the spot. I've never been in this position before, even at the club, there was always Steve or one of the other security guards around to help if needed. I'm at a loss as to what to do. I will my body to move, to do anything other than just stand here defenseless, my eyes wide with terror.

Dean Williams pulls out a chair in front of his desk and demands in a cruel tone, "Sit, Lauren."

My mouth is dry, but I force my legs to move, going and sitting in the proffered chair.

"Excellent." He claps his hands together and smiles coldly, like this is all a game to him, and perches on the edge of the desk in front of me, arms resting on either side of him. "You see Lauren, I've had my eye on you for a while now. You're a beautiful woman and I do so appreciate a woman with the, uh, *talents* that you possess."

"I-I do-don't fo-follow," I stutter, my sweaty hands clenched in my lap.

Dean Williams leans forward and runs a finger gently down my arm. "I first noticed you last year at that club, Strokes." He says 'club' like it's a dirty word. He gets a faraway look on his face as if remembering something.

I swallow, my words coming out more of a whisper. "I-I think you have the wrong person, and I'd like to leave."

"Leave? Absolutely not, my dear. Now I've shown my cards, I can't just let you just walk out of here. I have a reputation to uphold," he scoffs as he looks down his nose at me, his lips curved into a thin smile.

"I won't te-tell anyone," I whisper, my body trembling as I reiterate, "I'd like to leave. Now."

I go to stand and in an instant he's in front of me. I can feel his breath on my cheek, and I have to swallow back the bile that's risen to the back of my throat.

"Why? So, you can run back to *him*?" he hisses through clenched teeth, rage simmering in his gaze.

"Who?" I ask. Surely he can't know about Caleb.

The dean grabs my chin in his hand and tilts my head up to look at him, his face a mask of fury. "You think I don't know about you and Professor Anderson?" His laugh is humorless and cruel. "You underestimate my obsession with you. I know all about the two of you," he sneers. "So, if you want him to keep his... job and for you to keep your scholarship, you are going to do exactly as I say. Is that clear?" His grip on my chin tightens and I whimper.

The thought of anything happening to Caleb terrifies me and the dean appears to be so deranged that I wouldn't put it past him to do something to physically harm him. I have no choice. I won't let anything happen to Caleb if I can help it. I love him and will protect him the best I can.

*Fuck! Not the best time to realize you're in love with your professor, Lauren.*

With that thought I straighten my spine, my eyes ablaze with defiance as I shove his hand away from me, asking, "What do I need to do?"

"Good girl," he coos, and I think I just threw up in my mouth slightly. "Go home and wait for my call." He lets go of my arm and I take a step back, rubbing where he'd held me, anger simmering in my veins at the threat against Caleb. "Remember Lauren, not a word to anyone. You really don't want to see what happens when you cross me."

Bolting for the door, I open it so hard it hits against the adjacent wall with a thud, my heart pounding and the blood rushing to my ears as I quickly dash to the nearest exit, which is just off one of the corridors he brought me down. I burst out into the night air, taking in huge gulps of air.

"Fuck!" I exclaim. *What the hell just happened?*

I keep taking deep breaths in and out, trying to dampen down the rising panic. How do I keep getting myself into these situations?

Tipping my head back to look up at the night sky, my mind races with possibilities. But ultimately, what am I going to do? I can't tell Caleb, that's completely out of the question. I'm trying to protect him from that madman, not bring him into it.

The tears start flowing freely now, my face a complete mess. I wipe a hand under my eyes, but they keep coming. I need to think of a plan but first, I need to get home.

Taking in another large gulp of air, I will the tears to stop, give my face one more wipe and head inside. I find a waiter on my way back who's kind enough to show me the way. I left my bag and phone in Brad's truck, so I need to find him.

I notice Brad talking to a couple of other students, and begin my walk toward him, when a hand brushes my arm.

"Miss Taylor, are you okay?"

I pause at the sound of the low voice.

*Fuck my life. Not now. Literally anyone else.*

I paste a faux smile on my face before turning around. "Professor Anderson, I was just on my way to Brad. I need to leave, and he has my bag in his truck."

I can tell Caleb doesn't believe me by the tilt of his head, the way his jaw clenches and the look that says, *Yeah right*. This man knows me too well, and I was a fool to think I could keep something from him.

Sighing, I look around before saying quietly, "I need to get home. Please don't ask me any more than that right now because I can't give it to you," I plead.

Caleb isn't happy but he nods his head. "I'll meet you at the dorm, you're coming back to mine tonight," he whispers under his breath.

Both of us have pleasant smiles plastered to our faces, hoping anyone who's watching will see a student and their professor having an innocent conversation.

"No, Caleb. I need to be on my own. Please respect that," I force out, the tears welling up again.

*Not here. Do not cry here, Lauren.*

Caleb's eyes narrow slightly but he agrees with a nod of his head. A relieved breath escapes me as I say, "Thank you. I need to go. Goodbye, Professor Anderson."

With one last lingering look at the man I've fallen head over heels in love with, I turn and walk away to find Brad and get the hell out of here.

# Chapter Forty-Six

## *Caleb*

Something's wrong. I can feel it. That wasn't Lauren who left me earlier. Sensing eyes on me, I look over to see Dean Williams propped against the makeshift bar with a glass of whiskey in his hand. He lifts it in a salute with a smug grin.

*What has he done?*

For once I stay rooted to the ground, not following Lauren as my usual MO. Heading to the bar, I order a whiskey, leaning back against it, mirroring his posture.

"Such a shame Miss Taylor had to leave so soon," he drawls.

I shrug, feigning nonchalance. "Hadn't noticed."

The dean raises an eyebrow. "Oh? You two seemed quite... close. Considering she's a *student*." He emphasizes the word as if I don't already know.

I take a sip of my drink and put it on the bar, my stance relaxed but the rage simmers beneath the surface. "She asked if I'd seen Brad, you know, my TA."

"Hmm. Well, let's hope that whatever it was, that it's over with now." He gives me a pointed look.

I don't like what he's implying here. Does he know something? Does he know about me and Lauren?

"Not my problem. Like you said, she's a *student*," I confirm, hoping like fuck I can defuse this situation before it gets worse. This asshole has always acted with a dickish nature, so it's probably just another one of his games—one where he thinks he knows but doesn't.

I stand up, draining my glass before saying, "Excuse me."

I wait a good hour before I make my apologies and leave so it doesn't look too suspicious. One things for certain: I need to find Lauren and I need to find her quickly.

# Chapter Forty-Seven

## Lauren

I get back to the dorm room after nearly begging Brad to get me out of there. It wasn't my finest hour, but I needed to regroup and think. Pushing through the door I see Sydney's still up.

"Hey girl, how did it go?" she asks, not looking away from the TV. Syd's heavily into Criminal Minds at the moment, I keep teasing her that she's a stalker in the making.

"Erm..."

She must sense something in my tone as she glances up at me. I try to keep my features neutral, but I'm guessing by the way she nearly vaults off the sofa and comes rushing over to me, I fail miserably. Sydney pulls me into a bone crushing hug and I lose it. I burst into tears, sobbing on her shoulder.

I don't know how long we stand there for with me gripping onto her for dear life and her stroking my hair, alternating between shushing me like a baby and telling me everything's going to be okay.

Once I've calmed down slightly, Sydney pulls away, gently taking my face between her hands, and wiping away the tears.

"You gonna tell me what's got you all worked up like this?" she gently asks. Sydney isn't one to mince her words but I think even she can tell I'm about two seconds away from a mental breakdown and to tread carefully.

I laugh. "Where do I start?" Drawing back, I wipe my eyes and sit on the sofa, my head in my hands. "I fucked up, Syd."

She sits opposite me, curling her feet under her. "I'm sure it's not that bad, Lo," she says.

I lift my head up and look her in the eye as I mutter, "I've been sleeping with my English professor."

Sydney's quiet for a second before saying, "Yeah okay, that's bad."

I throw myself against the couch and lean my head back.

"I'm gonna need a bit more here, Lo. I get sleeping with your professor is bad, but to this extent?" she questions.

I think about how much to tell her and how much *not* to tell her, but after lying to her for so long, I'm tired. Tired of the lies. Tired of sneaking around. Just so. Damn. Tired. I start taking my hair out of the butterfly grip, trying to buy myself time before I either get the lecture of my life or I fuck up even more and potentially put Sydney at risk.

I run a hand through my hair before speaking, not entirely sure what's about to come out of my mouth—another lie or the truth. "Professor Anderson and I have been dating for months, in secret."

Sydney sits up, exclaiming, "Wait? Professor McHotStuff?"

"Sydney," I groan out.

She puts her hands up in surrender. "Okay, okay, not the point. But seriously though? McHotStuff?" She wiggles her eyebrows and for the first time since all this shit started, I laugh.

"Yes, Syd. McHotStuff."

"*Damn.*" She drags the word out in what I think is shock but mostly sounds like awe. She waves a hand in the air and says, "Continue."

I roll my eyes at her. "How magnanimous of you."

"Just get to the good stuff, because there's good stuff, right?" She raises an eyebrow at me.

"There's been plenty of good stuff." I sigh as I continue, "One of the things I didn't tell you about is this weird feeling I've been having. Like I'm being watched." Sydney's smile drops from her face and she leans towards me.

"It's been going on for a while and I thought that it was just my imagination." I shrug. "But tonight, at the party, the dean... I don't know... manhandled me? Into his office—"

Sydney gasps, tears beginning to form in her eyes. "No, Lauren—"

"Nothing like that, Syd," I rush out before she gets the wrong idea. "He manhandled me, told me that he'd been watching me for a while. That he knew about me and Caleb and if I don't want to lose my scholarship and for Caleb to lose his job, then I need to do as he says."

I didn't realize that the tears had started again until Sydney comes and sits next to me, handing me a box of tissues.

"That fucking bastard," she exclaims. "I'm going to kick that dickhead, right in—"

I cut her off, grabbing her arm. "Sydney. No. You can't say anything. He explicitly said that it had to stay between us. I shouldn't be telling you any of this, I could be putting you in danger." I sob harder at the thought of anything happening to my best friend, my sister.

"Fine. But we need to do something about this, Lo. I don't give a shit who he is, he can't go around threatening people." I love Sydney, but angry Sydney? She's in a league of her own and I wouldn't want to mess with her.

She gets up and starts pacing around, one hand on her hip and the other on her forehead—her thinking pose.

"Have you told McHotStuff?" she asks.

"No, I literally came straight here after getting out of the dean's house."

Sydney snaps her fingers and I know that what she's about to say is either going to be a genius idea or is going to get us into a world of trouble.

"Do you trust me?"

"What kind of question is that? Of course I do... just as long as we don't end up in jail like that time in Mexico." I cock an eyebrow at her, my lip quirking up in a small smirk.

Sydney claps her hands together. "Right, here's what we're gonna do."

# Chapter Forty-Eight

## *Caleb*

After getting back from the dean's party last night, I barely slept. Thoughts of what he could be implying and what had Lauren so spooked, messed with my head. I got up this morning and showered, trying to wake myself up before I headed downstairs and made coffee.

Sliding out my phone, I text Noah:

Me

> Need advice/help.

Noah

> Meet me at the diner. Thirty minutes.

*This guy never fails me.*

Walking to the door, I put my sneakers and leather jacket on before grabbing my baseball cap and putting it on backwards. I drive to the diner, *Hello Heaven, Hello* by *Yungblud* playing quietly on the radio.

I head inside the diner, the bell ringing as I open the door. Noah's not here yet so I grab a seat and wait for him. He arrives a couple minutes later, wearing his usual black T-shirt, black jeans, and black coat. I wouldn't put it past him to start wearing guyliner.

I stand up and we do one of those guy hugs.

"You good?" he asks as we sit down. A waitress comes over to take our order so I wait before replying.

"Something's up with the Dean of Admissions," I say as I lean back in my seat and cross my arms over my chest.

"I'm not following. What's that got to do with anything?" Noah questions.

I rake a hand down my face. *Queue the lecture.* "That girl, Lauren, that I was seeing?" He nods as I continue. "Something's happened and I've got a funny feeling he's the cause of it."

"And when you say something's happened..." He gestures with his hand in a 'get on with it' motion.

And so I explain everything from last night. Once I'm finished, Noah blows out a puff of air. "Something definitely ain't right there, man."

"I agree. We've been careful so maybe he hasn't found out about us?"

"Oh, he knows. There's no way he wouldn't, not with the comments he's made. What can I do?"

"You've changed your tune," I observe as I run a finger along my bottom lip. "You warned me off Lauren if I remember correctly."

"Things change," is all he says.

"Got something you need to get off *your* chest, Noah?" I smirk.

He looks out the window before mumbling so low, I almost don't catch it. "Let's just say I have my own student to deal with."

To say I'm shocked is an understatement. He's a high school teacher.

"Noah—" I start.

"She's legal, Caleb," he snaps. "She was held back a year."

"Fuck," I whisper shout. "We're really fucking things up for ourselves aren't we."

Noah nods his head in agreement. "So what are we gonna do about your problem?"

"I'm not sure yet. I need to talk to Lauren but she's not replying to my messages or calls."

"Let me know what the plan is, if there's a plan."

"Thanks, man. Appreciate you."

We finish up and I head home, still unable to get hold of Lauren. When I get home, I go straight into my office, trying to lose myself in work. Anything's got to be better than sitting here wondering what the hell's going on with her.

---

I've been working for the past four hours straight—my legs are numb and my back's killing me. I stand up, stretching out the kinks and head into the kitchen to order dinner. Grabbing my phone from the kitchen counter, I see a text message from Lauren. I nearly dropped the damn thing I'm so eager to open the message from her.

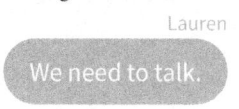

Lauren

We need to talk.

*Why doesn't that sound good?*

Me

> About what, baby girl? Are you okay?

I'm standing here like a simp waiting for her reply, watching the three dots appear to show she's typing, which only causes anxiety to claw at my insides. After what feels like forever later but was probably only a minute tops, her message comes through.

Lauren

> Meet me at Strokes at 7 p.m. I'll explain then.

I message her back telling her I'll be there and close down my phone. What does she want to talk to me about? To tell me about what happened last night?

I look at the time and see that I've got a couple hours before I need to leave. Going back to my original plan, I order dinner and put a film on in the background, trying to keep my mind busy so I don't start spiraling.

---

I turn up at Strokes five minutes before Lauren told me to meet her. It doesn't open for another hour so I stride into the bar area. She's sitting on a bar stool with her back to me and from what I can see, she's wearing her usual jeans and a hoodie, arms propped on the counter with her head hung low.

She must hear me approaching as she turns around, the smile that she normally graces me with not in sight. I lean in to give her a kiss but she puts her hand on my chest to stop me.

"Lauren?" I question as I take a step back, my brow furrowing. She's never pushed me away before.

She stands up from her seat, not making eye contact with me.

"What's going on, sweetheart? Talk to me," I implore. This not knowing is slowly killing me from the inside out. The feeling of dread is getting worse with every passing second. She's not...

"I can't do this anymore," she whispers.

And there it is. I feel like she's just punched me in the gut. In all honesty I think it would've hurt less.

"Why?" I grit out. Pain like I've never felt before engulfs my body, making it hard to breathe.

"You know my past. We've had this conversation before, this" —she gestures between us— "isn't going anywhere. You're my professor."

Confusion grips me. Yes we've had this conversation before, but I thought we were past it? That I meant something to her like she meant something to me.

I rub my chest, my heart aching, as I try again. "You don't know that it's not going anywhere, Lauren. We've been dating for a few months, you just need some more time to get used to the feelings."

Her head snaps up and I know it was the wrong thing to say. Fuck!

"Don't you dare try telling me what I *need* or what I *feel*, Caleb." The fire in her eyes tells me exactly how much I've just pissed her off. "We're done."

"'We're done?'" I exclaim, my own emotions taking over as I start pacing backwards and forwards in front of her, hands buried in my hair. I glance up at her. "I don't get a say in this?"

"No, Caleb, you don't. I've made my decision. Nothing you say will change that," she replies angrily.

"Lauren, please," I beg. This woman is the best thing that's ever happened to me so yeah, I'm gonna beg. "Don't do this," I whisper, tears in my eyes. I'm on the cusp of falling to my knees in front of her, to throw myself at her mercy because anything is better than this all-consuming loss, pain, and sickness that I'm feeling. She can't walk away from me, I honestly don't know if I'll survive it.

"Goodbye, Professor Anderson," she whispers back, finally looking up at me, tears shining in her eyes.

"No."

"No?" she repeats.

"No. I refuse for this to happen." I rush to her, placing my hands on her cheeks and my forehead against hers. "I love you," I breathe out. "I won't lose you, Lauren. I'm not letting you go."

Lauren lets out a sob, and it suddenly dawns on me that this is affecting her just as much as it is me. I just can't figure out *why* she's doing it.

"Whatever it is, we can work through it, sweetheart. Just let me in," I plead, placing a kiss on her forehead and breathing in her vanilla and strawberry scent, one I'm possibly about to lose forever if she has her way.

Lauren cups my hands in hers, squeezing them gently before removing them from her face. "Regardless of your…" She pauses, swallowing as if forcing out the words is causing her physical pain. "…feelings… this is over. I'm sorry, Caleb, I really am."

Lauren wrenches herself away from me, grabbing her bag from the stool and walks out, taking my heart with her.

# Chapter Forty-Nine

## *Lauren*

"*I love you.*"

The tears won't stop falling as I leave Caleb. My heart's ripping into shattered pieces that sprinkle along the ground as I walk. But it's all part of the plan.

'Phase one' is complete and I've never been so miserable in my entire fucking life. I can only hope he forgives me when this is all said and done. We needed to get the dean away from Caleb, so the easiest way to keep him safe was to 'break up' with him. But it had to look real, otherwise it wouldn't have worked.

"*I love you.*"

Sydney's waiting for me outside, she knew I'd need her afterwards. Coming round to the passenger side of the car, she hugs me, telling me everything will be okay. I nod but how can it be? I've lost the one person who stole my heart.

"*I love you*"

Those words are a permanent fixture in my mind. Every time I try to think of something else, those words are all I can hear. The look of utter devastation on his face as I broke both of our hearts.

The drive back to the dorms is quiet, Sydney giving me the space I need to sort through my thoughts and me not knowing what to say. I watch the world go by, my head leaning against the window as she drives.

Once we get back to the dorms, I head straight to the showers. I undress slowly, numb to everything around me. The tears that had slowed, begin again. I don't even have the energy to wipe them away, just letting them fall where they may. There's no one in here so at least I'm provided some privacy to the meltdown that I'm sure is coming.

I step under the spray and drop my head down. My tears mingling with the water and going down the drain. *Just like how my life feels right now.* A sob escapes me, a guttural cry of heartbreak that this is happening. That I finally learn to love someone, *really* love someone, for it to be dashed away before it had the chance to start.

I drop to the floor, bringing my knees to my chest, no longer caring if someone hears me or not. The pain is too overwhelming. The ache in my chest is so tight, I feel like I'm under water, unable to catch a breath, unable to feel anything but this deep all-consuming *pain*. I want it to stop. Because if this is what love is, I don't want it.

I'm not sure how long I sit and cry for, all I know is that the water has long gone cold and I'm shivering. The tears are slowly drying up, coming in short bursts rather than gut wrenching sobs. I slowly stand up, enjoying the pain of sitting in cold water that it brought to my body. The physical pain momentarily dulling the emotional pain and allowing me to sift through my thoughts.

Grabbing my towel, I move toward the mirror, wiping the condensation away to look at myself—red, puffy eyes. Check.

They say if you can look at yourself in the mirror for more than five seconds it's a sign you're confident in your body and the person that you are. I make it less than two before I'm turning my head away, disgusted at the sight of myself. Mad at the world for making me 'desirable' enough that a crazed man has taken it upon himself to ruin my life—or what feels like it—all because he woke up one day and said, "she's mine." I scoff internally at the idea that I would *ever* be his.

I get dressed, putting my sweats and hoodie on before grabbing my things, and heading back to my room. My feet shuffle slowly, as if my brain and body don't want to cooperate. The numbness traveling to every part of my body, refusing to work without my other half.

When I open the door, Sydney's holding a glass in one hand and a mug in the other.

"I'm not sure what you need right now, babe. Alcohol to numb the pain or coffee because... well, it's coffee." She laughs lightly, trying to make me smile but I don't have it in me.

"Alcohol. Lots and lots of alcohol," I mumble as I grab a blanket and curl up on the sofa.

"You got it. One glass of numbness coming right up."

Sydney comes over, handing me the glass and watching as I take a big gulp, almost downing it in one.

"I'm just... gonna go and grab the bottle," she says, wide eyed.

"Good idea."

Sydney comes back and sits in her usual seat opposite me, sipping her drink. "Have you heard from douchebag?" she asks.

We've dubbed the dean 'douchebag.' He needed a name that would make me fear him less, something that made him less of a threat—in my head, anyway.

"No, not yet. I'm not sure what's worse. What happened with Caleb today or sitting waiting for this 'call' I'm supposed to be getting." I take another healthy gulp of my wine before adding, "Right, one night..." Sydney raises an eyebrow at me wondering where I'm going with this. "One night of having a pity party. Then tomorrow it's back to it."

Sydney looks at me, pity filling her hazel eyes. "Lo—" she starts.

"Please, Syd," I implore her, tears filling my eyes again. "I can't live like this. I can't live with the pain I'm feeling right now. I need to focus on something else... *anything* else. I'm not going to be jumping into anyone's bed but I *can* work and I *can* concentrate on school, until each day starts hurting a little less." I plead with my eyes for her to understand. It's the only way I'm going to get through this without crumbling completely.

She nods her head. "While it's not healthy" —I go to interrupt but she holds up a hand, silencing me— "I will support whatever you need. I can see you care about him."

I give her a watery smile, the tears fighting to get out and for once in my life I stop fighting. I let them come. I embrace the emotions that I was always taught to hide, to stuff down because they were a sign of weakness. I let Sydney hold me as I cry for me, for Caleb. Vowing that one way or another Dean Williams will not win whatever *this* is.

# Chapter Fifty

## *Lauren*

It's been just over a week since *that* night. Caleb hasn't tried contacting me and I don't know whether to be upset that he hasn't reached out or relieved that he's respecting my wishes. I didn't bother going to class, emailing Brad telling him I was unwell and asking if he would send any missed assignments.

I've been true to my word—mostly—and haven't let myself dwell on the shoulda, woulda, coulda's. I've spent most of my time either at work or in the library studying, knowing that if I stayed in my room, I would most likely never leave it again.

I'm sitting in the library, finishing up an assignment when my phone goes off.

Unknown

Florence Hotel. 9 p.m.

*Fuck! It's got to be the dean.*

Calling Sydney straight away, I panic wondering if she'll answer as I know she's in class. It rings twice before she answers.

"Lauren." The alarm and concern in Sydney's voice is evident, as she rushes to add, "What's wrong?"

"Douchebag messaged," I whisper quietly.

You can hear Sydney's sharp intake of breath. "Shit! What did he say?"

"He wants me to meet him tonight," I whisper again.

My heart rate kicks up and my vision starts to blur at the thought of being in the same room as him again. But Sydney and I have a plan, one that, if all goes according to plan, will see the dean firmly where he belongs—behind bars.

"Okay. We both know the plan. Everything's fine, Lo. We've got this," she says, sounding more confident than I feel. "Everything's gonna be fine," she reiterates.

I nod but she can't see me so I take a deep breath and put my big girl panties on before repeating, "Everything's gonna be fine."

"I've gotta go but I'll see you back at the dorm in a little while, okay?"

"Sure. I'm just finishing up in the library then I'm gonna go to the Honey Pot before heading back. I'll see you soon."

We hang up and I grab my bag. I'm too restless to keep working so I make my way to the coffee shop, hoping the noise there will drown out the noise in my head.

# Chapter Fifty-One

# *Caleb*

I'm drowning. Drowning in a sea of emotions I can't fight my way out of. The pain I'm feeling, indescribable. In all of my thirty-six-years I've never had my heart broken—I've always been the one to break *their* hearts but this... this is too much for one person to handle.

It's been a week since I last saw Lauren. She's not been to class, having Brad send her the assignments that she needs. I haven't fought it, knowing she needed her space even though it killed me.

I've been like a walking zombie—going to class, teaching, marking papers and then coming home, only to sit until it gets dark, and I take myself to bed. If I even made it that far. Too many a night I've fallen asleep with an untouched bottle of beer or glass of whiskey in my hand.

*Wash. Rinse. Repeat.*

I ache, the tension in my body causing me to seize up with the emotions swirling around—sadness, anger, loneliness, resentment, then back to anger—not being able to think or function properly.

If the guys were to hear me like this they'd tell me to toughen up, to grow a pair. But for someone who's never felt this... loss, they just wouldn't understand. Hell, I don't understand it myself.

All I know is that I'm going to fight for Lauren. She's mine, and I'll be damned if I give her up.

I've been sitting in my home office, nursing a whiskey for the better part of the day, not moving, just lost, trying to figure out a way to get Lauren back. My gut is still screaming at me that the dean's got something to do with it.

I push out of my chair, my back and knees protesting, and walk into the kitchen, dumping the whiskey I poured but never drank down the sink. I put my hands on the counter and hang my head.

I need to get out of here.

Making my way through the quiet house, I grab my shit and head out. I look at my Mustang and decide to walk instead. Where to? I have no fucking clue. I just know I need to move.

I wander aimlessly through the streets until I end up on campus. Seeing that the Honey Pot is open I make my way across the path thinking a coffee might be a good idea. I pause at the window and see a familiar face inside. Freezing in place, my heart starts hammering in my chest at the sight.

*Lauren.*

My body's screaming at me to run in there, to scoop her up in my arms, and keep her with me where I know she'll be safe. But I don't. I just stand there, peering in, watching her through greedy eyes. I don't know why I don't go in, watching her from the window like some kind of stalker. Lauren's talking to Raven and she's never looked more beautiful, even with the bags under her eyes.

I bring a hand to my chest and rub as the phantom pain of her leaving runs through me. My fingers tingle at the reminder of what her skin feels like against mine, and I exhale harshly.

Lauren doesn't seem to interact much and Raven appears to pick up on it, placing a hand on Lauren's arm, a worried expression on her face. I keep watching the interaction, keeping to the shadows, hoping no one will notice and call the cops.

Lauren finally leaves, so I do what I do best—I follow her.

# Chapter Fifty-Two

## *Lauren*

I was longer in the Honey Pot than expected, doing my best to have a conversation with Raven but struggling. How do you have a conversation about the mundane when the unhinged university dean is threatening you and the person you love?

Grabbing my coffee, I head back to the dorm to get ready for tonight. The closer it gets to 9 p.m. the more my nerves kick in—the heart palpitations, the shaking hands, the struggling to breathe.

Sydney's in our room when I get back, and I breathe out a sigh of relief knowing I won't be doing this alone.

I meet her gaze and give her a small smile which she returns.

"Let's do this," she says as she grabs some stuff off the counter. I nod in agreement and follow her.

Sitting down at my vanity I let Sydney work her magic. The air around us is thick with tension, both of us worried about how tonight's going to go, but both wanting this to end. Once she's done my hair and makeup, she pulls out the clothes for tonight—a red body-con dress that leaves very little to the imagination.

The front is ridiculously low cut, only being held up with tit tape and a prayer. The back is also cut low, so low you can practically see the top of my ass crack. The sleeves are long, thankfully, giving me something to play with when my anxiety gets too much. We decided on heels, not my first choice seeing as I can't particularly run fast in them, but my trusty Converses don't go with the outfit.

As hare-brained as it is, neither Sydney nor I are fighters. I mean, Sydney loves to mouth off, but anything physical and she's out. But after watching one too many episodes of Criminal Minds, she decided that the best plan would be to catch him in the act—predictable? Yes. Will it work? Hopefully.

Sydney attaches a tiny camera, almost like a pin prick, and microphone to me, the tape pulling at my skin, before helping me into my dress.

If I can keep him distracted long enough we'll—hopefully—be able to get enough evidence against him to put him behind bars, discrediting any accusations about me and Caleb that he might throw out there. Thus keeping us both safe, seeing as it's his word against mine.

I didn't say it was a perfect plan, I just said we *had* a plan. An esteemed, 'happily married' Dean of Admissions versus a college age stripper—I think we all know how that would end.

Sydney puts her hands on my shoulders and I peer up at her through my lashes. "It's gonna be okay, Lo. If I could take your place, I would." The unshed tears in her eyes confirm what she's saying.

I put my hands on hers and lean into her. "I know. We got this, boo," I chuckle lightly and she gives me a small smile.

We take a minute to just breathe, the enormity of the situation not lost on us—this will either work or crumble around us. My money's on it going horribly wrong.

Sydney pulls back first. "Right bitch, let's get this show on the road."

Nodding my head, I follow her out. We make our way down to her car—Sydney fought me tooth and nail when I told her I was doing this alone. I basically got told to suck a hairy dick, and that she was coming with me as back up... needless to say, she won that argument.

The drive to the hotel is quiet, neither one of us speaking, and I'm not sure if that's making me feel worse or not.

Just as we're pulling up, I get a message:

> Unknown
> Room 316

The nerves ramp up and I start shaking as I read the message. I show Sydney the phone and she nods to say she's seen it. I get out of the car, taking in a deep breath as I stare up at the building.

*I can do this. I will do this. For myself. For Caleb.*

I force my legs to move, walking up to the automatic doors and into what will either make me or break me.

I walk in and automatically feel out of place. The opulence of the hotel not matching up with my stripper vibes. I feel like Julia Roberts in Pretty Woman, the only difference is that I broke the heart of my Richard Gere, and instead I'm walking toward Stuckey.

I ignore the random looks of disgust, heading toward the elevator that will take me up to the room, a ball of anxiety knotting in my stomach with every step I take. I press the button and wait. Once the doors open, I get in and head to the third floor. I know Sydney won't be far behind me. The plan was for her to wait for ten minutes, then come up, waiting outside for my signal to call the cops and get us to hell out of there.

Getting to the third floor, I step out into a deserted hallway and walk toward room 316, my knees wobbling with every step I take. Coming to a stop outside of the room, I brace myself for what's about to happen. I know that if I only think of worst case scenarios, I'll be prepared for anything. It doesn't stop the bile from churning in my stomach, though.

I knock on the door and wait. My heart's racing and my palms are sweaty as I gently move from one foot to the other, restless energy coursing through me. Trying to hide how terrified I actually am, I move my shaking hands behind the clutch I'm holding.

The door suddenly opens making me jump and I gasp at the person holding the door open.

"What are *you* doing here?"

## CHAPTER FIFTY-THREE

## *Caleb*

After I followed Lauren back to her dorm room, my gut kept telling me to get my car… that she was up to something and if I didn't move quickly enough, I'd lose her. Knowing she was safely tucked up inside—for now—I ran back home, vowing to myself to start adding cardio to my workouts.

Revving the engine, I pull out of my drive and head back toward campus, praying like fuck that I haven't missed her. Something's going down, I just know it.

Getting to Lauren's dorm in under ten minutes I sit and wait, tapping my fingertips on the steering wheel, restless, hoping I haven't got this wrong and end up looking like an idiot.

An hour later and I'm starting to regret my choices. My ass has gone numb, and my legs are aching. Running a hand through my hair, I decide that I've got this wrong, that I'm just being an overprotective asshole, and I need to go home, maybe book in a therapy session or something.

Just as I'm about to turn on the ignition, two figures emerge from the doorway, heads down and heading towards a Mini Cooper that's parked up outside.

*I fucking knew it.*

I smile at the fact I was right, normally I'm way off base, but then the apprehension sets in... where's she going in a hurry? And what *the fuck* is she wearing? Her dress—if you can even call it that—shows off every inch of her. A growl rumbles in my chest, and I clench my hands around the steering wheel, willing myself to calm down. There must be a logical explanation as to why my girlfriend is wearing next to fucking nothing.

Lauren and Sydney drive off and I quickly follow them, trying to keep as much distance between us as possible, but also being close enough that I can see where they're going. Weaving in and out of traffic, which is thankfully light, we turn off at an exit before heading farther into town. They keep driving for a few more minutes before pulling into the Florence Hotel.

*What the fuck?*

The car idles as I sit and wait to see what happens next. Luckily my windows are slightly tinted so I can see them but they can't see me.

Lauren gets out of the car, taking in a deep breath before heading inside, head down the entire time. I hear the engine start up on Sydney's car and watch as she goes to the parking lot opposite. Following suit, I do the same, parking a couple of spaces down.

I get out of my car and head over to Sydney. She's just closing her door when her head snaps toward the sound of me approaching and she looks at me with wide eyes. "Shit."

"The fuck is going on, Sydney? Why the hell has my woman just walked into that hotel all dressed up?"

"McHotStuff, I don't have time for this," she pleads, barging past me. "I need to get inside."

"Why? What's going on?" I gently clasp her arm to get her attention. Frustration that Lauren's put herself into a dangerous situation, and Sydney not answering my questions threatens to send me nuclear.

Sydney sighs. "Can we walk and talk? I need to get in there. Like, now." The urgency in her tone makes me stand up straighter.

"Start talking, Sydney," I grit out.

Sydney begins walking briskly toward the hotel and I fall into step beside her. "Dean Williams has been threatening Lauren," she whispers. "She was told that if she didn't do as he said, both of you would pay the price."

I blink, the words taking a second to sink in. "Are you fucking kidding me? Why didn't she tell me?" I whisper yell back. My strides getting quicker, needing to get to her *now*.

"She was trying to protect you," she snaps.

"From what?" I exclaim. "I'm a big boy, Sydney, I'm perfectly capable of dealing with the asshole without putting Lauren in fucking danger." I'm nearly shouting at this point, but concerned looks from other hotel goers causes me to lower my voice. "What the hell were you both *thinking*?"

The anger flooding my veins is enough to level a building. How fucking *stupid* can she be?

"We weren't thinking of anything other than trying to fix this. Lauren's first instinct might be to protect you, but *my* first instinct is to protect *her*," she replies angrily.

"If you think this is protecting her, Sydney, you still have a lot to learn." We get to the elevator as I ask, "What floor?"

"Third," she mutters.

The doors open and we step inside, I stab the button a little too hard and the doors close. I glance over at Sydney and some of the anger drains from me—she looks scared, terrified.

"What was the plan here, Sydney? Go in and seduce him?" I feel sick at the thought.

Sydney starts pacing around the small compartment. "To a certain degree. We wanted to get it on tape, to bury him, so that he can't do this again."

"For fuck sake, that's the stupidest plan I've ever heard," I shout.

"Well it seemed like a good idea at the time, alright?" she shouts back, tears forming along her lash line. "Caleb. She's my best friend, you think I want her in this situation?" she sighs.

"A good idea? That's the woman I love up there, going through god knows what," I exclaim as I run a hand through my hair.

*I swear to god, as soon as this is over I'm tanning my girl's ass a beautiful shade of red.*

Sydney's head snaps up, but we're saved from having *that* conversation as the elevator doors open.

We begin walking down the hallway when we hear, "Sydney" screamed.

I don't hesitate, I run.

# Chapter Fifty-Four

## *Lauren*

"Lauren, come in." Brad steps aside for me to enter but I furrow my brow at him, staying where I am.

"Brad, seriously. What's going on?" I ask. I take a quick glance at the door... yup, room 316. I look back at Brad, who's eyeing me like I'm his next meal, the intensity in his eyes making me swallow around the lump in my throat.

"Why don't you come in and I'll explain, hmm?" he says.

I steady my nerves and shuffle past him, leaning my body as far away from him as possible as I concentrate on putting one foot in front of the other. Trying to figure out why Brad's opening the door and not the dean.

I walk in as far as I dare, not wanting to be too far from an exit at any given moment. Much like the rest of the hotel, the rooms are done in an elegant way, the walls are cream but with blue accents. The living room is an open plan setting, two small couches facing a TV with a small table and chairs next to balcony doors.

Brad closes the door and comes up behind me, bringing me out of my perusal. "We're going to have so much fun together, my love," he whispers darkly in my ear. He goes to move my hair to the side but I step away.

"You need to start talking, Brad, right. The. Fuck. Now," I exclaim. "I'm so confused. You were the one that sent the message asking me to meet you here?"

Brad runs a hand through his blonde hair, a sinister grin playing on his lips before he replies, "Looks like the cat's out of the bag now. You met my father, his tastes—"

"I'm sorry. Your father?" I cut in, pacing around the room, one hand in my hair as I try and understand what the hell's going on. "Are you trying to tell me that Dean Williams is your father?" I laugh, because that's absurd, right?

"Yes, he's my father. We've been planning this for a while. We wanted it to look like he was after you the whole time. I guess it worked if you didn't know it was actually *me* who's been obsessed with you. Call it a... father/son bonding experience," he chuckles, but I stand there mouth agape, failing to see what's so funny as he continues, "The minute I saw you walking around in a black one piece at Strokes, I knew then that you were meant to be mine. Father just helped the process along until I was ready to show my hand." Brad shrugs like it's no big deal.

"Father/son bonding experience?" I scoff. "That's the most ridiculous thing I've ever heard. Why make it look like it was your dad, though? Why do *any* of this?" I pinch the bridge of my nose, none of this adding up and making sense.

"My father and I... This isn't the first time that we've become obsessed with the same woman, I'm just lucky that this time, another woman took his interest, leaving you all for me." Brad stalks closer to me and I move back, bumping into the sideboard behind me. "Every time you felt like you were being watched? That was me." Brad grins, almost like he's pleased with himself.

My mind and heart are racing at the thought that I've had this wrong the whole time. That I thought it was the dean who was pulling the strings, but he wasn't. It was Brad! I look at him, *really* look at him for the first time and I'm shocked to find the similarities in his features. *How did I not see this before?*

"But the party," I suddenly say, remembering. "You and the dean acted like you didn't know each other? His wife... your *mom* acted like she hated you."

He smirks, running a hand down his face. "Ah yes, acting at its finest. My mother hates me, always has. But that's more to do with the fact that I'm a result of my father having an affair, so technically... I'm not her son. I took my mother's name. Father and I don't go spreading our relationship for... certain reasons, as I'm sure you can understand." Brad brings his hand up, pushing a strand of hair out of my face and I flinch.

"All this time...?" I question.

He moves his hand down to his side and walks to the bar, pouring himself a drink, before downing it in one. "All this time," he mumbles before turning back to me. "All this time, I've wanted you. That lost look you had in your eyes called to my own. It called to the darkest parts of me. But then you had to get involved with *him* and I knew I had to do something sooner rather than later."

"We went on *one* date, Brad. I thought you were my friend?" I whisper.

"Friend? No, Lauren. I've never been your *friend*," he mocks. "Now, are you going to be a good little girl and do as I say? We wouldn't want anything bad to happen to Professor Anderson now, would we." His smile is all teeth, without actually smiling, and a shiver makes its way down my spine.

The deranged look in his eyes—so familiar to his father's, that the very little I'd had to eat before coming here was threatening its way back up. "You and your father are sick, you know that?" I shout, my body shaking as I deal with, not one but two, deranged men that are insistent on ruining my life, and threatening to harm Caleb.

Brad starts chuckling darkly, stalking toward me, and shaking his head. He snaps his hand out and grabs me by the throat, cutting off my air supply. I instinctively start clawing at his hands, trying to pry him off, as pure terror runs through me.

His pupils are blown wide and a dark, calculating look enters his eyes. "Do not test me, Lauren. I won't be held accountable for my actions should you deny me of what is mine."

He lets go, turning his back on me and I grab at my throat, rubbing where he squeezed as I take in much needed gulps of air.

"I'm not yours," I choke out, my throat sore from his grip.

He pauses mid step at my words, his body stiffening. Brad slowly turns to me, a murderous look on his face. "Tread carefully, my love. You. Are. Mine." He shouts the last part as if saying it louder it will make it true.

*Well, if I'm going to die today, I might as well make it count.*

I straighten my spine and channel my inner Sydney. "I will *never* be yours. You can delude yourself all you want, Brad, but I belong to no one. You disgust me," I sneer.

He advances on me, gripping my arm painfully, his nails digging in, the pain causing me to gasp. I want to call out, to shout for help but this is a turn in the plan that I didn't see coming.

"Why are you doing this to me?" I cry out, as he all but drags me towards the bedroom, my feet slipping along the floor in his haste.

Brad doesn't say anything as he brings me round and shoves me onto the bed. His cold eyes taking me in before saying, "I'm doing this because I can. I'll take what I want, and what I want is *you*, Lauren. To do exactly as I say, when I say. You have been a continued thorn in my side since I saw you a year ago. I have watched you, yearned for you, but I'm done waiting. I *will* have you. Mind, body, and soul."

"You may have my body, but you will never have my mind or my soul," I yell trying to get up off the bed, but he pushes me back down and climbs on top of me.

*Okay, this has gone on long enough now. I can't do this anymore.*

I take in as big a breath as I'm able to with a large, crazed, six foot something man on top of me, and scream at the top of my lungs, "SYDNEY."

Brad's head snaps up from where it was resting in the crook of my neck, anger pooling in his gaze. "Oh, Lauren. You shouldn't have done that."

I start fighting against him when suddenly pain explodes through my eye, and everything goes black.

# Chapter Fifty-Five

## *Caleb*

"Call 911," I shout to Sydney. Not caring about the damage I'm about to cause, I kick the door. It doesn't budge so I keep kicking until finally it gives way and opens.

Running in, with Sydney close behind me, I move quickly through the living room—nothing. I go towards the bedroom and take in the scene in front of me—Lauren passed out on the bed with... *Brad* leaning over her. *The fuck?*

I see red. Charging at him, I grab him by the shirt and pull him off her. He goes flying into the dresser, smacking his head on the corner. I stride over to him, kicking him repeatedly in the stomach, my emotions doing the talking for me.

"Mother fucking bastard cunt," I yell at his unconscious form, repeatedly kicking him before leaning down and punching him in the face, over and over again. "Wake up, asshole," I roar.

I can vaguely hear someone calling my name but I'm too far gone to notice who it is. This sorry sack of shit hurt the woman I love.

A hand gently lands on my arm and I look up, my vision blurred as I try to take in who's in front of me.

"It's okay, handsome. I'm okay. You need to stop now," the voice gently says, and fuck if that isn't the best sound I've ever heard.

The relief at seeing Lauren in front of me reduces some of my anger, and I abruptly stand up, hauling her into my arms, breathing in her vanilla and strawberry scent.

Lauren clings to me, sobbing in my arms as the cops and EMT's storm in. I grip her tighter, not wanting to let her go as the detectives start firing questions at us.

"Give us a minute," I growl. The detective nods and backs away.

Lauren lifts her head and I can see a bruise forming on her cheek, the relaxed feeling of having her in my arms quickly fading as I become enraged at the sight of it.

Gently cupping her face and running my thumb across the mark, I take a calming breath. Lauren's been frightened beyond all measure, she doesn't need me losing my shit. She needs my support. My attention. My *love*.

Remembering where we are and who we're surrounded by, I reluctantly pull away. I can see it in her eyes and by the tilt of her head that she understands why I've done it. She wraps her arms around herself and Sydney comes over, enveloping her in a hug.

One of the detectives comes back, a woman this time, and asks Lauren if she'll answer some questions. Nodding her head, she moves to follow with Sydney's arm still around her, giving me one last look before being led from the room.

# Chapter Fifty-Six

# *Lauren*

As I start to come to, I hear grunts and yelling. "Mother fucking bastard cunt."

*Caleb?*

"Wake up, asshole."

*What's he doing here?*

I groan as pain blooms across my cheek and I move my hand up to touch the skin there, wincing at the soreness.

"Lauren," I hear someone gasp. I open my eyes and see Sydney sitting next to me on... the bed?

*What the hell happened?*

Suddenly it all comes tumbling back to me and I frantically sit up—the hotel room, Brad. I look over to see Caleb leaning over Brad, punching him, I quickly scramble off the bed and move toward him.

Placing my hand on his arm I gently whisper, "It's okay, handsome. I'm okay. You need to stop now." He stills instantly, turning around to face me. The look of relief evident on his face. He doesn't say anything, just drags me into his body and holds me.

The tears start falling and I clutch onto him tighter, burying my face into his chest as the sobs wrack my body.

*It's over.*

There's a commotion behind me but I'm too exhausted to move and look at who it is. I hear the echoes of words spoken around me but I don't take them in, too busy breathing in the comforting scent of Caleb.

I pull away from him and he cups my cheeks, the fury clear as day in his eyes. I gaze up at him, taking in his handsome features knowing that this man has become so important to me in the short time that I've known him.

They say time isn't a measure, that when a soul meets another soul that it intrinsically *knows*, time means nothing—my soul knows Caleb's.

He drops his hands and takes a step back. At first I'm confused, wanting to chase him and his comforting embrace, but I quickly realize the voices I heard can't see us like this, so I tilt my head in acknowledgment.

Sydney comes over and puts her arms around me, offering me the comfort that I'm missing from Caleb. A detective asks for a statement, and I nod, allowing Sydney to guide me into the next room, giving Caleb one last glance.

I sit down on one of the sofas with Sydney next to me, her hand clutching mine, as a stern looking detective sits on the sofa opposite us.

"Lauren, I'm Detective Hernandez. Can you tell me what happened here?"

I nod and recount everything that happened, starting from the constant feeling of being watched, to the night of the dean's party and to now, with Brad. If it wasn't for Sydney's quiet strength, I don't think I would've gotten through it.

"Unfortunately, because this hasn't been called in before, and we have no evidence, this is going to be a tough one. It's your word against h—"

"We do have evidence," Sydney cuts her off. She looks at me, nodding towards my chest and says, "The tape."

Letting go of Sydney's hand I grab the wire and box from beneath my dress, ripping it from my skin, the pain lessening the brain fog, and hand it to the detective.

Detective Hernandez takes it from me, rewinding the tape and listening to it. She raises her eyebrows at certain points but otherwise keeps a stoic expression. "I'll take this, but because Mr. Moore wasn't aware he was being recorded, this might be inadmissible evidence." She gives me a pitying look before adding, "But I will do everything I can to make sure that doesn't happen."

I give her a small smile, grateful that going through all of this might lead to getting him convicted.

Someone walks into the living room, and my eyes dart up—Caleb's in cuffs and being led away by an officer.

I jump out of my chair as I exclaim, "What the hell? Why is he being arrested?"

All thoughts regarding me and what happened have fled. The only thing I'm concerned about right now is Caleb.

Putting out an arm to stop me, the officer says, "Ma'am, please step back."

I stop, eyes wide at Caleb. He gives me a small grin as he says, "It's all good. I'll be out in time to grade your next paper." With that he winks and lets the officer lead him away.

Gaping after him, I try to understand what just happened. I glance at Sydney, who's now stood next to me, but she just shrugs.

"Professor Anderson has been arrested for assault against Mr. Moore," Detective Hernandez says from behind us.

"What? Why?" I protest, spinning around to face the detective. "He was protecting me."

"Whether that is the case or not, he was seen assaulting another person by a member of law enforcement. He needed taking in for questioning."

*At least she has the nerve to look slightly contrite.*

"Can we leave now?" Sydney snaps. "Or are we being arrested as well?"

"You can leave," the detective nods, "but we might need to ask some more questions later."

After grabbing my clutch from the side, Sydney and I make our way out of the hotel as quickly as our feet will allow us without flat out running. We make it back to her car and get in.

I hit the dashboard in front of me as I shout, "Fuck."

I've been on a rollercoaster of emotions for the last twelve hours, caught between wanting to curl up into a ball and cry my eyes out or go on a murdering spree. I'm still in disbelief at the fact that it was Brad who was the mastermind behind all of this and not the dean.

Sydney pats my leg. "Let's get you home, babe. You'll feel better once you've had a shower and a large glass of wine."

I lean back against the seat and close my eyes. "A glass of wine sounds really good right about now," I agree.

After taking the world's longest shower and washing away the grubby feeling of Brad's hands on me, I settle on the couch with my drink, an ice pack attached to my cheek, while Sydney paces around tidying stuff away that she doesn't need to.

"What the fuck was that all about with Brad? I thought it was the dean?" Sydney suddenly says, looking up from her rage cleaning. "How the hell did that happen?"

"Honestly, Syd? I don't know. According to Brad, it was him who had been watching me, not his dad." It still feels weird knowing that the dean is Brad's father. "From what I could gather, this isn't the first time they've done this. I'm just glad it's over with now," I sigh, placing my head against the sofa and closing my eyes as Sydney goes back to her cleaning, silence settling around us.

I'm worried about Caleb and what'll happen to him. Voicing my concerns out loud, I mumble, "He's gonna be okay, right? They'll let him go?"

Sydney stops what she's doing, and braces her arms on the counter, glancing over at me. "Honestly? I have no idea. We can only hope that with our statements, they'll let him go."

I sigh, knowing that what she's saying makes sense, but it doesn't make me feel any better. I take a sip of wine, allowing the alcohol to relax me, lord knows I won't be able to sleep without being knocked out.

"Wait!" I sit up, a thought popping into my head causing the panic to rise again. "What did you tell the police about why Caleb was there with you?"

"That Caleb was in the hotel, saw me and how upset I looked and came over to check on me and I asked for his help."

"You're not one of his students though," I point out. "Didn't they think that was a bit off?"

"Apparently not." Sydney shrugs. "I guess the fact that they had a guy pretty badly beaten lying on the floor, and a woman who had been attacked, took precedence."

"Fair point," I agree as I sit back on the couch and place the ice pack back on my cheek. "Ow," I mutter and wince.

Pushing herself away from the counter, Sydney walks to the side table and starts fussing with it. "Have you heard from Caleb?"

I sigh. "No. I keep checking my phone but nothing."

Sydney nods, walking over and throwing herself down next to me. "Wanna watch a movie? I'm too wired to sleep."

"Sure."

She puts on the latest rom-com and I get as comfortable as possible, trying not to dwell on the shit storm of the night and what happened to Caleb.

# Chapter Fifty-Seven

## Caleb

"Thank fuck for having a best friend who's a lawyer," I laugh as I slap Theo's shoulder. "I owe you one, man."

"Sleeping with a fucking student." Theo pinches the bridge of his nose as he sighs. "I have no fucking words for you." He drops his hand and points at me adding, "I'm billing your ass for this."

I grin at him. "Yeah, yeah. You know I can't afford you." The air around us takes on a somber tone, the jokes gone as I say, "Seriously though, thank you. I lost my head for a minute."

Theo raises a brow. "Ya think, dipshit?"

We're standing outside the police precinct, Theo having got me out after spending a night in the slammer—one hundred percent, do not recommend. I'm still wearing the same clothes as last night, crumpled and bloodied from my rage fueled attack.

"You're lucky you got away with self-defense," Theo continues as he paces in front of me. "What were you thinking?" he hisses.

"I wasn't think—"

Theo rolls his eyes as he cuts me off. "Captain fucking obvious over there."

"Look, I wasn't planning on any of this. I wasn't planning on falling for her—"

"Heaven help me," Theo interrupts again. "You fell for her?"

"Hook, line, and sinker, my friend."

"Well shit," he says as he narrows his eyes at me. Finding whatever it is on my face that he was looking for, he mutters, "I need a drink," as he starts walking to his shark blue Porsche 911 GT3.

"Theo, it's 11 a.m., man," I call out, chuckling at him.

He flips me the bird, shouting over his shoulder, "It's five o'clock somewhere, asshole."

Laughing, I follow him and get into the passenger seat. "Where's my phone?" I ask as I start patting my pockets.

"Here." Theo passes me a bag with all the possessions I had on me before I was arrested—keys, wallet, and phone.

Turning it on, I see dozens of messages and missed calls. Some from students asking about extensions, and the rest from my girl. I smile as I read through her messages:

> Lauren
>
> Caleb, are you okay?
>
> Call me when you get out.
>
> I can't believe they arrested you!
>
> Don't drop the soap.

> Sorry, my nervous sense of humor's showing. How do you delete messages?
>
> I'm sorry.
>
> I miss you.

*She misses me.*

We pull out onto the main road, but before I can say anything, Theo cuts me off. "Before you go and do anything rash, as your lawyer, I'm advising you to stay low." He glances over at me, a serious look on his face. "A lot of questions are going to be asked, Caleb. Why you were in the hotel in the first place—"

"You know why I was there," I cut him off.

"Yeah, I know why you were there but that's because I'm your lawyer and one of your best friends, others do not." He gives me a pointed look before continuing, "You attacked your TA and were in a hotel room with two students." Theo runs a hand through his hair. "You need to keep away from her, Caleb."

"Fuck that," I snap. "She needs me."

"*What she needs* is to not have any more questions directed at her. For her not to lose her scholarship. I can only hope that Lauren and her friend have their stories straight."

"So what am I supposed to do? Carry on as normal? Ignore her? Act like she doesn't exist?" I exclaim, my heart pounding in my chest at the mere thought. "I can't do that, Theo."

"Well you're gonna have to," Theo snaps. "You need to lie low until this blows over. No contact other than in class, for nothing more than *class* related things, and hope like fuck that she forgives you come graduation when you can go and get your girl."

My head snaps to Theo. "Graduation? You can't be fucking serious? That's like…" I quickly do the math in my head. "…Four months away."

"Like I said, you better hope she forgives you."

"Can I at least call her to let her know?" Sarcasm drips from every word.

Theo sighs. "I would advise against it, but I can't stop you."

Leaning my head against the window, I mutter, "Can you just drop me back to my car?"

"Sure thing, man."

---

Theo telling me to stay away from Lauren was like a hammer to the heart—deadly. How can you stay away from the woman you love? The woman who consumes every fiber of your being? It's impossible is what it fucking is.

The only reason why I'm considering staying away is because I don't want this on her. She doesn't need that shit. I can move on, get another job somewhere else, but she needs her scholarship to finish school.

I'm pacing my house like a caged animal—call her? Don't call her? *Fuck!*

Finally picking up my phone, I call her. She answers after one ring.

"Caleb?" she breathes.

"Fuck it's good to hear your voice, baby girl," I mutter.

"What happened? Are you home? I'm on my way," she rushes out.

I can hear rustling in the background and I know I have to stop this fast. "Lauren, wait." *Fuck, I can't breathe.* "I need you to stay home, sweetheart," I grit out.

There's silence before she says, "What? Why?"

I take a deep breath before laying it all out there for her. "I need to lie low. I can't be around you until this all blows over."

I can hear her eyes roll from here. "Caleb, we've been sneaking around for months, there's no difference."

"Theo thinks—"

"Fuck, Theo, Caleb. Do you want to be with me? To keep doing what we're doing until I graduate and can go public?"

Rubbing my eyes and feeling a headache coming on, I know that's all I want. "Yes," I mutter.

"I can't hear you, Caleb. Say it louder for those of us in the back," she retorts and I can hear the smile on her face.

"Yes!" I shout, laughing at her.

"I'll be over in thirty," she says before the line goes dead.

Pulling my phone away from my ear, I look down at the black screen perplexed. *What the fuck just happened?* Did I just get railroaded by my twenty-year-old girlfriend?

Fuck. Theo is gonna lose his shit when he finds out.

True to her word, thirty minutes later Lauren's Uber is pulling up outside my house. I head to the door, opening it and lean against the doorframe, arms crossed taking her in. She's got her luscious blonde hair up in a ponytail, no makeup, and her usual sweats on. I don't think I've ever seen her look more beautiful, even with the giant bruise covering the right side of her face.

She gets out of the car, practically running up the path. Pushing off the doorframe, I reach for her and she jumps into my arms, wrapping her hands around my neck and her legs around my waist. I breathe her in as I take us inside, kicking the door shut. She lifts her head off my shoulder and takes my face in between her hands.

"God I missed you." She slams her lips against mine and I kiss her back, my tongue entwining with hers in a kiss that's all passion and heat.

Pulling back, I brush a hand over her bruised face, taking in every minute detail. She winces at my gentle touch. "Sorry, sweetheart."

"It's okay. I'd love to say I've had worse but this is legitimately the worst I ever had. I think it looks worse than it is though." She shrugs.

This woman is so strong. How does she do that? Just shrug things off?

"How are your hands," she asks, unwinding her legs from around my waist and slowly lowering herself down. "Let me see." Lauren grabs my hands and inspects them. They're battered and bruised, but I've had worse.

"I've had worse." I smirk as I haul her back into me, needing her close. I breathe in her intoxicating smell and just hold her. From the way Lauren is gripping my waist, I think she feels the same.

She peers up at me, a small smile playing on her lips as she runs her hands up my chest, goosebumps breaking out over my skin at her touch. "Well, now that's over with, Professor, I have more important things to attend to."

I grin. "Oh yeah, sweetheart. Like what?"

Lauren reaches up onto her tiptoes and grabs my hair gently, pulling me down to claim my lips with her own. I groan into her mouth, the taste of strawberries and vanilla flooding my senses as I pick her back up into my arms.

I grip her ass in my hands, caressing it as I walk us to the kitchen counter, putting her down and moving my hands to her waist, never once breaking the kiss. My cock is rock solid at this point, tenting my sweatpants, desperate to get to her.

Lauren starts pulling at my shirt and I get the hint immediately, drawing back from her and lifting it over my head. Her gaze is full of lust as she takes me in. Lauren places her palms on my chest and I'm sure she can feel how hard my heart is beating. Beating only for her.

Placing my hands on the bottom of her hoodie, I lift it up, my jaw practically hitting the floor when I see she's not wearing anything under it—not even a bra. I lower my head and capture one of her nipples in my mouth, sucking and biting until I'm leaving marks and then moving on to the next one. Lauren's panting and moaning at my not-so-gentle assault on her body.

Circling my tongue around her nipples one last time, I draw back and ask, "You wearing any underwear under these leggings, baby girl?"

Lauren smirks at me, a mischievous glint to her eyes. "Why don't you look and see."

"Don't mind if I do."

Lifting Lauren up slightly, I pull her leggings down and find that she is indeed *not* wearing any underwear. I nearly come at the sight of her bare cunt on my counter, glistening with her juices. I run a finger from her ass to her clit and back again. Lauren drops her head back, moaning, and opens her legs wider.

"Please, Caleb," she sighs. "I need you to fuck me."

I push a finger into her cunt and use my thumb to gently circle her clit. "Does this pretty little cunt want my cock? Hmm?"

"Yes, please. Don't tease me. Please, please," she cries.

*Well fuck me. I can't say no to that.*

Pulling my finger out of her pussy, I put it in my mouth, sucking the juices off, groaning at the taste of her.

I lock eyes with Lauren and she's watching me, a shy smile on her face. She grabs my face and pulls me in for a kiss, sucking my tongue as if it were my dick. I growl and reach for my cock, pumping it a few times before lining it up with her pussy, and thrusting into her.

"Shit, you're so big," Lauren gasps.

"Nah, you're just tight." I wink and she slaps my chest.

"Please move, Caleb. I really need you to fuck me, I'm so close to coming already," she pleads.

Not one to disappoint, I start thrusting into her, slowly at first but getting quicker and quicker as I start chasing my own release. Lauren's walls firmly gripping me, hurtling me towards the end before she's had the chance to come.

*We don't do that 'round here.*

Lifting my head from its thrown back position, I gather spit in my mouth and dribble it onto her clit, using my free hand that's not on her hip, to circle it.

"Fuck, yes. Right there, Caleb. Don't stop," she pants, as she clutches my shoulders tighter.

I lean down and take one of Lauren's nipples into my mouth, sucking hard and she comes instantly, screaming my name. Her pussy walls clench my cock so hard I follow behind her, roaring out my release.

Moving my head down, I capture her lips with mine in a slow kiss, our tongues tangling together as we breathe heavily. Lauren finally pulls away, gazing softly at me as she says, "Never let go."

My heart pounds in my chest as I look at the woman I love, who has become everything to me. Pushing back a strand of hair and kissing her forehead, I reply, "Never."

# Chapter Fifty-Eight

## *Lauren*

When Caleb called and tried breaking it off, I refused to accept it. We've been doing this for months now and—to my knowledge—we haven't been caught by anyone other than the dean and Brad. I won't lose him, we've been through too much to end it now.

After our impromptu fuck on Caleb's kitchen counter, we cleaned up and moved to his bedroom, both of us too exhausted to be anywhere else. We're lying in his bed, my leg thrown over his waist and my head on his chest, listening to the sound of his heart beating. Caleb's stroking a finger gently down my back, an arm behind his head.

"You okay, sweetheart?" he asks.

I gaze up at Caleb and smile. "Yeah, handsome. I am."

He looks at me with a worried expression, pulling me in tighter as he says, "You suffered a horrific experience last night and I fucked you on the kitchen counter without a second thought."

Sitting up, I look at Caleb head on. "Hear me when I say these words: if I didn't want you to touch me like that, I wouldn't have let you. This is my body; my choice, and I choose you. Every time, Caleb."

He cups my face gently, being mindful of the bruise on my cheek and I lean into him, bringing my hand up to cup his. "I love you, Caleb. You make even the darkest of days brighter. You make all the pain melt away. I refuse to let some asshole ruin what we have. To ruin what we can be."

I didn't realize I was crying until Caleb wipes a tear from my cheek. He grins at me. "What?" I laugh.

"You love me," he says, more of a statement than a question.

I roll my eyes. "That's what you took from all of that?"

"Yup," he replies as he tackles me to the bed, bracing himself on his forearms. "I love you, too, Lauren. So fucking much." Caleb leans down to give me a tender kiss and I sigh at the level of contentment I feel.

Never in my wildest dreams did I think I would find someone I wanted to share my life with. Even though I'm only twenty, there's no one else I want to be with, but I'm happy taking it one day at a time and seeing where it goes. I graduate in four months and after that? Who knows. But what I do know is that I want this man by my side every step of the way.

"Fuck knows why you want an old man like me, sweetheart, but I'll do everything I can to make you happy."

I slap his chest, laughing. "Shut up, Caleb. You're not old, you're just in your silver fox era." I wink.

Caleb groans and rolls off me onto his back, covering his face with his arm. "Fuck my life," he mumbles before pulling his arm down slightly and peering at me, one eyebrow raised. "Silver fox? Really?"

"What can I say? You've converted me."

"I guess I should say thank you for that."

"You're welcome," I retort.

Quick as lightning, Caleb jumps up and starts tickling me. "Brat."

I start thrashing around, trying to get him off me and laughing at the same time. "You love me... being a... brat," I gasp between breaths, before shouting, "Truce."

Caleb stops and gathers me in his arms, kissing my forehead. I snuggle into his chest and breath in his leather and cinnamon smell, knowing I'm exactly where I want to be.

# Chapter Fifty-Nine

## *Lauren*

The next four months fly by in a flurry of assignments, exams, work, spending time with Caleb, and acting as shocked as everyone else when they found out about Dean Williams and Brad.

Brad got a two year suspended sentence. That's it. The dean took a leave of absence from the university... indefinitely. They had no evidence against him, and Brad refused to testify against him, taking the blame solely on his shoulders. The last I heard they'd gone their separate ways. I just hope history won't repeat itself.

I continued working at Strokes, but my last shift is next week. Caleb and I are going traveling for the summer before I start my new job as an English teacher for dyslexic children. To say I'm excited is an understatement but it's bittersweet. I've been at Strokes for so long now, they're like my second family, so it's going to be hard saying goodbye to them.

The girls are all here today—Esme, Destiny, Sapphire, Sydney, and Raven—to cheer me on as I walk to the podium to graduate. Caleb's sitting with the other faculty members on stage.

The nerves start taking over and I glance over at him, instantly calming when he gives me a wink. *I should have known he'd know where I was.* I chuckle to myself at his possessiveness—the man knows no bounds.

My name's called and I make my way up to the stage, Caleb steps forward and I stop, furrowing my brow in confusion. He takes my diploma out of the chancellor's hand and whispers in his ear. The chancellor looks at me with wide eyes before turning and nodding his head at Caleb.

*What just happened?*

Caleb takes the chancellor's position and gestures with the diploma in his hand for me to come and get it. I smile at him and he smiles back, one so wide I'm not sure how his face isn't hurting.

Stopping in front of him, I lean in slightly and whisper, "Hi, handsome."

"Hey, sweetheart," he says before gently throwing my diploma behind his head and grabbing my hand, pulling me toward him.

I squeal as my hands come to rest on his chest. "Caleb." Breathless at being so close to him, I stutter out, "Wh-what are you doing?"

"Claiming my woman," is all he says before sweeping me up and kissing me in front of *everyone*.

The end

# Bonus Chapter

## RAVEN

I've spent my whole life in the shadows, watching but never seen. God, that makes me sound like a stalker but I swear I'm not. I'm the quiet one, the bookworm, the girl with the red hair that got picked on all through high school. And that's okay, I never minded. I've always been at my happiest surrounded by books.

My best friend, Mia, would always laugh at me whenever she saw me with a book in my hand, wanting to know about the latest damsel in distress that was being saved by a knight in shiny armor.

As I got older, the knight I always pictured took on the face of James Smith, my dads' best friend. I've been in love with him for as long as I can remember. What started out as an innocent child's love for her 'uncle,' turned into a teenage crush which turned into a first love, except he never stopped being my first love.

"Can I grab a black coffee to go," someone says, distracting me from my wayward thoughts.

Blinking, I shake my head and smile. "Sure, coming right up."

Busying myself with making a black coffee for the obviously rushed off their feet student, I shove all thoughts of James to the back of my mind.

Handing over the coffee, I say, "Have a great day," but all I get in reply is a grunt. Fabulous.

Swiping a cloth from the back, I head over to the tables and start clearing them away, wiping away sticky fingers and spilt coffee.

I've worked at the Honey Pot since it opened on campus a couple weeks ago, after desperately needing something to get me out of my dorm room.

Felicity, my roommate, loves men, which means my dorm has a constant flow of people in and out seeing to, uh, Felicity's... needs. If I could afford to be anywhere else, I would, but I can't. So, instead I bust my ass waiting on people, study in the library, and sleep when I'm dead.

The door opens and the bell chimes, alerting me to a customer. I glance round and notice Mia stomping through.

"Hey, lovely," I greet with a beaming smile.

Mia and I decided to go to the same university together, not being able to bear being away from one another. Mia and I met, like so many other kids, in kindergarten. We were lucky that our friendship withstood the drama of high school.

Mia gives me a hug as she says, "Hey, yourself."

"Usual?" I ask, walking back to the counter and grabbing her a cup.

"You need to stop memorizing people's orders, they'll start thinking you're stalking them," she says with a wink.

"Some people are into that sort of thing," I retort, passing Mia her drink. "I'm just going on my break, you wanna sit outside?"

Mia nods her head as she takes a sip of her coffee. "Yeah, I'd like to get the last of the rays before autumn really kicks in."

I hum in agreement, and we wander outside, placing our coffees down and getting comfortable on the white patio chairs.

The Honey Pot sits in an outbuilding on campus, having been freshly renovated over the summer, college kids having sent numerous complaints that they either had to get terrible coffee from the main cafeteria or they had to walk miles for the nearest Starbucks.

I sip on my coffee as I take in my surroundings, the warm sun beating down on my face, and the cool gentle breeze running through my hair.

Abingdon University is one of the top universities in the country and I was lucky to get a place here. As soon as I saw pictures of the old buildings covered with ivy, when I was ten, I knew I had to study here. That feeling hasn't lessened in the two years that I've been here.

"Have you heard from your dad," Mia asks, biting into a bagel that she snagged from behind the counter when I wasn't looking—I'll put the money back later.

I shake my head. "No, he's been busy with work. Something about him and James 'acquiring a new company,' I glazed over when he started talking," I chuckle. "I have my weekly phone call with him on Sunday though."

Mia smirks around the rim of her cup as she asks, "How is the lovely James?"

I roll my eyes at her. "Stop it. You know I don't see him much now." I glance down at my lap before adding, "Not since *that* night anyway."

"Hmm."

I shift my eyes to look at my best friend. "What?"

"Nothing. I didn't say anything."

Mia's always found my... fascination with James to be of interest. I'm not sure how or why but she's taken great delight in it.

"Don't you have somewhere to be?" I joke, trying to change the subject as I gather the rubbish on the table and stand up, break time over.

"Unfortunately, I do. I have class. I'll speak to you later though?"

I smile at her. "Of course."

Mia heads to class and I get back to work, thoughts of James—as always—on my mind.

# Acknowledgements

I have so many people to thank but like so many, the first one goes to my wonderful husband, Joe. If it wasn't for him saying to me on a dreary Tuesday morning, 'If you don't try, how will you know?' Never Let Go wouldn't be here. So thank you, my love. Thank you for believing in me when I didn't.

To my real life Sydney. Bitch, this book wouldn't be what it is without you and your crazy ideas. Thank you for holding my hand the whole way through. For pushing me when I doubted myself, and for basically being the complete bad ass bitch that you are. ILY.

Jinx. Thank you for your unwavering support and love for this book. Thank you for being a friend first and an author second. Your comments on how to shape this book were invaluable, and I can't thank you enough.

Jac. Thank you so much for all of your help and expertise when it came to adding more tension—trust me when I say this book wasn't half as good until she slapped my ass, told me to be a good girl, and get it done.

My betas, Luna, JJ, Amelia and Rynn. Thank you. Your comments made me laugh daily, and I'm so grateful for you.

To the first fifteen people who pre-ordered Never Let Go: Lauren North, Rachael Young, Kathryn Pettit, Stacy, Georgina Hannan, Nancy Brooks, Nicole-Jane Nevill, Katy Lofthouse, Emma Duncan, Step Furniss, Chelsea-Leigh Hartley, Jess Vale, Kristina Booker, Gina Tricoglus and Aimee Wakefield... Thank you. Thank you for pre-ordering this book without knowing anything about it other than the tropes. You guys are amazing.

And lastly to you, the reader. Whether you loved this book, hated it and didn't even get to this point, I thank you. Thank you for picking this book up and giving it a chance. You will never know how much I appreciate you.

# About the author

Luna Peters is an English author writing contemporary forbidden, age gap romances with dark themes. She lives with her real life cinnamon roll husband and two cats and can often be found curled up with her kindle supporting other indie authors.

# Stalk Me

You have my full consent to stalk me where ever you like to stalk your favourite authors.

Printed in Dunstable, United Kingdom